DEATH COMES
TO THE
NURSERY

Center Point
Large Print

Also by Catherine Lloyd and available from Center Point Large Print:

Death Comes to the School
Death Comes to the Bath

Death Comes
to the
Nursery

A Kurland St. Mary Mystery

CATHERINE LLOYD

CENTER POINT LARGE PRINT
THORNDIKE, MAINE

This Center Point Large Print edition
is published in the year 2020 by arrangement with
Kensington Publishing Corp.

This is a work of fiction. Names, characters,
organizations, places, events, and incidents are
either products of the author's imagination
or are used fictitiously.

The text of this Large Print edition is unabridged.
In other aspects, this book may vary
from the original edition.
Printed in the United States of America
on permanent paper.
Set in 16-point Times New Roman type.

ISBN: 978-1-64358-539-0

The Library of Congress has cataloged this record under
Library of Congress Control Number: 2019918616

Chapter 1

༺❦༻

Kurland Hall,
Kurland St. Mary, England, 1825

Lucy, Lady Kurland, looked up dubiously at the smiling face of the beautiful young woman standing in front of her, and then back at the letter in her hand.

"You're Agnes's cousin, Polly?"

"Yes, my lady." Polly curtsied again. "Agnes wrote and said you were looking for a new nursery maid, and as I was wanting to be leaving London, she told me to apply for the position." She nodded at the letter Lucy held. "That's from you, isn't it? Offering me a job?"

A note of uncertainty crept into Polly's voice, and her smile faltered. "Don't tell me Agnes was making it up, and you don't want me. I've sold everything I have to buy my ticket here."

Lucy set the letter to one side and considered Polly anew. Yes, she looked nothing at all like her cousin Agnes, but just because she was pretty didn't mean she wouldn't be a hard worker. Agnes had spoken very highly of her, and Lucy had an excellent opinion of her son's nurse.

"I understand that you are experienced with dealing with young children?" Lucy asked.

"Yes, my lady. I have two younger brothers and a sister. I always had to help me mum out, especially after me dad scarpered."

"Have you been employed as a nursery maid before?"

"No, but I'm willing to learn. And with Agnes telling me what's what, I'm sure I'll pick it up in no time." Polly must have seen the indecision on Lucy's face because she carried on speaking. "*Please,* my lady. Just give me a chance. I promise I won't let you down."

Lucy sighed and picked up the letter again. "Let's start with a month's trial, shall we? If you settle in well and prove to be satisfactory, I will consider hiring you for a full year."

Polly clasped her hands together on her bosom, her blue eyes sparkling. "Oh, thank you, my lady!"

Lucy beckoned to Foley, who had accompanied Polly into the morning room. "Will you take Polly up to the nursery, Foley? Ask Agnes to take care of her cousin. I will come up to see Ned at suppertime as usual."

"Yes, my lady." Foley smiled fondly at Polly and held open the door. "Come along then, young 'un. I'll get James to bring up your bags."

Lucy tucked the letter into her pocket and made her way slowly through the house to the study of her husband, Robert. It was a bright late-summer morning in Kurland St. Mary, and sunlight flooded through the windows, patterning the wooden floors. Lucy knocked on the door and went in. Her husband was sitting at his desk dealing with the account books and didn't look particularly pleased to be interrupted.

"Robert . . ."

"What is it?"

"I just interviewed Polly Carter for the position of nursemaid."

"And what does that have to do with me?" Robert asked. "Was Ned scared of her? Will she not suit?"

Lucy sat down in front of his desk. "I'm sure he'll love her. She's Agnes's cousin."

"As you are constantly telling me how wonderful Agnes is with our son, I'm wondering why you appear so doubtful about her cousin."

"She's . . . very pretty," Lucy confessed.

"So what?" Robert set his pen down. "Are you worried I'll run off with her?"

"Hardly." Lucy had to smile at that. "But I do wonder how the rest of the household will deal with her. Foley almost fell over himself being nice, and that isn't like him at all these days."

"He needs to retire," Robert said. "Have you reason to believe the girl will be incompetent?"

"None at all. Agnes recommended her," Lucy

7

said. "I've offered her a month's trial before I make up my mind completely."

"Then perhaps you might give her the benefit of the doubt. It's not like you to be worried about a pretty face, my love." Robert came around his desk and sat on the edge directly in front of Lucy. "Why do we even need a new nursemaid? We have three women in that nursery already. I don't want Ned smothered in petticoats."

"He is hardly smothered," Lucy objected. "He spends much of his time with you, and he also enjoys going down to the stables and Home Farm with James."

"Still . . . ," Robert said. "Why add another maid?"

Lucy looked down at her hands, which were folded together in her lap. "I thought you might have realized why by now."

"Realized what?"

"That I'm increasing again."

"Good Lord!" Robert stuttered. "But you've been so . . . well."

"As opposed to my last experience when I was not well at all?" Lucy asked, and Robert nodded. "Grace says that every pregnancy is different, and that this time I may suffer no ill effects at all."

"I damn well hope so. But Grace is an excellent healer and I trust her judgment. I hated seeing you so indisposed," Robert commented. "When is the little blighter due?"

"Just before Christmas, I think."

Robert came over, lifted Lucy out of her seat, and sat down again with her in his lap. He kissed her cheek and wrapped an arm around her thickening waist.

"How wonderful to think that Ned might soon have a little brother."

"Or a sister," Lucy reminded him.

"Even better." He kissed her again. "In all seriousness, my love, what delightful news."

"I haven't told anyone else yet," Lucy confessed. "But now that you know, I'll probably speak to Dr. Fletcher and my family."

"If you are happy to do so, then go ahead."

She cupped his chin. "Are you really pleased?"

"Why would I not be?" He raised a dark eyebrow.

"Because Ned isn't even three yet."

"Which is why you have my full permission to employ as many people as you want in the nursery, so that you, my dear, don't wear yourself out." He smiled at her, his dark blue eyes full of amusement. "Polly can't be that pretty, now, can she?"

Polly wasn't pretty.

Robert let out his breath as the new nursemaid curtsied and sent him a very saucy smile. She was beautiful. Her hair was gold, her eyes were blue, and her skin was perfectly tinted, like a porcelain ornament. She also had the figure of a goddess.

"Good afternoon, Sir Robert. Right pleased to meet you." Polly smiled down at her small charge, who was building a brick tower on the rug in front of the nursery fire. "Young master Ned looks just like you."

"Welcome to Kurland Hall." Robert finally managed a reply. "I do hope you are settling in well?"

"Yes, indeed, sir. Everyone has been so kind to me." She sat down on the rug, presenting Robert with an excellent view of her bosom, and offered Ned another brick to add to his tower.

Robert took the chair beside the fire and reached forward to ruffle Ned's hair. "Good evening, old chap."

Ned gave him a ferocious glare that reminded Robert rather too forcibly of himself and returned to constructing his fortifications.

"He's a lovely little boy, sir." Polly commented. "So polite! Not like my little brothers, who can curse with the best of them."

"I don't think Lady Kurland would approve of that," Robert murmured. "Ned certainly does seem to have a pleasant disposition."

He glanced up as Agnes came into the nursery carrying a supper tray. Dark-haired, tall, and thin, she looked nothing like Polly.

"Good evening, Agnes. How lovely for you to

have your young cousin working in the nursery with you now."

Agnes busied herself setting the tray down and did so with something of a thump. "I'm certainly glad to have another pair of hands, Sir Robert, what with Lady Kurland's news."

"Yes, another charge for you on the way," Robert agreed. "I am relying on you to keep an eye on Lady Kurland. She does tend to overexert herself."

"Don't you worry about that, Sir Robert. I know her ways."

Robert fought a smile. His wife did tend to be overly managing, even if she was often right about what needed to be managed.

The nursery door opened, and Lucy came in, her fond gaze immediately going to her son.

"Ned, are you ready for your supper?"

To Robert's relief, his son and heir ignored his mother just as completely as he had ignored his father and set another brick on top of the wavering tower.

Just as Robert was about to repeat Lucy's advice about his supper being ready, the tower crashed to the ground, and Ned's lower lip wobbled. Before Robert could react, Polly swooped the boy up and marched him over to the table.

"Never mind that, Ned. We'll build it even bigger next time. Now, come and eat your supper.

Cook said she had something special for you tonight."

Robert caught Lucy's gaze and shrugged. Whatever else Polly Carter might be, she certainly had a way with children. Knowing his wife, that would more than justify her staying on at Kurland Hall.

He held out his hand to her as he rose from his seat. "Everything seems to be in order here, my dear. Perhaps we should leave Ned to enjoy his supper?"

"I . . ." For once, Lucy looked conflicted, her gaze straying to the table, where Ned was chatting away to Polly as she cut up his meat.

"We have your father, my aunt Rose, and all the Fletchers coming to dinner tonight. Perhaps it would be a good opportunity to share our news with them?" Robert suggested. "And are you quite certain Cook will provide us with sufficient victuals?"

"Of course she will." Lucy finally came toward him. "But I suppose it wouldn't hurt to check."

Robert hid a smile as he bid his son and the nursery staff good night, and escorted his wife down the stairs. Polly would either succeed in becoming a good nursemaid or she wouldn't. His wife was clever enough to decide the matter without referencing Polly's looks, and that was good enough for him.

He went into his dressing room and allowed his valet to offer him a new cravat to replace the wrinkled one around his neck. He tied it neatly, without help, and secured it with the jet pin Lucy had given him for his last birthday. His valet assisted him into his new winter coat, which was dark blue and cut in the severe military style he still favored.

Since his visit to Bath and the hot springs, he'd installed a large bath in the dressing room, which meant he could indulge in regular hot soakings. It didn't quite replicate the healing power of the waters in the Bath spa, but it was certainly a help for his wounded thigh. He barely needed to use his cane these days.

Lucy had already changed for dinner, so he met her down in the drawing room, where his father-in-law, the Honorable Ambrose Harrington, rector of Kurland St. Mary and its outlying parishes, was warming himself in front of the fire.

"Ah! There you are, Robert. I was just telling Lucy that it's time to put young Ned up on his first horse."

"He's two years old," Robert pointed out. "He's still mastering walking."

"Which is why it's the ideal time to do it." Mr. Harrington was a keen horseman who loved to hunt. He turned to his wife, Robert's aunt Rose. "Don't you think so, Rose?"

"I think it is up to Robert, my dear," Rose answered him, her warm smile reaching out to both of them. "I didn't set my children on a horse until they were four or five."

"But you lived in the city. Here in the countryside, being a good rider is essential," Mr. Harrington asserted. "Present company excepted, obviously."

Robert tried not to let the rector's comment bother him, but it was difficult. Before his horse had fallen on him at the battle of Waterloo and almost killed him, he, too, had thought like his father-in-law. Now he could barely manage to be around a horse without a thousand fears engulfing him.

"You don't have to do it yourself, Kurland," the rector said encouragingly. "I'm sure one of your stable hands would be happy to help. Or even better, send the boy down to me, and I'll see that he's taught the proper way to do things."

"I know you would take great care of him, sir, but I'd rather wait a year or so until I am confident Ned will both understand and enjoy the process," Robert said firmly.

"And I agree with Robert." Lucy came up alongside him and linked her arm through his. "Ned loves visiting the stables with James, and that is quite enough for now."

"If you say so, my dear." Mr. Harrington sighed. "I'm only trying to make sure that my

14

first grandchild is properly prepared for his responsibilities."

To everyone's surprise, the normally selfish and indolent Mr. Harrington had taken quite a liking to his fearless grandson. His interest in Ned's progress and desire to be involved with his life had come as quite a shock to everyone, especially his daughter.

"I do hope young Ned will be coming down to pay his respects to his grandparents this evening?" Mr. Harrington asked. "Mayhap we can ask him how *he* feels about learning to ride a horse by himself, eh?"

Lucy caught Robert's gaze, and he shrugged. He had no issue with Ned coming down for a few moments before he went off to bed, but he knew his wife was less inclined to encourage any unnecessary attention on him.

"I'll ask James to check if Ned is still awake." Lucy headed out toward the hall. While she attended to the matter, Robert welcomed his old friend Dr. Fletcher and his wife, Penelope, who had just entered the drawing room. His land agent, Dermot Fletcher, also joined them and made polite conversation until Lucy returned. Robert wasn't the kind of man who enjoyed large gatherings, but the people invited to dinner were all well known to him and therefore quite acceptable.

"Was our son and heir awake?" he murmured

in Lucy's ear as she came to stand beside him.

"I believe he was. He'll be down in a moment. I told Agnes he should not stay above a quarter hour."

"In case his grandfather starts spoiling him?" Robert asked.

"In case Ned starts to think he can escape his proper bedtime every night," Lucy replied. "It is difficult enough to get him to go to sleep as it is without offering him too much excitement."

"Good Lord," Mr. Harrington murmured as he turned toward the door and raised his glass to his eye. "What have we here?"

Lucy sighed as a blushing Polly, who was holding Ned by the hand, curtsied to her father. "I assume Agnes was too busy to bring Ned down herself."

"One must assume so." Robert patted her shoulder. "Don't worry. I'll go over and make sure your father isn't saying anything too out-rageous."

Robert cast a quick look around the room and noticed that both the Fletcher brothers were staring at the beauteous vision that had descended among them. Dermot cleared his throat as Robert went by him.

"Is that Agnes's cousin, sir?"

"Apparently."

"She looks nothing like her."

"She is rather fetching, isn't she?" Rose, who

was standing beside his land agent, offered her own opinion of the nursery maid. She didn't appear concerned that her recently acquired second husband practically had his aquiline nose down Polly's rather excellent cleavage. "When did she arrive, Robert?"

"This morning."

"Ah, that explains why I didn't meet her," Dermot said. "I was out visiting the Home Farm."

"I'm sure you'll take the opportunity to introduce yourself to her fairly soon, Dermot," Robert said encouragingly. "You *are* the one who dispenses the wages and manages the household staff."

He went over to his father-in-law's side and rescued the blushing nursemaid from his attentions, directing them instead onto his grandson.

Polly curtsied to him. "Thank you, sir. I'll go and wait over there until Master Ned is ready to return to the nursery."

She retreated to the door. Robert returned to his wife, who was standing with Penelope Fletcher in the middle of what appeared to be an animated conversation.

"Well, if I were you, Lucy, I wouldn't allow that woman in my house."

"Why not?" Lucy asked mildly enough. "She appears to be an excellent nursemaid."

Lucy and Penelope had a somewhat fractious relationship. But Robert knew his wife would

17

always champion her employee against her friend's objections.

"She is far too pretty!" Penelope rolled her eyes in Robert's direction. "You would not want to give your husband *ideas,* now, would you?"

"Ideas about what?" Robert joined the conversation.

"You know very well what I'm referring to." Penelope sniffed. "Men can be weak and easily misled—especially when their wives are no longer in the first blush of youth."

Lucy raised her eyebrows. "As we are the same age, Penelope, are you suggesting that Dr. Fletcher will also stray?"

"Of course he won't." Penelope patted her hair. "I am still beautiful, whereas you, my dear Lucy, have never been much more than passable."

Robert hastened to intervene as his wife visibly drew herself up. "I can assure you that my wife has nothing to worry about. I am very content with my choice."

Penelope regarded him dubiously for a long moment and then nodded. "I will allow that, seeing as you turned down my beauty for her . . . average looks, maybe you aren't inclined to chase your nursemaid."

"Thank you, I think," Robert said. "But I believe you were the one to break our engagement, not me."

Penelope waved away his correction. "It hardly matters now, does it? We both ended up with the partners we deserved." She smiled fondly over at her husband, who was in deep discussion with his brother. "I, too, am well content with my lot."

Foley appeared at the door and loudly cleared his throat.

"Dinner is served."

Ned disappeared back up the stairs with his new nursemaid without making a fuss, and Robert turned his attention to the prospect of his dinner.

As the gathering was informal, after making sure that Ned was on his way back to bed, Lucy accompanied Robert into the small dining room. Penelope's comments about her husband becoming enamored of a pretty face hadn't bothered her. She'd known as soon as Polly appeared and every man in the room stared at her that Penelope would say something. As Penelope was accustomed to being the most beautiful woman in the room, she probably hadn't enjoyed being outshone.

Lucy took her seat and waited as her father said grace before dismissing the servants so that they could serve themselves. Robert much preferred to eat his meals in comfort, and with her current guests being so familiar, she was more than willing to accommodate him.

He caught her attention as he sat down and raised his eyebrows as he picked up his wineglass. Lucy offered him a tiny nod in return, and he cleared his throat.

"My wife and I are happy to announce that we are expecting an addition to our family at Christmastime."

Everyone turned to smile at Lucy, who felt herself blush.

"How lovely!" Rose said. "A little brother or sister for Ned."

"Indeed." Robert gave one of his rare smiles. "We are delighted."

Dr. Fletcher winked at Lucy. "I'll assume that Grace is caring for you, but don't hesitate to ask for my help if you need it, my lady."

"Gladly," Lucy replied. "In truth, I am feeling remarkably well this time."

"I'm pleased to hear it." Dr. Fletcher toasted her with his glass.

As everyone settled in to eat, Penelope leaned in close to Lucy.

"As you are expecting, I'll double my warning about allowing that young woman in your house. Even good men are known to stray when their wives are unable to accommodate their more physical needs."

"I have no concerns about that, Penelope." Lucy spoke as firmly as she could.

"Then let's just hope that your confidence in Sir Robert is justified," Penelope stated. "Because if *I* were in your shoes, Lucy Kurland, I wouldn't be *quite* so sanguine."

Chapter 2

❦

"*I'll* accompany Master Ned to the stables."

"That's my job, Mr. Fletcher."

"And I'm telling you that I'm doing it today."

"You bloody well are not—"

Lucy hastened toward the two men, who were nose-to-nose at the bottom of the stairs in the main hall, glaring at each other.

"What on earth is going on?"

Dermot Fletcher swung around, his expression that of a small boy caught in mischief.

"Lady Kurland! I do apologize for disturbing you. I was just offering to walk young Ned down to the stables."

"Which is my job, as you well know, Lady Kurland." James, who was the most senior footman at the hall, jumped into the conversation. "I was just about to go upstairs to collect him and Miss Polly when Mr. Fletcher decided to interfere."

"I was not interfering, I simply—"

Lucy stared at both men until they fell silent. "I think I will walk with Ned today, so neither of you are needed."

22

Mr. Fletcher took a step back and bowed. "As you wish, my lady."

He stalked off into the house. Lucy distinctly heard his office door slam farther down the corridor.

"I'm sorry, my lady, but that Mr. Fletcher is being right annoying to Miss Polly," James said. "And she ain't for the likes of him, I can tell you that."

"I didn't ask for your opinion, James," Lucy said severely. "And I'm fairly certain that Polly would not appreciate you wrangling over her like two dogs with a bone. When she is with my son, she is doing her job and not to be distracted by either of you."

"Oh, she does her job, my lady. Don't you be thinking otherwise, and the young master likes her very much, and does as she tells him," James hastened to reassure her. "Now, I'd best be going upstairs, my lady. The young lad will be worrying as to where I am."

Lucy held up her hand. "I told you that I am going with Ned today. Please return to the kitchen and find something else to occupy your time."

James looked crestfallen as he bowed and went back toward the servants' stairs. Lucy raised her eyes heavenward and walked up the stairs to the nursery. Penelope had been wrong about Robert being interested in their new nursemaid, but in the past three weeks, every other male in the household, from Mr. Fletcher downward, had been acting like fools over the poor girl.

And to be fair to Polly, she was nothing but pleasant to everyone. She performed her job well and encouraged none of the men dancing around her for attention. It wasn't the first time Lucy had found the men of the household squabbling over Polly, and she suspected it wouldn't be the last.

When she reached the nursery, Ned came running toward her, his smile so like his father's that she couldn't help but smile back at him.

"Horses?" he asked hopefully.

"Yes, indeed." Lucy glanced over at Polly, who had her cloak and bonnet on and was ready to go. "It is a beautiful sunny day, and we will all enjoy the walk."

"Yes, my lady." Polly curtsied and turned to Agnes, who had just come in with a load of fresh linen. "We're off then, cousin."

"Hmmph," Agnes said. "Take your time. I've got to get this bed done."

Polly hesitated. "If you wait until I come back, I can help you."

"No need," Agnes nodded at Lucy. "It'll get done much faster without you and Ned helping."

Polly didn't seem to take Agnes's sharp words too seriously as she took Ned's hand. "Come on, then. Let's go."

Lucy held the door open to allow her son and his nursemaid to precede her. Polly hadn't seemed bothered by the lack of a male escort on her walk, which indicated to Lucy that, despite all the attention, she wasn't pining after any one man in particular.

They went out one of the many side doors of the old Elizabethan manor house, through the formal gardens at the back that led down to the stables and the Home Farm. Ned skipped ahead, his countenance cheerful, and Lucy simply enjoyed watching him. After two miscarriages, the birth of her son had changed her in so many ways. She was almost embarrassed by the depth of emotion she felt for him and tried hard to conceal it.

"He's a lovely lad, Lady Kurland." Polly fell into step beside Lucy. She was wearing a plain blue dress that did nothing to detract from her beautiful figure. "Such a sweet nature."

"One hopes he will keep it," Lucy agreed. "The advent of a baby brother or sister might cause some jealousy."

"Oh, aye." Polly chuckled. "I remember that with my family, but with all the attention Ned gets, I suspect he won't worry too much."

"That would be wonderful." Lucy walked on and then cast a glance at her companion. "How are you adjusting to living in the countryside, Polly?"

"I like it, my lady." Polly took a deep breath. "The air is clean, and there aren't too many people bothering me."

"If anyone is bothering you, I would like to hear about it," Lucy said firmly.

"Oh, you know men. They like to make cakes of themselves over a pretty face. I try not to encourage them, and eventually they stop pestering me."

Lucy had never thought about that aspect of being beautiful before.

"Or if they don't stop, my lady, I'm not averse to giving them a swift kick in the bollocks to set them straight."

Lucy struggled not to laugh. "Indeed."

"I grew up in the slums. I know how to take care of myself." Polly shaded her eyes to check on Ned, who had stopped to admire a patch of daisies. "Some old bloke tried to buy me from me mum when I was around five."

"Buy you? Whatever for?" Lucy asked.

"What do you think?" Polly's smile was touched with bitterness. "Some men like 'em young and pure."

"That's . . . horrible."

Polly shrugged. "It taught me to take care of myself, my lady. I'm not just a pretty face."

Lucy stopped by Ned and turned to Polly. "If you wish to stay on here, you are most welcome."

"Let's see how the next week goes, shall we?" Polly grinned at her. "You never know, maybe a handsome prince will turn up and sweep me off my feet."

• • •

Robert cast a distracted glance at his son and beckoned to his companion.

"James, will you keep an eye on Ned? I don't want him running out into the stable yard when a coach is coming in."

"I've got him, sir. Don't you worry." James nabbed the back of Ned's collar and hefted him up onto his shoulder. "Come here, youngster."

Robert had accompanied his son, James, and Polly down to the coaching inn in Kurland St. Mary, where Lucy was expecting a parcel. He had also been instructed to pick up any correspondence for the house or the rectory. There had been no sign of the innkeeper, so Polly had gone inside to see if his wife was in the kitchens, leaving Robert to deal with his son.

It seemed that Ned had inherited his grandfather's love of horses, which was both a pleasure and a problem for Robert, who still struggled to go near them. No one would believe that he had once been in a cavalry regiment and had relied on his mount to see him through several engagements during the war. Since the end of his military career and almost his life at Waterloo, he'd lost his nerve, which wasn't a convenient thing at all for a county squire. The constant chaos of the arrival and departure of coaches, farmers' wagons, and people in the stable yard made him nervous.

Perhaps he might take up his father-in-law's offer to teach Ned to ride after all . . .

"I got the mail, sir." Polly came out with a pile of letters. "Mrs. Jarvis says she'll go and find her ladyship's parcel, and will be right out."

"Thank you." Robert took the mail and stowed it in the deep pocket of his coat. "Perhaps you might help James with Ned."

Polly looked over to where the mail coach was disgorging its passengers. James had Ned on his shoulder and was showing him the four horses harnessed to the vehicle. Polly went still, and an apprehensive expression dimmed her usual smile.

"If it's all the same to you, sir, can I wait until James stops talking to the ostler?"

"Why?"

Polly grimaced. "Because Bert Speers has taken to following me home every time I come to the village, and he won't leave me be."

Robert frowned over at the young ostler. "Is he, by Jove? I'll be speaking to his master about that."

"Don't you bother yourself, Sir Robert." Polly spoke fast, one eye still on the ostler and the coach passengers who were milling out into the yard. "It'll just make things worse if he thinks I'm complaining about him." She went on tiptoe and craned her neck to see around Robert's shoulder. "Oh dear, it looks as if James is giving him a piece of his mind again. I hope they aren't going to start fighting."

"Not with my son in the middle of it, they aren't," Robert said. "Polly, come with me, and get Ned out of the way."

Robert pushed his way through the crowded yard to where the two men were standing beside the mail coach. He grabbed hold of Ned and handed him over to Polly.

"Go and wait inside."

"Yes, sir." Polly took Ned's hand and ran with him toward the inn.

James didn't look away from the angry face of the ostler. "This blaggard is annoying Miss Polly, sir."

"Indeed." Robert turned his attention to the shorter man. His dark eyes, thick black hair, and ferocious scowl didn't inspire Robert to approve of him.

"If I find out you've been bothering a member of my staff, I will haul you up in front of the local magistrate—who happens to be me—and make sure you pay the price for your insolence," Robert snapped.

"You can't stop me asking a girl to walk out with me," Bert sneered.

"I can if the girl has repeatedly turned you down, and you still pursue her."

"Who says I'm doing that?" Bert glanced toward the inn, where Polly and Ned had retreated. "She's lying, sir. She lures us in and then laughs at us, and you expect us to do nothing? *Look* at her. She's a worthless whore who deserves everything she gets."

Robert shoved his finger in Bert's face. "If you say one more word, I will have you put into the county gaol."

"For what, sir?"

"For whatever I say you have done." Robert didn't like to use his privilege, but in this one instance, he was quite prepared to do so. "Who do you think they will believe? You stay well away from Polly Carter and keep off my land, and we'll say nothing more of this."

Bert finally stepped back and mumbled something that might have been an apology before disappearing into the stables. Robert let out an aggravated breath.

"Did you know about this, James?"

"I only found out yesterday when I was walking with Polly and Master Ned, sir, and Bert came after us." James shuffled his feet. "I was hoping to have a quiet word with him about it, but as you can see, he's not one to back down."

"Hopefully now he will," Robert suggested. "If he doesn't, I want to hear about it immediately."

"Yes, Sir Robert." James drew himself up to his full height, and Robert noticed the bruise on his cheek.

"Have you been *fighting?*"

"As I said, sir. Bert came after us yesterday. I sent Miss Polly and Master Ned on their way and waited for him to catch up." James rubbed a hand over his jaw. "We exchanged a few blows before he ran off, but nothing serious."

"This is not acceptable behavior where my son is concerned," Robert said severely. "What if you'd been knocked out and Bert had followed Polly home? What might have happened then?"

"I wouldn't have let that happen, sir. I'm twice the size of that little imp," James insisted. "I would give my life for the young master."

Robert shook his head and went back toward the inn, where Mrs. Jarvis was waving at him from the door. There was a lot he wanted to say to James, but he needed to gather his thoughts and speak to Lucy before he said something he didn't mean. His absolute fury at the thought of Ned being caught in such an ugly situation surprised him.

"There you are, Sir Robert!" Mrs. Jarvis smiled up at him. "And how lovely to see your little boy! And I hear Lady Kurland is increasing again, so well done on that score." She winked and elbowed him in the side. "I have her parcel of fabric and lace from London right here, sir. Although she probably won't be needing any new gowns in her current condition, will she?"

"Probably not." Robert finally managed to get a word in edgeways. "Well, we must be on our way. It's way past time for Ned's nap."

"Always a pleasure to see you, sir. Mr. Jarvis will be sorry he missed you."

Robert lowered his voice and leaned in toward the innkeeper's wife "Your ostler. Bert Speers."

"What about him, sir?"

"Tell your husband that if I hear that Bert has been chasing after my nursery maid and my son again, I will be most displeased."

"Bert?" Mrs. Jarvis looked over toward the stables. "He's a quiet one. He hasn't been here above a month. He doesn't seem to have any friends and keeps to himself, except when he's had a few pints."

"He's been following Polly home."

"Well, she is rather beautiful. Who can blame him for trying?" Her smile faded as she registered Robert's expression. "You're serious, aren't you?"

"I most certainly am."

"Then I'll mention it to Mr. Jarvis the moment he gets back." She nodded. "It's not fair on Polly, who's a respectable girl and not one to lay out lures to the boys, despite her looks."

"Thank you." Robert nodded and stepped back into the stable yard, where James, Polly, and Ned awaited him. "Good day to you, Mrs. Jarvis."

. . .

Lucy looked up from her sewing as Robert came into her sitting room, shut the door, and proceeded to pace up and down the room, a frown on his face.

"Whatever is the matter?" she finally inquired.

"It's Polly." He turned to face her, his expression grim.

"Don't tell me that you have succumbed to her charms and are planning on running away with her after all," Lucy teased.

"No." He sighed and sat opposite her, his hands clasped together in front of him. "She is a pleasant enough girl, but everywhere she goes, she causes chaos."

"How so?" Lucy set her embroidery aside.

"I went to get your package from the inn this morning and found out that one of the ostlers has been following Polly home."

"That is hardly her fault," Lucy pointed out.

"I know." Robert paused to ponder his words, which was rather unusual for him. "James got into a fight with the man yesterday when he was escorting Polly and Ned home. If I hadn't intervened today, I suspect James would have started another fight, warning this Bert Speers to stay away."

"Oh, *dear,*" Lucy sighed. "The other day I caught James and Mr. Fletcher arguing about who should be accompanying Polly and Ned on

33

their walk down to the stables. And it isn't the first time I've seen such quarrels between the male staff."

"You see?" Robert flung up his hands. "Chaos wherever she goes. I don't like it, Lucy. I don't like my son being placed in such a vulnerable position."

Lucy considered his impassioned words. "I cannot help but agree with you about Ned, but I am loath to blame Polly for the lack of respect the men around her are showing. She is excellent with Ned, gets along well with Agnes, and performs her duties well. It seems unfair for her to lose her job over something she cannot control."

"I agree. But surely Ned's safety has to be our priority?"

"Of course it is." Lucy hesitated. "Perhaps you could speak to James and Mr. Fletcher privately, and ask them to leave Polly alone?"

"I can certainly do that, but I have no control over Bert Speers or any other man who fancies his chances with the new local beauty."

"Polly wants to stay on after her month's trial." Lucy said. "And I . . . I practically assured her that the job would be hers for the next year." To her astonishment, her voice wobbled. "I was hoping she would be here when the new baby was born."

"*Why?*"

"Because I *like* her, and—" Lucy swallowed hard and couldn't continue.

"Lucy." Robert reached for her hand. "Are you crying over a *nursemaid?*"

"Yes." She searched frantically for her hand-kerchief. "I'm *sorry.*"

"It's all right." Robert considered her. "If Polly is truly important to your current state of well-being, then I'm loath to get rid of her."

"Thank you." Lucy dried her eyes. "Perhaps I could offer her a shorter term of employment—to next quarter day?"

"That's a good idea." Robert nodded. "In fact, let me speak to her so that she understands that it is my decision, and not yours."

Lucy stood and went over to put her hand on Robert's shoulder. "Thank you."

He looked up at her. "For what?"

"For being so understanding."

"Me?" His smile was pained. "Mayhap I'm mellowing with age."

She kissed his forehead. "One can only hope so, seeing as you will soon be worrying for two children instead of one."

"Understand me, though, Lucy." He met her gaze, his expression resolute. "If there is any hint of her bringing further trouble on Ned, or if he is caught up in any violence, she will be turned off."

Lucy nodded. "I wholeheartedly agree."

35

He reached up his hand to clasp hers. "Then let's just hope I can knock some sense into James, Dermot, and any other of my employees making sheep's eyes at Polly."

"I'm sorry, Sir Robert." Dermot Fletcher repeated as he faced his employer across his desk. "But I cannot agree with you on this matter."

"I *beg* your pardon?" Robert stared at the flushed face of his land agent. "You can't agree that it is improper of you to chase after my nursemaid?"

"Of course, that's not proper, sir, but it's not what I meant." Dermot rushed to speak again. "I respect Miss Polly!"

"Then you have a funny way of showing it," Robert shot back. "Arguing with other staff, following her around like a lost sheep, making excuses to visit the nursery at all times of day, sometimes when you should be doing your own work."

"She is surrounded by those who are far beneath her," Dermot insisted. "She is not what she seems, Sir Robert. She is very intelligent and well read."

Robert studied his land agent's face. "Are you trying to tell me you might come to care for her?"

"I *do* care for her," Dermot said earnestly. "I have already considered asking her to be my wife."

Robert sat behind his desk and gestured for Dermot to sit as well. It was not in his nature to be circumspect, yet he would try his best.

"With all due respect, Dermot, you have only known her for a few weeks, and she is hardly of your social class."

"What social class?" Dermot replied. "I'm an Irish Catholic who earns his living in the same house as she does."

"Has she given you any indication that she favors your suit?" Robert asked.

"Not yet, sir." Dermot frowned. "She is beset by many fools, and she tries to be pleasant to all of them."

"Then, perhaps you might allow her the chance to make up her own mind when she is ready," Robert suggested. "From what I have observed, she treats all men the same."

Dermot met Robert's gaze. "You think I'm being a fool, don't you?"

"It is hardly my place to suggest anything of the sort, but—"

"You do think I'm a fool." Dermot sighed.

"I think that you are lonely, and that since Miss Anna Harrington became engaged to Captain Akers, you need to find a relationship for yourself."

Dermot winced. "Is it that obvious?"

"Only to those who know you well." Robert paused. "I just think it is too early for you to declare yourself to Polly Carter. She will be here for at least another quarter. Perhaps you should wait and see if she truly wishes to reciprocate your affections before you jump in and scare her off."

Dermot nodded. "I will think on what you have said, Sir Robert. Thank you for your counsel." He stood up and tried to smile. "I'd better get back to work. I probably have been neglecting things of late."

Robert asked him to send Foley in and waved Dermot away.

When Foley appeared, Robert gestured for him to sit down.

"I wanted to talk to you about James."

Foley raised his eyebrows. "Has he displeased you in some way?"

"Yes. Fighting with one of the ostlers from the Queen's Head, arguing with Mr. Fletcher, and pining over Polly Carter come to mind."

"Miss Polly is a pretty lass."

"Indeed, she is, but that doesn't mean my staff should stop doing their jobs. James is so busy defending her honor that he appears to have forgotten that his primary objectives are to serve this household and, more importantly, to safeguard my son from harm."

"He is a mite hotheaded about Polly," Foley admitted. "I've never seen him anything but kind and gentle before. These days, he threatens to fight anyone who as much as looks at her."

"So I've noticed." Robert shifted in his seat. "I want to speak to him personally. I'd also like you to address all the male household staff about their behavior around the female staff. Our nursery will be increasing in a few months, which will mean even more women in the servants' hall. I do not wish to hear of any problems."

"I understand, sir." Foley went to rise, which took him some time due to his rheumatism. "I was thinking James might make a fine butler after I retire."

"Until the last few days, I would've agreed with you. But I can't have someone brawling with potential visitors," Robert said. "Are you finally thinking about retiring then, Foley?"

"I think so, sir." His oldest retainer bowed his head. "You've settled down nicely now."

"I do believe I have." Robert offered Foley one of his rare smiles. "Lady Kurland has me well in hand."

"She does, sir. Thank God, and with another youngster on the way, your line is assured, and I can retire happy." Foley bowed.

Robert cleared his throat, aware that his butler was the last remaining member of his staff who had also served his parents. "You won't have to move far, you know. I'll find you a cottage on the estate, or in whichever of the villages around here you wish. Just say the word, and it will be yours."

"Thank you, sir." Foley straightened with some difficulty. "I'll think on the matter over the next few weeks. I'd planned to retire at Christmas, which gives you plenty of time to find my successor."

"Well then, let's hope young James minds his manners and redeems himself, and is ready to step into your shoes," Robert commented. "Send him to me now, Foley, and ask Agnes if she can spare Polly for a few minutes."

"Yes, sir."

While he waited for James to appear, Robert attended to the mail he'd picked up at the inn.

"You wished to see me, Sir Robert?"

"Yes, come in and close the door behind you."

He looked up as James entered and gestured for him to come forward. James's apprehensive stance reminded Robert of the young officers he had bullied and counseled into staying alive during the recent war. He decided young James could do with some brutal honesty and looked him right in the eye.

"I will not tolerate you fighting when you are in my employ, or tasked with guarding my son, or any member of my household. Do you understand me?"

James gulped at his arctic tone. "Yes, Sir Robert."

"If there are any problems with Polly and other men, I expect you to ensure the safety of my son and his nursemaid without resorting to violence."

"Polly doesn't encourage other men, sir," James protested.

Robert raised an eyebrow. "I didn't say that she did."

"She's a good girl, and one day, I hope she'll marry me."

"Has Polly suggested that she reciprocates your feelings?" Robert asked for the second time that morning.

"Recipro—what, sir?"

"Has Polly suggested she returns your affection?"

"No, sir, she hasn't, but that's because she's a respectable woman who wouldn't offer false hope, despite what Bert Speers says."

"If Polly is a respectable woman, she will not take kindly toward any man who gets into fights over her."

James nodded. "Yes, sir. She told me that herself." He shifted his weight from one foot to the other. "I promise I won't let you down again, sir."

Robert met his gaze. "You'd better not, or I can assure you that you won't be employed in this house for much longer."

"It's just that she doesn't ask for all the attention, sir, and I hate to see her being treated like she's a barmaid in a tavern, or something worse," James said earnestly. "There are people who mistake a kind word from her as something else entirely. Like Mr. Fletcher, sir, he—"

Robert held up his hand. "Mr. Fletcher is none of your concern."

"Yes, sir, but—"

"Rest assured that if the need arises, I will deal with Mr. Fletcher or any other man in this damn house who thinks he has a right to force himself on Polly's notice." Robert stared at James. "Are we quite clear?"

James nodded. "Yes, Sir Robert."

"Then go about your business." Robert waited until James had left before getting up from his desk and pouring himself a stiff brandy.

"Good, lord," he muttered. "I feel as if I've been thrown into a Drury Lane farce!"

There was another knock on the door, and Polly Carter came in. She wore a plain blue gown with an apron over it. Her blond curls were drawn away from her face under a cap. She curtsied low.

"You wished to see me, Sir Robert?"

"Yes, please come and sit down."

He resumed his seat behind the desk and waited for her to settle into her chair.

"I am concerned about the effect on my son of having you as his nursemaid."

Polly blinked her beautiful blue eyes at him. "How so, sir?"

Robert was done with diplomacy. "The men

who hover around you and their tendency to fight."

"I don't know what you want me to say, sir." Polly pleated her apron with her fingers. "I do my best to be pleasant to everyone who speaks to me, but I don't tolerate no rudeness, especially in front of your son."

"I'm not accusing you of anything, Polly. I'm just saying that I don't want my son put in a position where he has to run for his life when fists start flying." Robert studied Polly's anxious face. "I am aware that Lady Kurland wished to offer you the position of nursery maid for a full year. Due to the current situation, I have decided to be more cautious, and offer you employment only until next quarter day."

Polly stared at him for a long moment, a thoughtful expression on her face. "That's perfectly acceptable, sir, and I quite understand your position on this matter."

Having braced himself for tears and maybe worse, Robert found himself nodding with relief. "Good."

"Mayhap I should stay more in the grounds of the hall and not venture into the villages?" Polly looked hopefully at him. "At least for a short while until things have calmed down."

"I suggest you discuss that with Lady Kurland and Agnes," Robert suggested. "I would hate to restrict your movements."

Polly rose, straightened her skirts, and offered him an appraising smile. "You are a good man, Sir Robert. Most employers would've turned me off without even bothering to hear my side of the story."

Robert held her gaze. "And I will do so if my son comes to any harm."

She curtsied. "I can promise you that he will not suffer at my hands, sir." She turned and went toward the door, her carriage erect and her head held high. She glanced at the clock on the mantelpiece and then at him. "It's usually my half day, sir. May I still take it?"

"Of course." Robert said. "As long as Agnes is aware of your intentions."

Polly's lips curved into a mischievous smile. "Agnes thought I was going to be dismissed, so she offered to pack my belongings for me. I'll make sure she knows that isn't the case before I go out."

Robert had noticed some tension between the cousins but had accepted it as usual between family members. Did Agnes resent the fact the Ned obviously preferred Polly?

After Polly left, it occurred to Robert that the nursemaid was rather adept at managing the men in her life—including him—and that he had better not forget it.

Chapter 3

❧

"What is it, Agnes?" Lucy looked up from her letter writing to find her son's nurse hovering at her shoulder.

"I can't find Polly, my lady."

Lucy put down her pen. She was in her private sitting room at the rear of the house where she always started her day by interviewing the cook and her housekeeper, and then attending to the matters in her daybook.

"Is she unwell?"

"I don't know. She's just disappeared."

Lucy pushed back her chair and stood up, arching her back. "When did you last see her?"

"Yesterday around noon, just before she was asked to attend Sir Robert in his study." Agnes paused. "Is it possible that he dismissed her from her position?"

"He certainly didn't mention it, and I would've told you if the nursery were to be shorthanded. From what I understand of their conversation, Sir Robert merely warned Polly not to involve Ned in any of her romantic entanglements and offered her employment until quarter day."

45

"She didn't have the decency to tell me any of that." Agnes frowned. "But it doesn't surprise me."

Lucy headed for the back stairs, Agnes behind her, and ascended to the very top of the house where the servants had their bedchambers. The floor was deserted, as all the staff were already up and about. Lucy paused on the landing to catch her breath and waited for Agnes to join her.

"Which is Polly's room?"

"It's down here." Agnes turned left into the woman's section, walked down to the third door, and pushed it open. "Her bed doesn't look as though it has been slept in."

"No, it doesn't, but her possessions are all present." Lucy surveyed the gowns still on their hooks on the wall and the open chest full of petticoats, stockings, and undergarments. A tray of pins was scattered over the dressing table, along with a hairbrush and a discarded ribbon. Lucy also spied a half-filled bag.

"Yesterday was Polly's afternoon off," Agnes said. "When she returns, she usually pops her head into the nursery to say good night and to check on Master Ned, but last night she didn't come in at all."

"Mayhap she didn't return to the house," Lucy mused. "Is it possible that she spent the night somewhere with a friend and merely overslept?"

"She's only been here a month, my lady,"

46

Agnes pointed out. "She's hardly made any acquaintances except those in the house and on Kurland land."

Lucy turned a slow circle, trying to understand what had become of Polly, her thoughts flying in so many directions that she felt quite unwell. "I must speak to Sir Robert."

"Yes, my lady." Agnes hesitated. "Do you think she ran off?"

"I don't know," Lucy said. "She's your cousin. Do you think that is likely?"

"She seemed to like it here." Agnes grimaced. "Maybe it was too quiet for her, and she decided to go back to London."

"If that was the case, why would she not just pack up and go rather than agree to stay on for another three months?"

"I have no idea, my lady." Agnes headed for the door. "I need to get back to the nursery. Ned's upset enough as it is, what with Polly disappearing without a word . . ."

"Please go ahead."

Lucy paused to gather up a blue dress that Polly had thrown onto the floor and shook it out. There was a large mud stain on the hem of the skirt, which perhaps explained why she had discarded it rather than hanging it up. Her cloak was missing, as was her best bonnet and her stout boots—all things that she had probably been wearing as she left for her afternoon off.

But where had she gone?

Deep in thought, Lucy went down the stairs and found Robert in his study. He glanced up as she came in and immediately went still.

"What's wrong?"

"Polly's missing."

"As in has left entirely, or has not returned from wherever she went on her afternoon off?"

"Most of her possessions are still here, but she isn't." Lucy bit her lip. "Did she seem agitated when you spoke to her yesterday?"

"Not at all. In truth, she was remarkably understanding about the whole thing."

"Did you give her money?"

"No, of course not." Robert looked affronted. "We always pay our staff in arrears."

"Which means she was only paid last week for the first month of her service." Lucy frowned.

"An amount that I doubt would take her very far."

"I agree," Lucy said as she took a quick turn around the room. "Then I wonder where she is?"

"Perhaps she stayed overnight with someone and has forgotten the time?" Robert suggested.

"I had the same thought, but Agnes says Polly had not made many acquaintances outside the hall." Lucy looked over her shoulder at her husband. "Did Polly indicate to you that she planned to meet someone yesterday?"

48

"No, after our discussion, she asked me if it was still all right to take her half day. I told her to carry on. That was the last I saw of her."

"That's the last anyone saw of her." Lucy sighed and resumed her pacing.

"Didn't she go back upstairs to tell Agnes she was leaving?" Robert asked.

"Not according to Agnes. And she didn't pop her head in and say good night to Ned when she returned, either."

Robert frowned. "I told Polly to make sure Agnes knew she was going out, and she promised she would do so." He paused. "I got the distinct impression that she and Agnes were not getting along. Perhaps Polly decided not to tell her cousin out of spite, because Agnes had assumed she was about to be dismissed and had offered to do her packing for her."

"Agnes didn't mention any of this, but I had wondered if all was well between them." Lucy frowned. "Ned is very taken with Polly, and I don't think Agnes particularly cares for it."

Robert rose to his feet. "Let's find Foley and begin a search of the house and grounds."

He strode ahead of Lucy and entered the door that led to the kitchens and the butler's pantry. By the time she caught up with him, he was already speaking to his butler and the cook. From what she could tell, everyone was surprised by his announcement and was shaking their head.

"Where's James?" Robert asked, his sharp blue gaze scanning the kitchen.

Foley scratched his head. "I haven't seen him this morning. Have you, Mrs. Bloomfield?"

The butler and the cook exchanged glances before she replied in the negative.

Michael, the second footman, stepped forward. "Shall I go up and check his room? Maybe he's ill."

"Yes, please do that," Robert replied. "And come back here. I'll need you to go to the stables for me."

"Yes, Sir Robert."

Lucy leaned in and whispered, "I wonder if James is with Polly."

"I damn well hope not," Robert replied, equally quietly. "But the odds aren't looking good, are they?"

Dermot Fletcher came in through the back door, whistling, and then stopped dead as he saw his employers in the middle of the kitchen.

"Is something the matter?" he asked cautiously.

"Well, at least you are here," Robert said. "Polly is missing."

"Missing?" Dermot paled. "I saw her yesterday walking down the drive toward the village."

"At what time?"

"Just after midday. I heard the church clock chiming."

Michael came clattering down the back stairs

and came over to Robert. "He's not in his room, sir, and his bed hasn't been slept in."

Lucy pressed her hand to her rounded stomach and briefly closed her eyes as the room swirled around her. Had James and Polly impulsively left together without a stitch of extra clothing and none of their possessions? Or had they simply gone off and would return when they felt like it? Either scenario annoyed her.

"Miss Polly wouldn't—" Mr. Fletcher started to speak, and Robert cut him off.

"Mr. Fletcher, I need you to go into the village, alert the rector, and make sure that James and Polly are not availing themselves of anyone's hospitality."

"James's parents have a farm about a mile away, sir," Michael said. "They could've gone there."

"Yes, of course." Robert nodded. "Go down to the stables, Michael, and alert Mr. Coleman as to what is going on. Ask him to send the grooms out to search the parkland. When you have done that, please come back here with a gig so that I can go to Mr. Green's farm and ascertain if James has turned up there."

"Yes, Sir Robert." Michael hurried out through the scullery.

While Robert issued his stream of orders and went off with Mr. Fletcher, Lucy sank down into a chair and helped herself to a cup of the strong, fortifying tea Cook kept ready in a teapot on the table. She knew that in her current condition, Robert would not allow her to rush out and search for Polly. Not that she felt like rushing anywhere when it was hard to breathe and she still felt nauseous.

"Are you all right, my lady?" Cook asked.

"Yes." Lucy summoned a smile. "I'm just worried about Polly and James."

"Do you think they've run off together? The boy did think the world of her."

"It certainly seems possible." Lucy sighed as Cook dropped a crushed lump of sugar in her tea. "Thank you."

As the kitchen returned to normal, she sipped her tea and contemplated what to do next. It was morning, and it was quite possible that Polly and James would come back to Kurland Hall. What they expected to happen next was hard to contemplate, as Robert would no longer wish to employ either of them. Perhaps they would simply collect their things and leave.

Was it possible that James had somehow found Polly in distress and saved her from Bert, the ostler? Perhaps, at that point, Polly had realized that she cared for James and had confessed her love. James might have taken her to his parents' farm to receive their blessing and they had stayed the night.

Even to Lucy, such a scenario sounded like it

had been taken right out of a gothic novel, but then again, Polly did look like the perfect damsel in distress . . .

Lucy finished her tea and glanced over at the kitchen clock. There was little she could do at this time but speculate, and she refused to sit around worrying any longer. Agnes would be shorthanded in the nursery, and there was no one to take Ned out for his daily walk. She would change into her stout walking boots, find her cloak, and take her son to the park. Not only would she be getting some much-needed exercise, but she would also spend time with her son, who always required her full attention.

Robert put on his riding boots and thickest greatcoat and went out to the front of the house where Michael awaited him. He climbed up into the swaying gig.

"Do you know the way to the Greens' farm?" Robert asked as he settled onto the seat.

"Yes, sir." Michael gathered the reins and clicked to the single horse. "Just sit tight, and I'll get you there in no time."

"There's no need to rush," Robert stated. "I'd rather get there safely than not at all."

"Right, sir." Michael glanced over his shoulder as he carefully turned the gig around. It was fairly obvious to most of Robert's household that, unlike most country squires, their master was not comfortable around horses. Robert had long ago given up any pretense that he would ever be like the wild, horse-mad youth he'd once been.

He gripped the bench seat with one gloved hand and determinedly stared out over the flat fields that composed the bulk of his estate. Drainage was a major issue; it was a constant battle during the months when the Kurland River overflowed its banks and saturated his fields. Robert and Dermot had recently visited the estate of Coke of Holkham Hall in Norfolk to observe his methods of farming and gained some valuable insight into ditch digging and the power of water channels and windmills. They'd already started preparing the land closest to the river for new drainage.

The light dissipated as the overhead trees closed over the road like gnarly, interlocked fingers to form a green-tinged tunnel that darkened into an impenetrable gloom as they passed through the middle of a copse of oak trees.

"Not far now, sir," Michael said as they emerged once more into the light, leaving Robert blinking. "It's just past the Prentice farm."

"Thank you." Robert hadn't been out to visit the Green family for almost a year. They tended to come to see James at Kurland Hall and meet with Robert there, or to seek him out in Kurland St. Mary during market day.

There was no sign for the farm, but Michael seemed confident that the narrow track where he turned off was the correct one. Robert held onto his hat as the wind blew over the fields, making the growing wheat and corn rustle and sigh like a thousand whispers. The signs were that the harvest would be good, but one never knew what might happen with the weather. A week of rain could destroy the crops, and a week without it could have just as much of a devastating effect.

Such was the joy of farming . . . Robert was heartily glad that the main part of his income came from his family interests in the industrialized north, which continued to prosper even while his farming income waxed and waned.

He shaded his eyes as the farmhouse and outbuildings of the Greens' farm came into view. The stone-and-brick cottage had been re-thatched a year ago, and looked sturdy and well kept. Even as the gig drew to a stop among a cacophony of honking geese and barking farm dogs, the front door opened, and Mr. Green came out.

"Sir Robert!" He strode over to the horse and held its head while Robert stepped down to the ground. "I was just about to drive over to Kurland Hall."

"Why is that, Mr. Green?" Robert asked after a hearty handshake.

"Well, come in and see for yourself." Mr. Green walked back to the front door and bellowed down the hallway. "Sir Robert's here himself, Gwen! No need for us to worry."

Robert followed him into the farmhouse and down the hall to the large, sunny kitchen at the rear of the building, where he discovered Mrs. Green tending to her son James, who lay on a settle covered with a blanket.

"Good morning, Sir Robert," Mrs. Green said. "Did you come seeking my son?"

"Indeed I did, Mrs. Green. Good morning to you," Robert removed his hat and sat down near James. "What happened?"

James sighed heavily and turned toward Robert. "Someone hit me, sir."

"Were you fighting again?" Robert asked quietly.

"*No,* sir. I was just walking to the village from the hall. Someone came up behind me and hit me hard enough to knock me off my feet."

"In broad daylight, Sir Robert!" Mrs. Green interjected. "What is the world coming to?"

"I have no idea, Mrs. Green," Robert said politely, and then returned his attention to James. "Then, how did you end up here, over a mile away from where you fell?"

"I don't know, sir." James groaned. "The next thing I remember was Nell, my dog, sniffing and pawing at me, and then I heard my father's voice."

Robert looked up at Mr. Green, who had sat on the trestle by the kitchen table, hands on his spread knees. "Where exactly did you find him?"

"Near the bottom of the track up to the farm, sir." Mr. Green patted one of the dogs that had gathered around him. "Not that I found him by myself. If it hadn't been for the dog, he could've lain there all day, seeing as I wasn't planning on going out." He nodded at his son. "I was up at five, milking the cows, when Nell practically dragged me out there by grabbing hold of my sleeve with her teeth."

"Clever dog," Robert said. "So none of you know how James came to be lying on your land after being attacked somewhere close to Kurland Hall?"

"I know it sounds odd, sir, but that's the truth of it," Mr. Green assured him. "We're just glad the boy is all right."

"Thanks be to God," Mrs. Green murmured.

Robert continued to study James, who was struggling to meet his gaze. "Would it be possible for me to speak to your son alone for a moment?"

Mr. and Mrs. Green exchanged puzzled glances. "If you wish, sir. We can go into the parlor."

"Thank you."

Robert waited until they left and then turned to James.

"I understand that you might not wish to reveal the truth of your actions in front of your parents, but I would ask for a full accounting now, please. Did you get into a fight with Bert Speers?"

"No, sir. I swear it."

"Did you see Polly yesterday?"

James's hand crushed the patchwork quilt in his fist. "I got off work just after she did, so I was . . . following her to Kurland St. Mary."

"Did you speak to her?"

"No, sir." James vigorously shook his head and then winced. "She was too far ahead. I tried to shout out to her, but I doubt she heard me."

"Or she chose to ignore you. Go on."

"Go on with what, sir?" James blinked at him. "I didn't catch up with her. Just before I reached the church, someone jumped me from behind, and that's the last thing I remember."

Robert contemplated his footman, who did look rather worse for wear and had a bloody wound on the side of his head.

"Did you see where Polly went when she entered the village?"

"No, sir. She was blocked from my view by the church."

"And you remember nothing since yesterday afternoon until your father found you early this morning?"

"That's correct, sir." James hesitated. "Did Polly say something different? Is that why you're asking me all these questions?"

It was an interesting thing for James to ask—almost as if he feared to be blamed for something. Robert considered his young footman and decided to be blunt.

"Polly has disappeared. I was rather hoping I'd find her here with you."

Lucy sat at her dressing table as Betty redid her hair. It was a windy day, and Lucy suspected that her loose curls would not fare well in the breeze when she ventured out on her walk. She'd instructed Betty to braid her hair tightly to her head so that she could fit it under her bonnet.

"That's much better." Lucy admired her reflection. "Thank you."

"You're welcome, my lady." Betty slid another pin into place. "Have you any news about Polly?"

"Not yet." Lucy sighed. "I can't believe she has just run off."

"Mr. Foley did say that James was missing, too." Betty paused hopefully. "Mayhap they are together. That will really put Agnes's nose out of joint. She's always been sweet on James."

"I didn't know that." Lucy turned in her seat so that she faced Betty. She wasn't normally one to gossip with the staff, but Betty had been with her since she'd lived in the rectory and was a trusted confidante. "Did you think Polly and Agnes got along well?"

"Not at all, my lady. Agnes is right jealous because Master Ned prefers Polly, and so does James." Betty set about tidying the pins. "Agnes wasn't pleased by that, and she let her cousin know it." She tutted. "The arguments those two had after Ned had gone to bed."

"They argued a lot?"

Betty nodded vigorously. "Yesterday morning, when I went up to the nursery to look for your missing book, my lady, I heard them through the wall. Agnes was insisting Polly was going to be dismissed, and that it was her just comeuppance. Polly would have none of it."

It occurred to Lucy that this must have been just before Polly went down to speak with Robert, never to be seen again.

"Agnes said that it would be a blessing if Polly left, and Polly accused her of being jealous." Betty straightened the bed coverings. "Polly didn't half slam the door on her way out down the stairs."

"Oh, my goodness," Lucy said. "Perhaps that is why Polly decided not to come back."

"I suppose it's possible, my lady, but why would she leave without her possessions?" Betty looked doubtful. "Do you remember when Mary went missing from the rectory? She took everything with her."

Despite the seriousness of that occasion, Lucy almost smiled. She would never forget that particular incident, which had drawn her into an uneasy alliance with a bedridden Robert and eventually ended up in their marriage.

Betty came over and patted her shoulder. "Now

don't fret too much, my lady, especially in your condition. Sir Robert wouldn't like that at all."

"You're right," Lucy agreed. "But I do feel somewhat responsible. Polly is in my employ, and she seemed to want to stay on at least for the next quarter."

"Perhaps she's as flighty as she looks, and got a better offer, and decided to play us all for fools." Betty went toward the door. "That girl always struck me as a deep one, my lady."

Lucy considered Betty's opinion as she readied herself to go up to the nursery. It was all so confusing. Polly hadn't told her cousin that she was leaving for her half day; Agnes hadn't mentioned that she and Polly had been arguing just before Polly left. But who was telling the truth?

Lucy decided not to say anything to Agnes until Robert returned from visiting the Green family. If Polly and James were found together, there would be plenty of opportunities to discuss the matter further.

Chapter 4

I found James at his parents' farm." Robert came into Lucy's sitting room and shut the door behind him. "He has no idea where Polly is."

Lucy frowned. "Then where has he been? Foley told me that James only had a half day yesterday and did not have permission to stay the night at the farm."

"James claims that someone hit him on the head, and that he woke up the next morning in his father's hay cart with his dog next to him," Robert commented.

"You don't sound as if you believe him." Lucy studied her husband's face.

"Because it is quite fantastical! How can he not know how he ended up at his parents' farm?" Robert asked. "If he really was hit on the head, then why would his attacker pick him up and deposit him nearly a mile away where he was sure to be found?"

"I agree that it does sound somewhat strange," Lucy said slowly. "It makes one wonder why the person who supposedly attacked James knew him well enough to know where he lived."

"James lives here now, Lucy, and has done so for several years," Robert reminded her. "Why didn't his attacker drop him off at our front door?"

"Perhaps because he would've been found too quickly?" Lucy looked up at her husband. "If the person simply wished to get James out of the way, then the longer before he was discovered, the better."

"Mr. Green did say he wouldn't have found James so quickly if it hadn't been for his dog." Robert shoved a hand through his hair and sat down opposite Lucy. "And I'm still not convinced he was even attacked."

Lucy stilled. "Do you think he was fighting over Polly again?"

"Or fighting *with* Polly." Robert sighed. "He says he saw her walking ahead of him into the village, but that she was too far ahead to notice him."

"I suppose that is possible." Lucy bit her lip. "Robert, are you really suggesting that James is lying about everything?"

"I dealt with a lot of young men in my time in the cavalry, Lucy, and I'm fairly good at spotting the liars, the bullies, and the cowards." Robert hesitated. "I don't think James is telling me the truth, but I don't know why."

"Perhaps he argued with Polly, and she was the

one to knock him out, and he's too embarrassed to admit it."

"It's possible, but how did he end up at his parents' farm?"

"He could've walked there," Lucy pointed out. "If he truly was dazed, he might have forgotten that."

"True." Robert was still frowning. "He did seem genuinely shocked when I told him that Polly was missing." He raised an eyebrow. "I assume she hasn't been found yet."

"Not yet. I was thinking I might go down to the Queen's Head and see if she bought a ticket on the mail coach." Lucy said.

"I'll go. I haven't had a chance to change yet, and the gig is still outside." Robert went to stand. "You stay here and rest."

"I'm not an invalid, Robert." Lucy sat up straight. "I'm not even tired."

"I am quite aware of your capabilities, my love, but I'd rather you coordinated our efforts to find Polly from *here*." Robert went toward the door. "If Polly is discovered before I return, send one of the grooms to find me."

With that, he was gone, leaving Lucy feeling mildly aggrieved at his display of high-handedness. In moments of stress, he had a tendency to order her around as if she were of inferior rank. Too restless to return to her book, Lucy went out into the hallway and toward the main entrance, which was in the oldest part of the house and led into the medieval hall.

She'd asked Foley and Mrs. Bloomfield to organize a search of the manor house, which, because of its construction, contained many unexpected nooks and crannies, staircases that went nowhere, and dark cellars. Polly wouldn't be the first member of her staff who had accidentally wandered off and gotten lost.

Mr. Fletcher had gone down to the rectory, and Aunt Rose had volunteered to check all the houses in the village. Lucy's father had ridden out to the outlying parishes of Kurland St. Anne and Lower Kurland to make sure Polly hadn't gotten lost on her walk and sought shelter somewhere.

On one of their shared walks with Ned, Polly had confided to Lucy that she found the countryside a confusing and somewhat frightening place—what with the open fields and lack of light. It was possible that she had just lost her way.

Lucy paused at the bottom of the stairs, for once unsure how to proceed. She could go up to the nursery and see Ned again, but she would be disrupting the routine she had very firmly put in place purely out of her own restlessness. Her certainty that Polly hadn't merely gotten lost and that something was truly wrong consumed her.

"Lucy?"

She blinked and turned to the now-open front

door, where her sister Anna was smiling at her.

"Anna!" Lucy hurried toward her sister and embraced her. "How lovely! I was not expecting you back until next week!" She took her sister's hand. "Come and tell me all about your visit with the Akers family. How was Harry?"

Anna laughed and patted her shoulder. "Goodness me, Lucy. So many questions when all I want to do is run upstairs and see how my adorable nephew is!"

"You may go and see him later," Lucy said firmly as she gestured to Foley, who had come into the house behind her sister. "But, first, we will have some tea."

"As you wish." Anna untied the ribbons of her bonnet to expose her natural blond curls held in a loose bun on the top of her head. "I only just arrived back at the rectory, and no one was there except Cook. I decided to come up to the hall to see you first and tell you my news."

Anna pulled off her gloves and held out her left hand for Lucy to inspect. "I married Captain Akers."

Lucy gasped and pressed a hand to her chest. "You are *married?*"

"Yes." Anna blushed adorably. "I know you will wonder at such haste when we had decided to wait, but while I was staying at his home, he received new orders that will take him from our shores for almost a *year.*"

Anna's bright smile dimmed. "Harry tried to pretend that everything was all right, but I knew that in his heart he was worried that another year of delay would make me forget him entirely." She shrugged. "Not that such a thing is possible, but you know how men are."

Lucy couldn't imagine Robert even thinking such a thing, but she nodded encouragingly.

"He asked me if I'd consider marrying him before he left, and I said yes," Anna continued somewhat breathlessly. "He managed to obtain a special license, and due to the necessity of speed, I was unable to invite my friends or family to join me. I do hope you will forgive me for that, Lucy."

"Of course!" Lucy agreed. She was disappointed not to have been present, but she was so surprised Anna had gone ahead with the marriage that her emotions were a mere nothing. Her sister had always been averse to marriage because of her fear of having a child.

Captain Harry Akers had not only gained Anna's love, but had convinced her that he was willing to do everything in his power to protect her from her own fertility. Lucy knew such intimate details only because she had inadvertently overheard a private conversation when she'd visited the Akerses and Anna had sought her advice.

"Where is Captain Akers now?" Lucy asked.

"He had to report to Southampton at the earliest opportunity." Anna looked as if she was trying not to cry. "His mother asked me to stay with her while he was gone, but I wanted to come home first and share my news with everyone."

Lucy took Anna's hand in hers. "I'm so happy for you, my dearest sister. Father will be delighted."

"He will certainly be surprised." Anna hesitated. "Do you think his feelings will be hurt that he was not able to officiate at the wedding?"

"I suspect his pleasure at your wedded state will easily outweigh his disappointment, Anna," Lucy said robustly. "When Captain Akers returns, perhaps Father can hold a ceremony blessing the marriage in Kurland St. Mary church."

"I'm sure he'd love to do that." Anna nodded. "And I'm quite certain Harry would not object at all."

Foley appeared with a tray of tea that he placed in front of Lucy.

"Apologies for the interruption, my lady, but I wished you to know that we have completed the search of the house and have found no trace of your missing maid."

"Thank you, Foley." Lucy busied herself pouring tea as Anna unbuttoned her pelisse. "Did you walk up here, Anna?"

"Yes, because there was no one at home, which was most odd, because I sent a letter ahead announcing the time and day of my arrival." Anna took her cup. "Is something amiss?"

"My new nursemaid didn't come back after her afternoon off yesterday," Lucy said as she offered Anna a biscuit. "The whole village and hall are out looking for her."

"The poor girl!" Anna exclaimed. "That explains why Aunt Rose was not at home and Father's favorite horse was missing from the stables."

"They should be back soon enough," Lucy said. "I can send someone down to tell them that you are here at the hall if you wish."

"I told Cook. I'm fairly certain she will tell Aunt Rose when she returns, so there is no need to worry." Anna looked over at Lucy and smiled. "You look very well."

"Thank you." Lucy's hand came to rest on her rounded stomach. "I'm expecting another child in December."

"Oh!" Anna's smile dimmed. "Are you . . . happy about that?"

"I am." Lucy smiled to reassure her. "It's wonderful news."

"Yes, of course. How selfish of me not to immediately congratulate you." Anna reached for Lucy's hand. "You must think me such a shrew."

"Not at all." Lucy well understood her sister's fears. Losing their own mother in childbed had put its mark on both of them. "Robert is also pleased. He believed we would all spoil Ned rotten if he remained an only child."

"If you wish, I will stay with you until the birth, and then return to visit the Akers for the remainder of Harry's voyage," Anna offered eagerly.

"That would be lovely," Lucy said. "Otherwise, you will leave me with Penelope, who will tell me not to be silly about the pain of childbirth after she sailed through it with barely a squeak."

Anna rolled her eyes. "I would not wish ill on any woman having a child, but Penelope has been rather obnoxious since the birth of little Francis."

Lucy poured more tea, more grateful than she could've imagined to have her sister back with her at Kurland Hall to gossip with. "*And* she warned me that my new nursery maid was too beautiful and would encourage Robert to stray."

Anna spluttered into her tea. "She did not."

Lucy nodded. "Unfortunately, it is that particular maid who is missing. I'm rather surprised Penelope hasn't been up here to inquire whether Robert is still in residence and to remind me that she said that the girl would be trouble."

"I do hope she is found." Anna set her cup back on the table. "Perhaps I should stay here at the hall for a few days before I return to the rectory. I can help you manage the nursery until she returns."

"I would appreciate that greatly." Lucy smiled

at her generous sister. "As long as Aunt Rose and Father won't object."

"They will understand." Anna waved away Lucy's objections with a chuckle. "After I tell them about my unexpected wedding, they might kick me out altogether!"

Robert sent Michael around to the stable yard with the gig and went directly into the Queen's Head, where he found the proprietor, Mr. Jarvis, behind the bar.

"Afternoon, Sir Robert."

"Good afternoon." Robert nodded. "Do you have a moment to speak to me privately?"

"Of course, sir." Mr. Jarvis beckoned Robert to follow him into the back of the old inn and through to the kitchen. "I'll get Mrs. Jarvis. She won't want to be left out."

Inwardly, Robert sighed, as Mrs. Jarvis tended to be rather garrulous and was very fond of speaking her mind.

He waited in the small snug room to the right of the kitchen, with its low black beams and white wattle and daub walls, until they both joined him.

"Polly Carter didn't return from her afternoon off yesterday," Robert said. "Did she purchase a ticket for the mail coach here?"

The husband and wife looked at each other and then at Robert. "Not that I know of, sir," Mr. Jarvis answered for them both.

71

"Is it possible that she obtained a ride from another source without paying for it?"

"With her pretty face, I have no doubt that any number of men would've been willing to take her up," Mrs. Jarvis said. "But I can't say that I saw her here at all yesterday. Did you my love?"

"No, but I'll go and ask at the stable if you'll wait here for a moment, sir." Mr. Jarvis looked askance at Robert.

"I'd appreciate that."

Mrs. Jarvis decided to keep Robert company after her husband left. It didn't take her long to start talking again.

"If Polly had bought a ticket for the mail yesterday afternoon, she would've had to wait until this morning to leave, and she didn't stay here last night."

Robert grimaced. "I hadn't thought of that. Thank you."

"It's more likely that she smiled at some young farmer and he took her wherever she wanted to go. Where's she from?"

"London, I believe," Robert replied.

"Then the mail coach would have been the most sensible route." Mrs. Jarvis nodded. "If she could afford the ticket."

"She received her first month's wage last week."

"Was she not content up at the hall?"

"As far as I am aware, she was well settled."

"She was a nice girl, always happy to chat, and very respectful of her betters," Mrs. Jarvis commented. "Perhaps she got some upsetting news in that letter she picked up when you came in the other day."

"Perhaps she did." For once, Robert was glad that the landlady was willing to gossip and had noticed that Polly had received mail, which he certainly had not. "Her family is still in London."

"Then maybe that explains it." Mrs. Jarvis smoothed down her apron. "She waited for her money and left at the first opportunity. You'll probably get a letter as soon as she gets home."

"I would've preferred it if she'd just given her notice in the traditional manner," Robert commented. "Leaving without a word to any-one—even her cousin—is highly irregular."

"The young rarely think of these things, Sir Robert, do they?" Mrs. Jarvis heaved a sigh that almost dislodged her bounteous bosom from the low-cut bodice of her gown.

"Is Bert Speers still employed here?" Robert asked.

"I believe so," she said cautiously. "Mr. Jarvis had a word with him the other day about Polly, and he insisted that she was deliberately enticing him." Mrs. Jarvis chuckled. "As if a girl like that would be interested in plain old Bert. I told him so as well."

Robert picked up his hat. "Perhaps I will make

my way out to the stables and find Mr. Jarvis. I'm probably keeping you from your work."

"It's no trouble talking to you, sir." She winked as she opened the door. "Although we wouldn't want any gossip flying around the village about the two of us, would we?"

"No, we would not." Robert excused himself and hurried toward the door that led into the coach yard and stables that sided onto the old inn. He'd already overcome one misunderstanding with his wife over the landlady of the Queen's Head, and he was reluctant to incite another incident.

Mr. Jarvis was already stepping out of the stables and came over to where Robert was standing.

"No one remembers seeing Polly Carter here yesterday, sir."

"Thank you." Robert paused. "What about Bert Speers?"

"He's not here today."

"Why not?"

"It's his day off, Sir Robert." Mr. Jarvis gestured at the half-empty yard. "We're never that busy on a Tuesday. I need them all here on market days and Saturday."

"Will you let me know when he returns?" Robert asked

"You think Polly might be with him?"

Robert noted the incredulity in the landlord's

voice, but he wasn't prepared to ignore any possibility, which stopped him worrying about much worse scenarios.

"One never knows the way a woman's heart works, Mr. Jarvis." Robert replied. "Just let me know when he returns. I wish to speak to him."

"Yes, sir. I'll do that."

Robert found Michael and climbed into the gig. After they drove out into the village proper, he turned to his servant.

"Did you hear any gossip about Polly while you were in the yard?"

"None, sir. No one had seen her, either." Michael shortened the reins. "I asked most specifically."

"Then where is the damned girl?" Robert muttered to himself as they retraced their journey back to Kurland Hall.

If Polly hadn't purchased a ticket to leave on the mail coach, had she persuaded someone to drive her all the way to London? It was possible that some besotted fool might have done so, but in that case, who had dealt with James? Was it possible that the two incidents were entirely unrelated? Past experience told Robert that they must be inextricably entwined.

He set his gaze on the horizon and attempted to order his thoughts as the two men approached the gates of Kurland Hall. Mrs. Jarvis had also mentioned that Polly had received a letter. Had she not needed to buy a ticket because someone had sent her money or driven down to Kurland St. Mary to pick her up? If they had, that might explain why James had been knocked out. Had he witnessed something? Gotten involved in a scuffle with Polly and some unknown man?

Robert was heartily glad when the gig drew up in front of his home. If there was anything he needed right now, it was a conversation with his eminently sensible wife.

Chapter 5

❧

S ir Robert?"

Lucy looked up as Foley came into the breakfast parlor, his expression anxious. After she had discussed everything with Robert the previous evening, Lucy's sleep had been disturbed by violent dreams that had kept her awake half the night.

"What is it?" Robert lowered his paper.

"Giles Durley is here and wishes to speak to you urgently."

Robert dropped his newspaper onto the table. "I'll come at once."

Lucy rose, too, and Robert looked back at her. "You don't need to disturb yourself, my dear."

She raised her chin. "I am coming with you."

He didn't bother to object again but set off at a fast pace, leaving her rushing along behind him. The Durley family were farmers on the side of the Kurland estate that sloped down toward the river, and had been there for several generations.

"Sir Robert, Lady Kurland." The farmer took off his hat and bowed to them both.

"Good morning, Mr. Durley. What do you need to see me about?" Robert asked.

Giles grimaced. "We were working on the new drainage ditches, sir, like you told us to do, and we found a body at the bottom of one of them."

Lucy pressed her fingers to her lips while Robert instinctively stepped in front of her as if to shield her from the horrible news.

"Do you think it might be Polly Carter, our missing nursemaid?"

"Yes, sir. Me and the missus met the lass the last time we were in Kurland St. Mary." Giles cleared his throat. "We covered her up all decent like, and I have her in the back of my cart."

"Thank you." Robert nodded. "Perhaps you might take her body down to Dr. Fletcher's house in the village, where she can be properly laid out."

"If you wish, sir." Giles put his hat back on. "The poor lady. May she rest in peace."

"Amen," Lucy whispered as Giles bowed and left them in the study. She turned to Robert and struggled to clear her throat. "We should go to Dr. Fletcher's."

"*I* will go." He held up his hand. "Please don't argue with me."

"I am not going to argue with you. I am going to fetch my cloak!" Lucy responded and whisked herself away before he could say another word.

• • •

Robert didn't say anything as Lucy climbed into the gig with him, her expression resolute. He'd learned over the years that his wife was almost as stubborn as he was, and that he must choose his battles wisely. She might look frail, but she was never one to shirk her responsibilities, and he respected that, even though it sometimes made him worry.

Before he left, he told Foley to keep an eye on James, who was now recuperating in his room, and not to let anyone in to visit with him. As Foley had guessed what had happened to Polly, he was quick to act on Robert's orders and sent Michael upstairs to sit outside James's door.

Robert didn't bother to make conversation as he drove the gig down the drive of Kurland Hall and along the country road to Kurland St. Mary village. There weren't many people out at this time of day, but those who saw the gig raised their hats or curtsied as they progressed past the farm cottages, the small collection of shops, and onward toward the duck pond, where the village school sat opposite Dr. Fletcher's house.

The children were out playing in the school-yard, watched over by the new teacher and one of her assistants. Robert acknowledged the school-mistress's wave as he circled the pond and came to a halt outside the doctor's house. Unwilling to encounter Penelope, Patrick's acerbic wife, he assisted Lucy down from the gig and entered the house from the side door where his friend welcomed his patients.

The room Patrick used to concoct his medicines and perform surgical tasks was beyond his study, and Robert headed toward that door.

Patrick glanced up as Robert appeared, looked past him, and raised an eyebrow.

"Lady Kurland? Perhaps you might go and speak to Penelope. She is remarkably upset by this matter and could do with the benefit of your sound advice and calm counsel."

"It seems as if you are both determined to keep me away from the body," Lucy said. "I will go and speak to Penelope, but do not expect me to remain with her for the rest of our visit!"

Robert came in and closed the door; the smell of cleaning fluids and other unpleasant substances weaved around his nose, making him close his mouth tightly. There was a body laid out on the large marble slab Patrick had somehow obtained from a butcher's shop and used for his examinations.

"It's definitely Polly Carter," Patrick said.

"Do you have any idea how she died?" Robert asked.

"She was strangled. That much is obvious already." Patrick lightly touched Polly's waxen cheek. "See the mottled purple of her skin and the bruising around her throat?"

Robert leaned in to observe more closely. In death, Polly looked like a beautiful, sculptured angel.

"She obviously tried to fight off her attacker." Patrick gestured at her hands. "She's even broken some of her nails, and there's blood as if she scratched his face . . ." He paused. "She's even got a handful of the bastard's hair clutched in her fingers."

Robert's gaze traveled down from Polly's damaged throat to the disarray of her clothing. One of her boots was missing, and her dress was muddied and torn at the hem.

"Was she raped?" he asked abruptly.

Patrick didn't flinch at the brutally direct question. They'd worked together during the worst military campaigns in France and Spain. This wasn't the first dead woman they had seen or had to deal with in their official capacities.

"I don't know yet." Patrick straightened up. "I'll need to remove all her clothing and take a closer look at everything."

"Are you quite certain that the injuries couldn't have been caused by her simply losing her way and falling into the drainage ditch?" Robert asked.

"Unless she had her hands around her throat and was attempting to strangle herself when she fell, then no," Patrick said dryly. "I assume she attempted to fight off an attacker who ended her existence."

"I wish this hadn't happened right now," Robert muttered. "Lucy will insist on getting to the bottom of it, and I'd much rather she stayed home, put her feet up, and looked forward in peaceful anticipation to the birth of our second child."

Patrick chuckled. "If that is what you truly wish, then I believe you married the wrong woman. With all due respect, if Lady Kurland chooses to involve herself in this matter, no one is going to stop her."

Robert took a seat at Patrick's desk. "As I suspect you are correct, I intend to stay here and watch you work before I venture forth to issue a full report to my wife."

"Well, I won't say I didn't tell you so." Penelope poured Lucy a cup of tea and then sat back in her chair.

"Tell me what?" Lucy wasn't in the mood to be helpful, while Penelope was oozing smugness.

"That it was a mistake to hire Polly Carter."

"You told me that she would run off with Robert," Lucy pointed out. "As far as I can tell, she didn't run off anywhere and has probably been murdered."

"Lucy, when you employ a girl like that—"

"Like what?" Lucy asked. "Polly was extremely hardworking and well-liked by all the staff up at the hall."

Penelope waved away her reply. "She was far too beautiful, and you know it. Girls like that *always* bring trouble on themselves."

"I hardly think that her being beautiful means that she deserved to be murdered," Lucy said stubbornly. "You are quite beautiful, and no one has murdered you, yet."

Penelope sat bolt upright. "Because I understand that being beautiful is a burden, and that I have to be very careful not to be *over-familiar* with any man."

"Polly was not over-familiar, and even if she was, it doesn't mean that she deserved to be killed." Lucy put her cup down with such force that the saucer rattled.

Penelope tutted. "Please don't get angry, Lucy. It is bad for the baby."

"I am *not* angry, I am simply—"

"Attempting to defend the indefensible," Penelope spoke over her. "Perhaps Polly did something that enraged her attacker? Mayhap she had more than one lover, and was playing the odds, and got caught?"

"And maybe she was just walking down to the village on her afternoon off and was attacked by a crazed madman for no reason whatsoever!" Lucy realized her voice was rising with every word, and that she *was* now shouting, and was, in fact, quite angry after all.

She shot to her feet, almost knocking her cup

over. "I am going to speak to Dr. Fletcher. Please excuse me."

Penelope stood, too, her hand outstretched. "Lucy, please don't do that, Patrick said—"

Lucy marched toward the door, Penelope at her heels, and went into Dr. Fletcher's empty office. Robert appeared at the interior door and blocked her view of whatever Dr. Fletcher was doing to the body on the marble slab.

"Perhaps you might wait until Dr. Fletcher has finished his examination, my dear."

Lucy glared at him. "I would prefer to see Polly now."

He came toward her, and his fingers closed gently on her elbow. "And I would prefer it if you waited. You are obviously upset."

"I am upset because Penelope has been regaling me for the past quarter of an hour with her *opinions* of how Polly should've been more careful."

"That's not what I said at all, Lucy!" Penelope exclaimed. "I merely suggested that she might have inadvertently caused what happened."

"Which is what my wife just said." Robert motioned for Penelope to step back from the doorway. "Will you allow me to come into the parlor and explain what Dr. Fletcher has discovered so that he may get on with his work?"

"If you must." Lucy was aware that she

sounded grudging, but she wasn't prepared to moderate her tone.

"I will go and see if Francis is enjoying his midday meal." Penelope excused herself after one last reproachful glance at Lucy and stomped up the stairs, her head held high.

Robert drew Lucy into the parlor and closed the door behind them.

"You were rather rude to Penelope."

"She was being insufferable," Lucy replied. "She immediately assumed that poor Polly had done something to deserve to be murdered!"

Robert leaned up against the door and regarded her carefully. "One cannot completely discount the notion that Polly's death was not a random act of violence, though."

"What are you suggesting?"

"I'm saying that it is unlikely there was a murderer roaming the Kurland lands who luckily came across Polly and killed her."

His calming tone steadied her, but she was still not willing to give up the fight. "Then you do think she caused her own death."

"No!" He frowned at her. "Stop jumping to ridiculous conclusions, and look at the facts. We know that Polly was attracting a lot of attention from men. We also know that she was afraid of one of those men."

Lucy nodded. "Bert Speers."

"Exactly. And James was attacked yesterday,

which is another strange coincidence, wouldn't you say?"

"I suppose you do have a point." Lucy moved restlessly around the room. "But Penelope—"

"Often says things that are insensitive and rude." Robert interrupted her. "And thus her opinion, in this case, can be discounted."

Lucy went over to Robert, who immediately wrapped his arms around her.

"I'm sorry."

He kissed the top of her head. "For getting annoyed with Penelope? It's hardly the first time you've done that."

"I'm . . . a little emotional at the moment," Lucy confided, her cheek settled comfortably against the dark blue of Robert's waistcoat.

"I can't say I've noticed," he said dryly.

Lucy placed the palm of her hand on his chest and burrowed even closer. "When my mother was pregnant with the twins, one of our maids was let go because she was with child."

He stilled. "I don't understand what—"

"Anna and I were upset because we'd liked her very much. Cook said she had deserved her fate, and that it wouldn't have been right to have a fallen woman in a good Christian household with innocent girls around." Lucy slowly raised her head to look at Robert. "But how could that be true when it was my father who had sinned with her?"

"Lucy, my dear love . . ." Robert cupped her cheek. "I had no idea." He gently kissed her nose. "Did your father know the child was his?"

"I assume so, seeing as he sent money to her family every year for the child's upkeep." Lucy took a deep, shuddering breath. "I'm sorry. I have no idea why I felt the need tell you that particular family secret."

"Probably because you are with child, and because you are worried about Polly."

"Precisely." She found a smile somewhere, glad for his prosaic answer, and tried to appear reasonable. "Now, what were you going to tell me about Polly?"

Robert's brow creased. "Are you sure you want to know what Patrick told me, or would you prefer not to hear the details?"

"I'd like to know. Polly is—I mean, was—one of our servants."

"She was strangled," Robert said flatly. "She obviously attempted to fight off her attacker, but whoever it was prevailed."

"My goodness," Lucy whispered.

Robert took her hand and led her to sit by the fire. "One thing I learned from my days in the cavalry, investigating such matters, was to look at my men's faces to see if anyone had been scratched or hit." He grimaced. "It narrowed the field of suspects considerably and often proved a good indicator of the culprit or culprits."

Lucy shuddered. "Did James have a scratched face?"

Robert shifted in his seat. "Yes, but he had been fighting with Bert Speers and was left in a bramble patch on his parents' farm."

"Do we know where Bert Speers is?"

"Presumably, still at the Queen's Head. After we leave here, I'll go down and speak to Mr. Jarvis."

"Poor Polly," Lucy murmured. "I need to return to Kurland Hall and let Agnes and the rest of the staff know what has happened."

"We'll go as soon as Dr. Fletcher has finished his examination," Robert promised. "I really would prefer it if you let me deal with this. I promise I will tell you everything he says."

"As you wish." Lucy realized she was far too tired to argue with him. The thought of seeing Polly's dead body made her uncharacteristically nervous.

"Thank you." Robert reached over to squeeze her fingers and gestured at the tea tray. "Do you think Penclope would mind if I helped myself to some tea? It's rather too early to start on the brandy."

When Patrick came to find him, Robert followed him back into his surgery where Polly's body was now decently covered with a sheet.

"As far as I can tell, she wasn't raped," Patrick

88

said. "But she did receive several blows to her body that resulted in bruising and cuts."

"With a weapon?" Robert asked.

Patrick grimaced. "No, just someone's fists." He went to wash his hands. "Poor girl didn't stand a chance."

"I assume you can keep the body here until we find out what Polly's family wants to do with it?"

"Yes, of course. Our cellar is very cold." Patrick gestured at a box on his desk. "Do you wish to take her clothing?"

"I suppose I should." With some reluctance, Robert picked up the box. "I know that my wife will wish to keep everything for Polly's family."

"Do you have any idea who might have done this, Major?" Patrick asked, instinctively reverting to Robert's old cavalry rank.

"Seeing as every man in Kurland St. Mary thought Polly was the most beautiful woman they'd ever seen, the list of suspects is quite wide," Robert commented. "But I have a few ideas."

Patrick dried his hands and opened the door into his study. "I saw her with James, your footman, a few times in the village."

"Indeed." Robert wasn't going to be drawn on the possibilities quite yet.

"I also heard that James was knocked out the other day."

Robert paused to look back at his friend. "Who told you that?"

Patrick shrugged. "Just the usual village gossip. Remember, I go in and out of people's homes every day. They tell me some very interesting tales."

"I'd appreciate it if you kept your suspicions to yourself."

Patrick had the gall to laugh. "As if that would make a difference in a small place like this, where everyone knows everyone else's business. Something as sensational as a murder will only encourage more gossip."

"Unfortunately, due to our past experiences in this matter, I know that all too well." Robert sighed. "Thank you for your help."

Patrick offered him a mock salute. "You're most welcome, Major."

Robert went across to the parlor and discovered that Penelope had brought her son down from the nursery. He had nothing against the boy, who had the sweet nature of his father. He also had no interest in amusing any child but his own.

Lucy had already risen and was coming toward him, her expression expectant.

"Do we need to leave, my dear?"

"Yes, if we are to speak to Mr. Jarvis at the Queen's Head and alert our staff to this dreadful occurrence." He bowed to Penelope, who was feeding her son a biscuit from her plate. "A pleasure to see you, Mrs. Fletcher. Thank you for the tea."

"You are most welcome, Sir Robert." Penelope's glance slid toward Lucy, and she lowered her voice. "One can only hope that your wife will recover her temper soon."

"My wife is entitled to her own opinions," Robert said. "And she is more than capable of speaking for herself." He offered Lucy his arm. "Shall we go, my lady?"

Lucy was smiling as he handed her into the gig.

"What is so amusing?" Robert asked.

"You are." She patted his cheek. "You might not agree with a word I say in private, but in public you are always on my side and my staunchest defender."

"Which is just as it should be." He walked around and hauled himself up into the gig. "Do you wish to accompany me to the Queen's Head before we go back to the hall? It is on our way."

"That would suit me very well." Lucy settled her skirts around her and drew her cloak closed at the throat. "Did Dr. Fletcher have anything more to add to his conclusion that Polly was strangled?"

"Only that she was beaten," Robert said, his gloved hands curling into fists. "I wish I had the bastard who did that to her in front of me now."

"I am not one to revel in violence, but in this

instance, I cannot help but agree with you," Lucy said.

"Dr. Fletcher mentioned that he had seen Polly out walking with James."

"Oh, dear." Lucy sighed. "If Dr. Fletcher noticed them together, then everyone in the village will immediately leap to the obvious conclusion."

"That James murdered Polly?" Robert frowned. "He grew up here with a family who are well known and liked. Do you really think people will believe that about him?"

"Whether they believe it or not is hardly the issue, is it? They will talk about it. James had better stay up at the hall until we have cleared this matter up."

Robert negotiated the turn onto the village high street. "But what if it was James?"

Lucy was quiet for some while before she answered him. "We already know that love can turn ugly—that reasonable people can do unthinkable things when they feel threatened."

"Agreed." Robert slowed the horse down and nodded to one of the local shopkeepers who had stepped out to watch them go past. "Don't forget, we still have to speak to Bert Speers."

He drew the gig up in the enclosed courtyard of the Queen's Head, glad that it wasn't market day and that the mail coach had long since gone. One of the ostlers ran out to hold the horse's head.

"Morning, Sir Robert."

"Good morning, Fred. We'll only be here for a short while, so there's no need to stable the horse."

"As you wish, sir. I'll get one of the lads to hold onto him for you then."

"Thank you." Robert helped Lucy down, and they went through the side door that led directly into the inn.

Mr. Jarvis came to greet them, his expression troubled.

"If you're here for Bert Speers, sir, he didn't come back last night."

"Did he not?" Robert glanced down at Lucy before returning his gaze to the landlord. "Are his possessions still here?"

"Yes, sir. I checked his room." Mr. Jarvis grimaced. "I heard about what happened to Polly Carter. If Bert does turn up, I'll lock him up myself."

"If you would, I'd appreciate it greatly." Robert nodded. "And let me know immediately, because it is imperative that I speak to him."

"Understood, sir." The innkeeper nodded.

Robert escorted Lucy back to the gig, and they rode home in silence along the narrow cow-parsley-lined lane until they turned in through the gates of Kurland Hall.

"I'd best speak to Agnes first." Lucy visibly braced herself.

"We'll speak to her together." Robert briefly clasped her hand. "I assume she has an address for Polly's mother?"

"Yes." Lucy lapsed into silence again as they pulled up in front of the main door.

"Are you feeling quite well?" Robert asked as he walked around to help her down. "Would you prefer it if I spoke to Agnes alone?"

"I'd prefer it if we both talked to her." She flashed him a tired smile. "And then I might take a restorative nap."

He ushered her straight through the hall and into his study, where he asked Foley to make them some tea and to fetch Agnes. While they awaited her arrival, Robert paced in front of the fire.

"You wished to see me, Sir Robert, my lady?" Agnes spoke from the door.

She looked her usual immaculate self, her lace collar ironed to perfection and her petticoats rustling with starch.

"We have some sad news about your cousin, Polly," Robert said. He strongly believed in getting straight to the point when being the bearer of bad news. "Her body was discovered in a drainage ditch on the Durley farm."

Agnes gasped and pressed her hand to her mouth. "Oh, my lord."

"I'm sorry for your loss, Agnes. I can assure you that Lady Kurland and I will do everything in our power to find out what happened to Polly and, if necessary, to bring the wrongdoer to justice."

"What have I done?" Agnes whispered, her eyes wide and her words barely audible. "Why did I ever allow myself to get caught up in this terrible muddle?"

Robert raised an eyebrow and looked over at Lucy, who approached Agnes.

"I'm not quite sure what you are trying to say, Agnes. No one is blaming you for what happened," Lucy said.

"If I hadn't allowed *that woman* to come here . . . and bring such grief to this family—"

"As I just said, Agnes, no one is blaming you," Lucy said firmly. "I know that you and Polly didn't always see eye to eye, but that's often how it is with one's family. It doesn't mean that you didn't care for her or that you should feel guilty in any way."

"But she *wasn't.*" Agnes was openly sobbing now.

"Wasn't what?" It was Lucy's turn to offer Robert a puzzled glance.

"Part of my family." Agnes gulped hard. "I'd never clapped eyes on her in my life before she turned up at Kurland Hall."

Chapter 6

As Agnes continued to cry, Lucy led her to a seat by the fire, offered her a new handkerchief, and waited patiently for the storm to pass. When Agnes appeared to have sufficiently composed herself, Lucy met her gaze.

"I thought Polly was your cousin."

"She *is,* ma'am—well, Polly Carter is, but that wasn't her."

"I don't quite understand. Are you saying you were duped?"

"No, my lady."

"If the Polly we met wasn't your cousin, then why didn't you mention it when she arrived bearing a letter from me offering her a position in my nursery?" Lucy asked.

Agnes swallowed and stared down at her apron. "Because when she came upstairs after meeting with you, she handed me a letter from my cousin Polly explaining what had happened, and why she was here instead."

"And yet you didn't think to mention it to me or to Lady Kurland?" Robert intervened, the irritation in his voice quite apparent. "Did it not occur to you that introducing a complete stranger into our household, one who was to care for our *son,* was perhaps something that we should have been made aware of?"

Agnes dissolved into tears again, and Lucy frowned at Robert. He was far too used to dealing with military subordinates to have the finesse necessary to coax answers out of a distraught female.

She curbed her own impatience until Agnes composed herself.

"You said that your cousin Polly sent you a letter. What did she say?"

"She asked me to let the Polly you know take up her position."

"Did she explain who she was sending in her place?"

"No, my lady. I don't even know her real name. My cousin Polly said that the deception was necessary, and that she would vouch for her friend."

"And that was sufficient for you to allow this fraud to take place?" Robert asked.

Agnes's worried gaze flicked toward Robert, who had retreated to the window seat but was still staring at her intently.

"She gave me money," Agnes whispered. "A lot of money—more than two years' wages."

Lucy attempted to conceal her surprise and disappointment with her son's nurse, but feared she made a bad job of it as Agnes again began to weep.

"I'm so sorry, my lady, sir. I don't know what I was thinking. She promised me 'Polly' would be gone in a month, which didn't seem long enough for her to cause any mischief." Agnes looked up. "And she was good at her job, respectful to me for the most part, and Ned liked her. If that hadn't been the case, I would've told you earlier, I *swear* it."

"But Polly agreed to stay on for another quarter," Lucy said slowly. "Is that why you were arguing just before she disappeared?"

"Yes, my lady. I told her I would reveal the truth if she stayed on."

"And what was her response?"

"She laughed and told me to go ahead and see how long I kept my own job. She said she liked it here." Agnes dabbed at her eyes. "I knew she was right. I wished with all my heart I had never allowed myself to get caught up in something so wrong."

Robert cleared his throat. "Don't we all?" He walked back over to the fireplace and stared down at Agnes. "Perhaps you might return to the nursery. My instinct is to let you go without a reference, but Ned has had enough disruptions in his life this week without depriving him of his nurse. We will reconsider your employment at the next quarter day."

Agnes stood and bobbed a curtsey. "Thank you, Sir Robert. I am so sorry, my lady."

She rushed out of the room, and Robert turned to Lucy.

"Please don't suggest that I was too harsh with her."

"I won't. I have never been so shocked in my life! What on earth possessed her to do such a foolish thing?"

"Money, of course," Robert said grimly. "Two years' wages for what she thought was going to be one month of a different Polly Carter in our house? I can almost understand her reasoning—except this concerns *my* house and *my* son, and I can't help but be enraged by such a deliberate deception."

Lucy let out a slow breath. "If Agnes was desperate enough to conceal what she had done, was she desperate enough to kill Polly?"

"I hadn't thought of that." Robert paused before continuing, his gaze assessing. "But I doubt she would've had the strength to strangle Polly."

"Perhaps she paid someone to do it for her?" Lucy suggested. "She certainly had the money to do so."

"It is still rather unlikely, but I will not discount it," Robert said. "Should we get rid of Agnes immediately, then?"

"My instinct is to agree with you, but if we do suspect her of murder, then it would be better if we knew where she was," Lucy said. "I'll ask Anna to supervise the nursery and pay close attention to everything Agnes does."

"I suppose it will have to suffice." Robert moved restlessly around the room. "But I have to tell you, Lucy, that the mere idea that Agnes and Polly were around our son *appalls* me."

"I'm sorry, too." Lucy met his gaze squarely. "As I was responsible for hiring Agnes in the first place, the blame lies squarely with me."

He waved away her concerns. "She isn't the first person to be corrupted by money, and she won't be the last. You did everything you could."

Lucy rose to her feet. "I'll go and speak to Anna, and then I'll go to Polly's room, and see if I can find any evidence of who she really might be."

"That's an excellent idea. I had Foley take up the box of her possessions Dr. Fletcher gave me to her room as well. Let me know what you discover." Robert went over to the door.

"What are you going to do?" Lucy inquired.

His face settled into grim lines. "I'm going to have another conversation with James."

Robert went up to the top floor of the house, where Michael was sitting patiently outside James's bedchamber. Michael jumped up when he saw Robert and stepped back from the door.

"Morning, Sir Robert."

"Good morning, Michael. You may go down to the kitchen. I'll let you know when you should return."

"Yes, sir."

Robert went into James's small room, bending his head to avoid the blackened beams that formed the structure of the Elizabethan roof. James was sitting up in bed, a Bible at his side.

"Sir Robert, I'm feeling much better today. May I resume my duties?"

"Not quite yet." Robert sat on the only chair and stared at his footman. The bruises and scratches on his face were less vivid now, but still obvious.

"We found Polly Carter."

The relief on James's face was immediate. "Is she all right?"

"No. Her body was recovered on the Durleys' farm."

James briefly closed his eyes, his hand fumbling to find his Bible. "I . . . don't know what to say."

"Perhaps the truth?"

"I *told* you what happened, sir," James blurted out and then stopped, a look of horror transforming his expression. "Do you think—I *killed* her?"

Having learned the value of silence early on in his military career, Robert continued to study James.

"I *loved* her! Why would I want to do that?"

Robert shrugged. "Love is a very strong emotion, and closely akin to hate."

"I didn't kill her." James's mouth set in a firm line.

"Then who did?"

"Bert Speers? Mr. Fletcher?" James shook his head. "Anyone but me, sir, I *swear* it."

Robert let another long moment elapse before he replied. "I am the local magistrate, and I'm responsible for investigating and prosecuting crime in this vicinity. It is therefore my duty to find out who killed Polly Carter. I will carry out that duty without regard to whether I know the murderer or his family."

"You're saying that if it is me, you'll send me to hang."

"Yes." Robert held James's anguished gaze. "Now, is there anything else you wish to tell me about what happened when you last saw Polly Carter?"

Lucy went into Polly's bedchamber and surveyed the contents of the room. On her instructions, no one had entered or attempted to clean it since Polly's disappearance had first been discovered.

She started by stripping the bed linen and found nothing but a small, tattered piece of shawl tucked under the pillow that looked as if it might have belonged to a child. Ned had a blanket that he loved to curl his fingers into while he slept.

Lucy wondered whether Polly had kept her own keepsake. Not that it had helped to keep her safe from the monsters . . .

Lucy dropped the dirty bed linen outside the door and turned her attention to the trunk in the corner. She sat on the chair and methodically emptied out the contents, checking pockets and the insides of shoes and handkerchiefs as she went. A faint smell of perfume permeated the garments along with another, more oily scent Lucy couldn't identify. At the bottom of the trunk she discovered a set of playbills for a theater in London and took them over to the window to read.

The playbills featured a variety of theatrical experiences, including recitations of Shakespeare, dancing, comedy, and tragedy, which was fairly standard for the more popular theaters in London. Two of the bills were for a theater called the Corinthian, which apparently was located close to Covent Garden, and the third was for the Prince of Wales.

Lucy hadn't visited London very often and couldn't remember attending a performance at either of the establishments. Had Polly kept the playbills because she had enjoyed the shows, or was there a closer connection? At this point, that could be anything. Lucy could only hope that closer inspection would reveal more clues as to Polly's real name and previous occupation.

She laid all the garments on the bed and lined up the shoes on the floor beneath it before turning to the dressing table. She tidied up the hairpins, spare buttons, sewing thread, and needles into their respective containers. Opening the first drawer, she checked and then rolled up the woolen stockings before placing them on the bed along with Polly's spare petticoats and underthings.

The second, smaller drawer held Polly's spare handkerchiefs, neckerchiefs, and mittens. There was also a garish red lip color in a tin that smelled as strongly of oil as the trunk. Lucy reached farther into the drawer and discovered a small velvet box tucked right at the back.

"Goodness me," Lucy murmured as she turned the key to reveal the contents. "I wonder where this jewelry came from. It is rather fine." She carefully lifted out a diamond necklace and two rings and checked beneath the satin lining of the box. There was a single card wedged into the box with distinctive slashing handwriting on it.

"To Flora Rosa, with my continued devotion." Lucy read the words out loud. Unfortunately, the final signature was impossible to decipher.

Lucy kept the playbills and the jewelry box on the dressing table and packed everything else away. She would take her findings to Robert and see what he had to say on the matter.

Before she left, Lucy's gaze lingered on the trunk.

"Is that your real name? Flora Rosa?" Lucy whispered. "It doesn't sound real, but I wish you peace, and I swear that I will do everything I can to get you justice."

She closed the door behind her and went down the stairs to find Robert.

He was sitting in his study, a frown on his face as he massaged his forehead.

"Ah, Lucy, come in."

She shut the door and went over to his desk, placing the items she'd found on the surface.

"What did James have to say for himself?"

"He insists he didn't kill her, but he did admit to catching up with her before she reached the church."

"My goodness." Lucy brought her hand to her mouth.

"He says that they argued, she told him to leave her be, and he let her walk away from him."

"I assume this was before he was hit on the head?" Lucy asked.

"Yes." Robert grimaced. "He's now saying that he thinks he saw her with Bert Speers just in front of the church. I'm not sure I believe him."

"Because now that he knows Polly is dead, James needs to make sure he is seen as innocent?" Lucy suggested. "And implicating Bert

Speers is the easiest way to clear his own name?"

"Yes, that's exactly what I thought." Robert let out a frustrated breath. "Am I being too cynical? I've known James all his life. He's never struck me as the kind of man to murder someone and then blatantly lie about it. I've known people to kill in a moment of anger, but they are usually so overcome with guilt and remorse after the fact that, when confronted with the evidence, they usually confess."

"I think you are dealing with him in exactly the right way," Lucy hastened to reassure him. "You are attempting to be fair but not allowing your natural tendency to defend someone you have personal knowledge of to override your judgment."

"I can try and find out if anyone in the village saw Polly walking with another man that day," Robert suggested. "That would help to corroborate James's story. But until then, I think he'd do better to stay in his room."

"I agree." Lucy nodded. Have you heard anything from Mr. Jarvis at the Queen's Head?"

"Not yet." Robert shoved a hand through his hair. "Did you get Polly's mother's address from Agnes?"

"Yes. I will write to her immediately and get Michael to take the letter directly down to the mail coach so that it will be received as quickly as possible."

"Good," Robert said and gestured at the items Lucy had placed on his desk. "What have we here?"

Lucy handed him the playbills and opened the jewelry box to reveal the card. "I think that Polly's name might be Flora Rosa. Somebody wealthy must have given her these jewels."

"Then why was she working here as a nursery maid for a pittance?" Robert asked.

"She did say that she was glad to get out of London," Lucy said slowly. "Maybe she was running away from something or somebody?"

"And decided to bring her problems into my household?" Robert demanded.

"It didn't make any difference, though, did it?" Lucy reminded him. "She still died."

"And embroiled us in yet another case of murder," Robert grumbled.

"The card is addressed to Flora Rosa." Lucy attempted to regain her husband's attention and draw him away from his personal grievances. "The signature is unreadable."

Robert picked up the card, put on his spectacles, and squinted at the handwriting. "It's a single word. That's all I can make out. Flora Rosa sounds like the name an actress might use."

"I didn't think of that." Lucy pointed to the playbills. "Is she listed in them?"

Robert started reading, discarding the first two bills from the Corinthian and pausing as he ran his gaze over the long list of players at the Prince of Wales.

"Ah. Here she is. It doesn't say what part she plays, but there is definitely a Flora Rosa listed."

"I suppose our Polly could've worked for this actress and stolen the jewelry," Lucy pointed out.

"But our Polly was certainly beautiful enough to have enjoyed some success on the stage and to have gained herself an admirer."

"As I have no knowledge of such things, I will assume that you are correct." Lucy gave him a rather sharp gaze.

Robert shrugged. "As a young man, I did loiter in the green rooms of some theaters."

"I am aware of that—seeing as that's how you met Mrs. Jarvis from the Queen's Head."

Lucy would rather not discuss his youthful appreciation of the ex-actress, who had remembered him rather too well for Lucy's liking when she'd given up the stage and married the landlord of the local inn.

"I wonder if Mrs. Jarvis might still have contacts with the theater in London?" Robert said. "She might even have heard of Flora Rosa."

"I doubt it, but I am quite happy to ask her," Lucy offered. "But if we really want to find out what happened to send Flora Rosa running to Kurland St. Mary, we will have to go to London and investigate the matter for ourselves."

Robert put the jewelry and the playbills in his desk and locked the drawer.

"Before we get ahead of ourselves, my dear, perhaps we should discuss what else we can discover here. Bert Speers is still missing, and James is not telling me the whole truth. The only suitor I can completely clear of murdering Polly is Dermot Fletcher, who spent the last two days at my side catching up on his work."

"We don't know exactly when Flora Rosa was murdered. Dermot could've trapped her somewhere and killed her later," Lucy demurred.

"We did go out and speak to the Durleys, so perhaps you have a point." Robert groaned. "Maybe Dermot saw her wandering around their fields with another man and was overcome with rage."

"I agree that it sounds unlikely." Lucy paused. "I forgot something."

"What?"

"To examine the clothes Flora was wearing when she died."

"I told Foley to leave the box in her bed-chamber. Wasn't it there?"

Lucy rose to her feet. "I think I moved it to strip the bedclothes. I'll go and find it right now. I am so forgetful!"

Robert had no desire to poke through his murdered nursemaid's garments, but he waited patiently for Lucy to return with the box.

When she did, she extracted Flora's gown and wrinkled her nose at the creased fabric before setting it aside.

"Is there anything in a pocket?" Robert asked.

Lucy gave him a patient look. "Her dress doesn't have pockets." She delved in the box and brought out a long strip of narrow fabric with two bags attached to it. "Here they are."

She frowned as she explored the interior of one of the bags. "I haven't found her coin purse yet, or her wages, and they don't appear to be here, either. Perhaps it was just a robbery."

"I doubt that, but please carry on," Robert said.

She undid the string on the other bag, which produced a crackling sound, and withdrew a letter that she held up to Robert.

"Mrs. Jarvis said she'd received a letter. That must be it." He gestured at Lucy to read it.

Lucy unfolded the single sheet and held it up to the light.

"My dear friend, all is not well here. Your flight has been discovered, and your destination is known. Be very careful."

"Well, that isn't very helpful," Robert said.

"It does indicate that Flora was in danger," Lucy pointed out. "And that Polly Carter was trying to protect her."

"We don't know if that letter was from Polly," Robert countered.

"Who else would be writing to her?"

"Her protector?"

"Surely, if she had a powerful or wealthy man 'protecting' her, she wouldn't have felt the need to run away in the first place." Lucy held up a finger. "Unless that was who she was running away from."

Robert took the letter and read it for himself. "The handwriting is quite crude and probably not that of a gentleman, which might indicate that you are correct about the letter being from Polly."

"Thank you." Lucy looked at him expectantly. "Now when do we depart to London to find the real Polly Carter and ask her what on earth is going on?"

Chapter 7

⁕

Lucy made her way to the kitchen, the box containing Flora's possessions in her hands. She would ask the housekeeper to launder the clothing and return everything to Flora's bedchamber.

Robert had avoided answering her question about the necessity of a trip to London by claiming he had to meet with Mr. Fletcher and leaving his study before she could stop him. As it was unlike him not to be honest with her, she had a suspicion that his reluctance to engage on the matter was because he didn't want her to come with him.

"Of course, he doesn't want you to come," Lucy murmured to herself. "Why would you even doubt that?"

"Excuse me, my lady?"

Lucy looked up to discover Foley holding the door into the kitchen open for her.

"Good morning, Foley." Lucy stepped past him. "Is Mrs. Bloomfield here?"

"I believe she's out at the Home Farm this morning, my lady," Foley said. "I told her to take one of the footmen with her. We don't want what happened to young Polly happening again, now, do we?"

Lucy nodded and took the box through to the scullery. "Will you ask her to have these clothes laundered and returned to Polly's room?"

"I will, my lady." Foley followed her back into the kitchen. "I was just about to take this message to Sir Robert." He held out a folded piece of paper. "It came from the Queen's Head."

"Thank you." Lucy scanned the letter. "Will you bring the gig around to the front of the house and *then* take this to Sir Robert?"

By the time her husband emerged from the house, she was already sitting in the gig awaiting him. His steps slowed as he approached, and he raised an eyebrow.

"You're coming with me?"

"Indeed." She offered him a challenging smile. "Have you not yet learned that I am not very biddable?"

"I knew that before I married you." He stepped up into the gig and took the reins from her. "I did have hopes that vowing to *obey* me might curb your impulses, but it seems that I was mistaken."

She bristled at his words—and then realized he was smiling, and contented herself with pinching his arm instead.

"You will not stop me coming to London with you, either."

"I'll certainly try." Robert set off. "But perhaps we should call a truce and deal with Mr. Jarvis at the Queen's Head before we commence hostilities?"

The journey down to the inn didn't take long, and they were soon pulling up in the busy stable yard. Robert got out and handed Lucy down, and one of the ostlers moved the gig out of the way.

Mr. Jarvis met them in the hall, his expression grim.

"He arrived back here this morning on the mail coach. He wasn't very cooperative, so I put him in the cellar and locked the door."

"Thank you." Robert touched Lucy's shoulder. "Perhaps you could ask Mrs. Jarvis if you might examine Bert's possessions while I go with Mr. Jarvis and deal with this matter?"

For once, Lucy decided to humor him. She had no desire to be stuck in the cellar with an angry or violent man.

"As you wish." She smiled sweetly at Robert.

"See how easy it is to obey one's husband?" he murmured into her ear before turning back to Mr. Jarvis and following him into the public bar of the tavern.

Lucy sniffed and went to find Mrs. Jarvis, who was more than willing to allow her access to Bert's shared room above the stables.

". . ."

"I'll come in with you, sir, if you don't mind," Mr. Jarvis said.

"I don't mind at all," Robert replied as Mr. Jarvis picked up a large cudgel propped against the outside of the locked and barred door.

Like a lot of the older buildings in Kurland St. Mary, belowground the inn had remnants of the monastery and church that had once stood in its location. The elegant, curved ceilings of the cellar, with their stone pillars, looked somewhat out of place among the barrels and dusty bottles.

The second they entered the room, Bert Speers sprang up from his cloak-covered bed and came toward them. His hair and clothing were disordered, and his chin was black with stubble.

"What the bloody hell is going on? Why am I being held here and treated like a criminal?"

"I was hoping you could tell me that," Robert said. "Where have you been for the last three days?"

"I don't have to answer to you," Bert sneered.

Robert turned to Mr. Jarvis. "As his employer, I'm fairly certain you have the right to ask the same question."

"Aye, you can't just disappear for days without telling anyone where you've gone, Bert."

Bert rolled his eyes, which did nothing to endear him to Robert. "I had to go home. My mother needed me."

"You didn't think to ask my permission?" Mr. Jarvis asked. "Why not?"

"Because I had to go immediately! I told Jeremiah."

"Strange that Jeremiah didn't mention it to anyone, then."

"That's not my fault, Mr. Jarvis, now, is it?"

"Where exactly did you go?" Robert inquired.

"Back to London," Bert said. "Where else? I bought a ticket and got on the mail coach. If you don't believe me, ask Henry Haines next time he's here."

"I will ask him," Mr. Jarvis said. "Don't you worry about that."

Robert leaned back against one of the upright casks of ale and regarded Bert carefully. "Perhaps you might clarify something else for us. When did you last see Polly Carter?"

Bert frowned. "What's she got to do with anything?"

"Please answer the question," Robert ordered, his tone hardening.

"Why? Has she been telling tales about me again?"

"She hasn't said a word." Robert kept his gaze on Bert's face. "When did you last speak to her?"

"That's none of your business."

"Don't you be disrespectful to Sir Robert." Mr. Jarvis brought the cudgel up toward Bert's face

116

in a menacing manner. "You answer his question or I'll wallop you."

"I spoke to her the day before I left," Bert said grudgingly. "I told her to stop playing silly games and getting me into trouble, or I'd make her pay for it."

"Did you now?" Robert let the silence fall around them.

"Did I what?" Bert frowned.

"Make her pay?" Robert continued to stare until Bert started to shift his feet.

"I might have tried to shake some sense into her, but if she's saying anything different, then she's lying."

"She's dead," Robert said flatly. "Perhaps your attempt to 'shake some sense into her' turned violent and you *inadvertently* murdered her."

A red flush rose from Bert's throat to suffuse his face. "I didn't bloody kill her!"

Mr. Jarvis glanced at Robert. "I'd lay odds on who the liar is here, sir."

"I didn't kill her!" Bert shouted, the sound echoing off the low stone ceiling. "Why would I do that?"

"Because you are a violent jealous man?" Robert asked. "The kind of scoundrel who would rather beat a woman who chooses not to care for him than find someone else?"

He straightened up and met Bert's furious

117

gaze. "You'll stay here until I can speak to Henry Haines."

"You can't do that!" Bert growled.

"I damn well can." Robert stepped closer. "As I've already told you, I'm the local magistrate, and it's my job to investigate local crime and prosecute offenders."

He nodded to Mr. Jarvis. "Let's leave him to think about his choices, shall we? Perhaps a period of quiet reflection will make him more forthcoming."

As Robert and Mr. Jarvis left, Bert spun away to repeatedly smash his fist against the wall.

"I don't care what he says, Sir Robert. It's as clear as day that he's guilty," Mr. Jarvis observed as they mounted the stairs back to the bar.

"That remains to be seen, but he didn't do himself any favors behaving like that, did he?" Robert agreed. "No wonder Polly was afraid of him."

"Well, as to that, sir . . ." Mr. Jarvis paused to shut and lock the cellar door behind them. "I *did* see her talking to him once or twice without there being any trouble. Which was why when Mrs. Jarvis told me that he'd been following her home, I wondered what was going on."

"I didn't realize that," Robert said. "I received the distinct impression from Polly that she was afraid to go near him."

"Maybe they were in the middle of a lover's

tiff, and Bert lost his temper with her when she didn't want to make up?"

"What time does the mail coach usually arrive?" Robert asked.

"Around eight in the morning, Sir Robert." Mr. Jarvis poured two pints of ale and handed one to Robert. "Do you want to speak to Henry yourself?"

"I think I'd better," Robert said. He took a grateful sip of his beer and then another, more appreciative swallow. "I think I'll sit here, finish my ale, and wait for Lady Kurland to find me."

Mrs. Jarvis cast a disgusted look around the small cramped room and wrinkled her nose.

"It smells like a fox's den in here and looks like one as well. I'm right sorry about that, Lady Kurland."

Lucy remained in the doorway as Mrs. Jarvis stomped through the mess, picking up garments and throwing them randomly onto the two beds.

"Which side belongs to Bert Speers?" Lucy asked.

"This side. The one that looks like he emptied out his entire possessions on the floor before he left us in the lurch for three days."

"Maybe he did empty everything out," Lucy said slowly. "Perhaps he wanted to make sure that there was nothing here to incriminate him if he didn't return."

"Which begs the question of why he came back," Mrs. Jarvis said.

Lucy slowly raised her head from her contemplation of the mess. "I suppose we'd better look through everything and see if we can find that out."

Breathing carefully through her mouth, Lucy delved into the pile of clothing and checked pockets and straightened garments until there was a neat pile on the bed. She picked up one of the discarded boots and gingerly turned it upside down. A small leather purse fell out, and she picked it up.

"That doesn't look like a man's purse, does it, my lady?" Mrs. Jarvis commented.

"No, it doesn't." Lucy released the leather string and counted the coins that fell into her palm. "I wonder where he found this?"

"And why he hid it in his boot." Mrs. Jarvis held out a folded letter to Lucy. "This was folded up, real small-like, in his waistcoat pocket."

Lucy read the letter and frowned. "I can't make much sense of it."

"Give it here." Mrs. Jarvis whisked it out of her hand. "Looks like lots of numbers to me. Maybe bets he intended to place? He did like to gamble, that one."

Lucy reclaimed the grimy piece of paper, put it aside with the purse, and contemplated the pile of clothing. What had brought Bert Speers back to Kurland St. Mary? She would take the things they had found back to Robert and see if he had gained any information from Bert that might help uncover his reasoning.

Mrs. Jarvis set about tidying Jeremiah's side of the room while still muttering about both men and their lack of cleanliness. Lucy waited until she'd finished and then stood up herself.

"I would appreciate it if you kept what we found to yourself, Mrs. Jarvis. I don't want Bert knowing we've been through his possessions."

"I won't tell a soul." Mrs. Jarvis drew a cross over her bosom. "Except for Mr. Jarvis, that is. I can't keep anything from him."

"As he accompanied Sir Robert down to the cellar, I think he will have his own secrets to keep, don't you?" Lucy opened the door, letting in a welcome blast of fresh air. "You have both been very helpful."

"If Bert was the one to murder that poor girl, then he deserves everything he gets," Mrs. Jarvis said fiercely. "I'll be the first one at his hanging if he's guilty." She sighed. "He did seem to be really sweet on her at first, but seeing her with James set him off in a black mood, and he never recovered from it."

Lucy reentered the inn and found her husband ensconced on a stool, enjoying a pint of ale with the innkeeper.

"Are you ready to depart?" she asked.

In reply, Robert drained his tankard, offered Mr. Jarvis some coin, which was declined, and came over to Lucy.

"Bert will be residing in the cellar for at least another night while we investigate his claim to have been in London for the past three days." He nodded to Mrs. Jarvis and led Lucy out to the coach yard. "Did you find anything interesting?"

"Yes, indeed. I'll show you when we get home." Lucy allowed him to assist her into the gig, and they set off.

Robert waited in his study for Lucy to go upstairs, take off her bonnet, and check in on Anna and Ned. Dermot had left some correspondence on his desk for him to sign, so he occupied himself with that until his wife reappeared.

"Is everything all right in the nursery?" Robert asked.

"Ned is rather ill-tempered. Anna says he is missing his Polly and his James." Lucy sighed. "Agnes is not herself, either."

"I'm quite glad to hear she at least has a conscience," Robert replied as he poured them both some coffee. "If she was happy as a lark again, I might reverse my decision about keeping her on."

"It is just so unsettling for Ned," Lucy said. "I promised to take him down to the stables later, but he cried and said he wanted to go with James."

"I'll take him," Robert said abruptly.

His wife studied him for a long moment. "Mayhap we could both go."

"I'm quite capable of dealing with my son for an hour or two."

"I know you are, but he does tend to get rather excited around the horses, and—"

"You wouldn't want me panicking and making things worse." Robert finished the sentence for her.

"I wasn't going to put it quite like that, but—"

"It's all right. I am well aware of my limitations." Robert scowled at her. "Take him yourself."

She reached for his hand, his gaze steady. "Come with me. Ned would be thrilled."

"Perhaps tomorrow after I've spoken to the mail coach driver." He finished his coffee in one gulp and refilled his cup. "Now, would you like to hear what Bert Speers said, or do you want to tell me what you found in his room?"

Lucy brought out a small leather purse and placed it on the desk. "I found this wedged in one of Bert's boots."

Robert opened it and allowed the coins to spill out. "It's hardly a fortune, is it?"

"It's exactly what we paid Polly for her first

123

month of service," Lucy said. "And I just showed the purse to Agnes, who confirmed that Polly had one that was very similar."

Robert counted the coins. "You didn't find Polly's purse with her, did you?"

"No, which makes one suspect that this might well be hers, and that Bert took it from her at some point."

"He claimed he saw her in the village and warned her not to make up stories about him, or she'd be in trouble."

"He *admitted* that?"

"Yes, which I found quite remarkable. When I told him Flora was dead, he lost his temper, insisted he hadn't killed her, and that he'd been in London for the past three days visiting his sick mother."

"How very convenient for him," Lucy sniffed

"Indeed." Robert paused. "He didn't seem particularly surprised, either. But if he did kill her, why on earth did he come back to Kurland St. Mary?"

"Mrs. Jarvis had the same thought." Lucy nodded. "Everything in his bedroom had been turned upside down as if he'd departed in a great hurry. Perhaps he came back because he realized he'd left Flora's purse here and feared it would be discovered."

She offered him a much-folded piece of paper. "He also had this in his pocket. Mrs. Jarvis thought it might have something to do with his betting on the races."

Robert frowned at the list of numbers. "I'm not sure what it is. When one bets on a horse, one usually has the odds *and* the name of the runner, and this is just a jumble of numbers."

He placed the paper on the desk and flattened it out with his palm. "It could be anything at this point."

"The fact that Bert kept it in a safe place, and had obviously been doing so for a while, might indicate that it is important, yes?" Lucy asked.

"I'm not discounting it in the least," Robert assured her. "I'm more interested in seeing what he has to say about having Flora's purse in his possession."

"Perhaps he stole it from her to teach her a lesson." Lucy sipped her coffee and ate one of the biscuits Foley had provided on the tray. "He did admit to speaking to her, didn't he?"

"He said he gave her a good shaking." Robert grimaced. "Perhaps her purse fell out while he was doing so."

"I doubt that if it was in her pocket under her skirts," Lucy objected. "Unless she had it in her hand." She set her cup down and leaned forward. "It almost sounds as if you are trying to find excuses for Bert's behavior."

"Not at all. I'm attempting to think of every possible explanation before I get ahead of myself and start casting blame where it doesn't belong."

"But Bert practically admitted to killing her!"

"No, he didn't. He flatly denied it."

"Then he obviously lied."

"Mr. Jarvis told me that he'd seen Flora and Bert talking perfectly amicably at the inn on several occasions, and he was surprised when I'd asked him to keep Bert away from her."

"That was probably when Bert was attempting to court her."

"I suppose so." Robert crossed his arms and stared out over the parkland. Something was nagging at him, and from his wife's expression, he was conscious that he was failing to adequately address what it was.

"What about James?" he asked abruptly.

"James saw Bert and Flora together, was hit on the head, and was deposited at his father's farm," Lucy said firmly

"So if Bert was with Flora, who hit James?"

Lucy's mouth formed a perfect O as she stared at him. "Maybe Bert saw James watching them, ran back to knock him out, and then took James to the farm."

"Leaving Flora alone?"

Lucy's brow creased. "This is all getting remarkably complicated, isn't it?"

"That is one thing we can agree on completely," Robert said. "If James is telling the truth, who hit him on the head? Is there someone else involved that we do not yet know of?"

"Mr. Fletcher?" Lucy suggested. "Have you spoken to him about any of this yet? He did say he saw Flora walking down to the village that day."

Robert frowned. "As I already mentioned, he was with me the day Flora was killed."

"All of it?" Lucy asked. "Can you absolutely swear that he couldn't have gotten away from you at some point?"

Robert relapsed into silence, his booted foot tapping impatiently against the floor.

"I can't possibly conceive of Dermot being a murderer."

"I agree, but if he saw Flora, perhaps he saw James or Bert or some other person of interest," Lucy suggested.

"I'll talk to him after I've spoken to James again."

"Thank you." Lucy sighed. "I asked Foley to send a message down to Mr. Snape to collect Flora's body from Dr. Fletcher's."

"Mr. Snape does have excellent storage facilities. I'll pay for the coffin and for his time." Robert finished his second cup of coffee. "I'll wager Patrick will be glad to release the body into the care of the undertaker. He says that his wife objects to him storing bodies in her cellar."

"She would," Lucy remarked rising to her feet as she smothered a yawn. "I hope the real Polly

Carter's mother replies to my letter soon. I sent her enough money to cover its delivery to us."

"You'll probably never see that again." Robert rose and went to open the door for her. She paused to look up at him.

"Which gives us all the more reason to go to London and speak to her directly!"

Chapter 8

Having made no headway with James, who was stubbornly sticking to his story that he'd only seen Bert Speers with "Polly" and had not spoken to either of them afterward, Robert turned his attention to his land agent. He had invited Dermot to accompany him down to the Queen's Head early the next morning and now sat beside him in the gig. He'd promised Lucy he would return by eleven so that they could take their walk with their son.

"Do you think Bert Speers is the culprit, then, Sir Robert?" Dermot asked as he expertly turned the corner onto the country road.

"He certainly seems to have some grievance with Polly." Robert glanced over at his land agent. "Did you ever see them together?"

Dermot took a while to answer, his gaze fixed on the road in front of them. "I saw them."

"Mr. Jarvis suggested that not all their encounters were acrimonious."

"No, they weren't." Dermot relapsed into silence again.

Robert was just about to prompt him with

another question when his companion rushed into speech.

"She seemed quite friendly with him at first. Then, later, she confessed that he was angry because she was spending time with me, and that he thought she was getting above herself."

Robert pondered that interesting information. It mirrored almost exactly what Polly had apparently said to James.

"I have begun to wonder whether Polly was just"—Dermot paused—"playing with all of us."

"What makes you say that?" Robert asked.

"Mayhap she enjoyed us fighting over her."

"It's possible."

"It seemed like it was all a big game to her sometimes. That she didn't take any of us seriously."

"Maybe she didn't."

It occurred to Robert that if Flora had indeed been an actress and a dancer, her ability to play a role might have stood her in good stead in the unfamiliar world of Kurland St. Mary. Being agreeable to all had its advantages.

"Not that she derived any pleasure from seeing us fight over her," Dermot said. "In fact, she found it extremely annoying and told me in no uncertain terms to stop."

"Which perhaps validates your observation that her heart wasn't really involved in any of her interactions."

"Sadly, yes." Dermot grimaced and sighed heavily. "She never really cared for me, did she? She just reflected back my own desire for her."

Remembering how easily Flora had calmed his own fears and made herself amenable to his orders, Robert found some truth in that.

"When you saw her that last morning walking down to the village, did you follow her?" Robert asked.

"As I was intending to visit the Queen's Head to send a letter to my sister in Ireland, I had no *choice* but to follow her."

"Did you see her with anyone?"

"James, who was ahead of me, caught up with her, and they had a somewhat animated discussion before she stormed off toward the High Street."

"What did James do after that?"

"He followed her for a little while, and then I lost sight of him." Dermot fumbled with the reins as he turned into the coaching inn. "I saw Polly meet with Bert, though." His expression darkened. "He grabbed hold of her arm and thrust his face into hers. I yelled at him to stop, but I don't think either of them heard me because I was too far away."

"Did they leave together?"

"Yes. I don't think Polly had much choice in the matter, seeing as Bert had hold of her arm and was dragging her along behind him."

Robert turned to stare fully at Dermot. "Forgive me, but I find it hard to believe that a man who professed to be in love with a particular woman would make no effort to intervene when she was accosted by another man."

A flush of color stole up from Dermot's collar to cover his face. "You . . . ordered me not to get involved with her, sir. I tried to do as you said."

Robert continued to stare at his subordinate until Dermot jumped down from the gig and spoke to one of the ostlers. Perhaps Lucy had been right, after all, and his land agent was not averse to lying about what had happened, either.

Unwilling to let the matter drop, but aware that he needed to speak to the driver of the mail coach before he left the inn, Robert got down from the gig and headed out into the crowded yard. A collection of passengers was boarding the coach, and one of the ostlers was putting up their baggage on the roof.

Robert sidestepped around two chickens in a crate and narrowly avoided standing on a small child almost obscured in his mother's skirts.

"Excuse me, ma'am." He briefly raised his hat and concentrated his attention on the elderly man sitting on the box, who was shouting out instructions as to the loading of the coach.

"Are you Henry Haines?"

"Yes, sir." The man touched the brim of his old-fashioned tricorn hat. "You must be Sir Robert Kurland. Mr. Jarvis said you'd be wanting a word with me." He checked the time on his pocket watch and beckoned to Robert. "Climb up here so I can hear you proper. We don't have much time at this stop."

Robert gave one harried glance at the four horses harnessed to the coach and vaulted himself upward to sit beside the driver.

"One of Mr. Jarvis's ostlers, Bert Speers, claims he rode with you to London three days ago. Is that correct?"

"Aye, he did." Henry nodded. "I brought him back, too."

"Did he stay on the coach until it reached London?"

"I didn't see him leave." Henry turned to bellow something to one of the ostlers about the placement of a bag. "Sorry, sir."

"Whereabouts in London did you drop him off?"

"Whitechapel."

"And you picked him up there three days later?"

"I picked him up in Mayfair, sir, which was something of a surprise, but he paid me the extra fare." Henry checked his watch again. "I didn't see that pretty young nursemaid of yours going back to London, either."

"So I understand." Robert grimaced.

"I do remember her traveling down here, though. She was sitting up top, and she got to talking with Bert, who was just starting his new job as an ostler here."

"They arrived on the same coach?" Robert made sure to clarify the coachman's words.

"Aye. They chatted all the way, merry as larks." Henry shook his head. "God rest her soul."

"Amen to that," Robert said.

Henry put his watch away and reached for his horn. "We'll be leaving in a minute, Sir Robert, so unless you fancy a trip to London, you might want to get yourself off the coach."

"Thank you for your help." Robert contemplated the jump and decided that dignity be damned. He would sit on his arse and slide down carefully. "I wish you safe passage to London."

"Thank you, sir."

As soon as Robert reached the ground, Henry blew on the horn, and the activity around the coach redoubled, their actions reminding Robert of a frenzied swarm of bees.

"Last call!" Henry shouted as the final passenger scrambled up to the roof and the ostlers slammed the doors and stood back. "Next stop Clavering!"

Robert held his breath as Henry maneuvered the impossibly laden coach beneath the arched entrance to the stable yard and out onto the road. As a child, he'd loved to come down to the inn with his father to see the teams of horses. Back then, he would've been up on their backs, examining every horse and asking a thousand questions. He already suspected Ned would be the same.

So Bert had been to London, which still didn't absolve him of murdering Flora but did, at least, corroborate his account of not being in the vicinity of Kurland St. Mary for three days. Robert paused at the door. But if Bert had been away when Flora's body was discovered, when had he learned that she was dead?

He sought out Mr. Jarvis and found him in the kitchen, eating a hearty breakfast.

"Morning, sir. Fancy something to eat before we go and speak to Bert?"

Robert studied the huge slab of sizzling gammon and four eggs on Mr. Jarvis's plate, and his mouth watered.

"That would be most welcome."

"Then sit yourself down, sir."

Mr. Jarvis pulled out a chair as his wife placed a clean plate in front of Robert and dished him up a succulent piece of ham and two eggs.

"Thank you, Mrs. Jarvis."

She winked at him as she returned to the stove and refilled the pan. Robert spent the next few minutes indulging his more physical appetites by slowly chewing the home-cured and -smoked gammon, which had been fried to perfection.

Eventually, after downing half his ale, he turned to Mr. Jarvis, who was on his second plateful of food.

"Did you tell Bert that Polly was dead when he arrived back here?"

"No, sir. I left that to you."

"But you said he was in fighting humor when he got off the coach."

"He was, sir, but that might have been because he'd taken three days' leave without telling me and knew I was going to be angry with him."

"Did he ever mention that his mother was sick before?"

"He never mentioned he had a family. Said he grew up in an orphanage and was sent to work in the stables of some London toff before he took up boxing."

"He boxed?"

"He used to, sir. When he applied for the position, he said he'd lost his taste for fighting and wanted a more secure job."

Recalling Bert's broken nose, broad frame, and pugnacious expression, Robert could absolutely imagine him in the ring. If he still followed the sport, the piece of paper Lucy had found in his belongings might be a list of betting odds for fights.

"And he started here about a month ago? Henry Haines said he arrived on the same coach as Polly Carter."

"That's right!" Mrs. Jarvis entered the discussion. "I'd forgotten about that. Bert helped her off the roof of the coach and brought her bags down."

Robert drank his ale and declined Mrs. Jarvis's offer of more food. When the innkeeper finished eating and set his plate to one side, both men descended into the cellar again. This time, Robert halted outside the door.

"I need to speak to Bert alone. Can you wait out here and only come in if I shout for you?"

Mr. Jarvis frowned. "Are you sure about this, sir? He's not afraid of a fight."

"Obviously." Robert took out his pistol. "I do have some protection, Mr. Jarvis. I won't allow him to overcome me."

"As you wish." Mr. Jarvis didn't look happy as he unlocked the door. "But don't hesitate to call out if you need me. There's no shame in needing reinforcements, sir."

Having been in the military, Robert was fully cognizant of that fact. He went into the room to discover Bert sitting against the opposite wall, his cloak around his shoulders and his dark gaze fixed on the door. Robert set his pistol on the top of the nearest beer barrel, within easy reach of his hand.

"Good morning, Bert."

His companion didn't reply.

"How did you know Polly Carter was dead

if you were in London when her body was discovered?"

"I didn't know she was dead until you told me."

"Yet you didn't seem shocked by my disclosure."

Bert shrugged. "Some might say she had it coming."

"So you weren't surprised that she had been murdered?"

"I didn't say that, sir." Bert met his gaze. "I told her to be careful. She wouldn't listen, and she ended up dead."

"For a man who professed to be in love with her, you seem remarkably pleased that she died."

"It's not my fault if she wouldn't bloody listen, now, is it? I did my best to warn her."

"To warn her not to talk to any other man but you?"

Bert opened his mouth as if to reply and then closed it again.

"After you accosted Polly on the street, where did she go?" Robert asked after a lengthy silence.

"I didn't notice, sir. I had to get back to work."

"She didn't follow you to the inn?"

"Not to my knowledge."

"And you didn't drag her off with you?"

Bert scowled. "I wish I had. Maybe she'd still be alive if I'd locked her in my room for a few days."

"You were seen by more than one person

arguing with Polly and then forcing her to accompany you away from public view. Where did you take her, and what did you do with her?"

"I didn't do anything that she didn't deserve, sir," Bert responded. "You can ask me as many questions as you like, and you'll still get the same answer!"

"Did she deserve to be killed?" Despite his growing frustration, Robert pressed on. "Did she, perhaps, refuse to accept your ultimatums and you accidentally killed her in a fit of rage?"

"I didn't bloody kill her!" Bert snarled.

Robert reached inside his pocket and drew out the blue purse Lucy had found.

"Then how did Polly's purse end up hidden in the toe of your boot?"

Bert shot to his feet, his gaze on Robert's palm. "Where the bloody hell did you get that from? I—" He stopped and breathed out hard through his nose. "That just *proves* it wasn't me."

"How so?" Robert asked.

"Because if I'd murdered the silly cow, I wouldn't have been stupid enough to steal her purse and leave it in my possession!"

It was Robert's turn to shrug. "Most murderers make mistakes. Isn't that why you returned to Kurland St. Mary? To rectify your error?"

"I came *back* because—" Bert closed his mouth and sat down again, his arms crossed over his chest.

"Because what, Bert?"

"Someone is trying to make me look guilty, sir. Someone wants me to be blamed for this. *That's* the man you should be looking for, not me."

"Does this man have a name?" Robert asked mildly. "Because from what I can see, all the evidence of this crime points to you. You were seen arguing with Polly, you even admit to doing so. You were seen dragging her off, and *you* have her stolen purse in your possession."

"You're wrong, sir. Polly herself told me that she'd seen the man, which was why we were arguing in the first place! If you'd just let me out of here, I could prove it in an instant!"

"Of course, you could." Robert put the purse back in his pocket. "I'm afraid you'll have to stay right where you are for now. If you suddenly remember the name of the man you say we should be looking for, then please let me know."

Bert made a frustrated sound. "If you let me out, I can find him for you."

"If you tell me his name or give me a description, I can find him myself." Robert reclaimed his pistol. "If there is such a man in Kurland St. Mary, he should be easily recovered."

"He's probably gone back to London by now."

"And you foolishly imagine I'll let you go to London to find him?" Robert turned to the door. "You must think I'm a complete flat. Good day, Bert."

"You can't keep me here forever!"

Robert knocked on the door and looked over his shoulder at Bert. "I am aware of that, but as the local magistrate, I can send you to the county town to await trial for murder whenever it suits me."

Bert glowered at him. "If you do that, you'll be condemning an innocent man to death."

"Then you'd better come up with the name of the man you insist is the real murderer before I do so, hadn't you?"

Robert waited until Mr. Jarvis secured the door behind him before heading for the stairs.

"Did he admit it yet, sir?"

"No. He's insisting that someone else is responsible."

Mr. Jarvis's disbelieving snort echoed Robert's thoughts.

"If he doesn't change his tune soon, I will be sending him off to await trial at the county assizes," Robert said as he emerged into the hallway of the inn.

"Aye, sir. But don't you worry in the meantime. I'll keep him safe for you here."

"I appreciate that." Robert shook the landlord's hand. "Are there any letters to take up to the hall?"

"No, sir, are you expecting something in particular?"

"Just a letter from London." In fact, Robert was

fairly certain they would never hear from Polly's mother, but he refused to give up hope.

"I'll send one of the boys up if we get anything later, sir." Mr. Jarvis walked through to the yard with him, his keen gaze settling on his ostlers, who were standing around with very little to do.

"Get Sir Robert's gig out, Fred!" Mr. Jarvis bellowed.

As Dermot had walked into the village to speak to some of the tenants, Robert climbed up, took possession of the reins, and left the inn, his mind full of the complicated conversations he'd had that morning. James and Dermot were not being honest, and Bert Speers was intent on denying what would seem to be a clear case against him.

Robert heaved a sigh. There was no way around it. If he wanted to find out exactly what had happened to the real Polly Carter and why his nursemaid had been murdered, he would have to go to London. Probably with his wife, because unless he incarcerated her in the cellar alongside Bert Speers, she would never allow him to leave without her.

Lucy smiled as her son ran ahead of them, his gaze fixed on the distant stables. He had all his father's determination, and she had no doubt that if left to his own devices, he would prefer to spend his days with the grooms and horses. She glanced over at her husband, who was walking alongside her, his expression thoughtful, his blue gaze turned inward.

"Did you manage to convince Bert to confess his crime?"

"No." He grimaced. "*He* tried to persuade *me* that there is another man involved in the matter—a man he conveniently refused to name."

"Yet you still seem troubled."

"You know me too well." His slight smile warmed her. "As I told Bert, he is the one who was seen threatening Flora—something he admits—and he was seen dragging her off somewhere. He then ran off to London to see a 'sick mother' when Mr. Jarvis told me he was raised in an orphanage."

For once, Lucy remained silent as Robert continued to talk.

"And then we have the mystery of what James was up to, and Dermot telling me that he saw Bert with Flora and did nothing to stop him because he didn't wish to disobey my orders."

"That sounds highly unlikely," Lucy conceded.

"I don't like all these loose ends, Lucy. As the local magistrate, I should assess the evidence and immediately send Bert to the assizes, but my instinct tells me I'm missing something important."

"I'm not sure what," Lucy pointed out. "It seems quite clear to me. Bert was obsessed with

Flora, disliked her enjoying the company of other men, and strangled her in a fit of jealous rage."

Robert stopped walking and flung his arms wide. "Then why in God's name did he come back to Kurland St. Mary?"

Lucy frowned. "Perhaps he felt guilty and *wanted* to be found out?"

"Then why not confess everything instead of stubbornly insisting that he didn't kill her, and that someone else is making it look like he did it? None of this makes sense."

"And I haven't heard from Polly's mother, either," Lucy reminded him.

Robert resumed walking again. "There's no escaping it, my love. We're going to have to go to London, speak to Polly's mother, and try to find out what happened to the real Polly Carter."

Chapter 9

Confident that, in her absence, Ned would be well looked after by Anna and a very repentant Agnes, Lucy was looking forward to her visit to London. She hadn't been there since her marriage and was eager to explore the shops, visit the theaters, and enjoy the new fashions. Robert gave her a substantial amount of pin money that she rarely spent in the village. She had funds at her disposal and a long list of requests from Anna and Rose to satisfy.

Her only concern about the whole journey was currently sitting opposite her in the carriage . . .

"I am so looking forward to staying with your uncle, the earl of Harrington, Lucy! I'm certain that your family move in the very best circles, and that, as we both know, *is* where I belong."

Lucy caught Dr. Fletcher's attempt to stifle a grin as his wife expounded on her own family connections and her conviction that she would've been greatly missed by the ton.

When Robert had informed her that he intended to bring Dr. Fletcher with him, Lucy had accepted the need for a strong man to accompany her husband into the somewhat dangerous area around Whitechapel, where Polly's mother lived. She had *not* anticipated that Penelope would insist on joining them, leaving her own son in Lucy's nursery "to keep Ned company."

It was, however, quite like Penelope to blatantly ignore Lucy's sensibilities in order to further her own plans. It was also why Penelope had ended up spending six weeks in Bath at the Kurland town house and had given birth to her son there.

Sometimes one just had to accept one's fate, but Lucy was getting somewhat tired of it.

"Where exactly is the Harrington residence, Lucy?" Penelope inquired.

"Portland Square."

Penelope sighed blissfully. "How lovely! And are all your cousins still living at home?"

"Both of them are still there. I believe Julia is engaged now and will be marrying next year. Max is unlikely to be allowed to move out until my uncle decides he is mature enough to do so."

"Do they entertain much?"

"I have no idea." Lucy faked a yawn and settled into her seat. "I do hope you will excuse me, Penelope, but I am rather tired."

Robert, who could sleep anywhere, was already dozing, lulled by the motion of the carriage. It would take them at least two days and four changes of horses to get to London in a timely manner, with stops at inns along the way. Lucy could only hope that Penelope did not intend to question her about her family for the entire journey.

Eventually, they drew up outside her uncle David's imposing mansion in Portland Square, and Lucy allowed Robert to help her out of the carriage. The front door of the house opened, and a stream of liveried servants came down the steps and immediately started unloading the baggage. Robert surreptitiously stretched out his injured left leg, which never did well on long carriage rides, and started haltingly up the stairs.

He waited for Lucy and the Fletchers to join him in the grand black and white tiled hall where an imposing butler greeted them.

"Sir Robert, would you care to follow me? Lord and Lady Harrington are awaiting you in the drawing room."

The butler turned to ascend yet another flight of stairs, and Robert grimaced. Lucy went to his side and offered him her arm, and they made their laborious way up the steps. Robert shared his muttered opinion that town houses were the very devil, necessitating endless stair climbing, sometimes over seven floors.

"Lady Kurland, Sir Robert Kurland, Dr. Fletcher, and Mrs. Fletcher." The butler announced them and stood aside to allow Lucy to enter the room.

"Lucy, my dear!" Lucy's uncle David came forward and drew her into an embrace. "You are looking very well, my girl, very well indeed."

"As are you," Lucy smiled up at him. He looked quite like her father, but was far more forthright and always full of energy. "Thank you for allowing us to stay with you for a few days."

"It's our pleasure." He turned to Robert and shook his hand. "How are you, sir?"

"Very well, thank you, my lord." Robert turned and gestured toward the Fletchers. "May I introduce you to the earl of Harrington, Mrs. Fletcher, Dr. Fletcher?"

Penelope curtsied low. "A pleasure, my lord."

"Dr. Fletcher and I served together in the Hussars, and he was single-handedly responsible for saving my life," Robert said.

The earl exchanged bows with Dr. Fletcher and offered Penelope an appreciative smile. "You are both most welcome." He looked over at his wife, who was speaking to Lucy. "I believe we have arranged a dinner party for the night after this to celebrate your arrival. Is that not correct, Jane?"

"Indeed we have." Lucy's aunt Jane, who was a formidable society hostess, smiled at them all. "You will have the opportunity to meet Julia's intended, and Max has promised me that he will attend."

"Has he?" The earl raised an eyebrow. "Good, because I've been meaning to speak to him about overspending his allowance."

Aunt Jane slid her hand through Lucy's elbow

and turned toward the door. "I am sure that you are all quite exhausted by your journey. I will show you to your rooms and will expect to see you at dinner at promptly six o'clock."

After a sumptuous dinner and some animated conversation, Robert retired with Lucy to their bedchamber. With the help of his valet, Silas, he set about changing his best coat for an older one and put on a sturdy pair of boots.

"There is no need to tell your uncle where Dr. Fletcher and I are going, my dear." Robert slid his pistol into his pocket, along with a small sharp knife. "Let them think that all of us are having an early night after our travels."

"You forget that in a house this size there are always servants on call. My aunt and uncle will be perfectly aware that you went out, but I doubt they will ask *me* about it."

He flashed her a conspiratorial smile. "They'll probably think we're off to a gambling hell or a brothel."

"Which is exactly why they will not inquire!" Lucy sat forward. "Please be careful, Robert."

"We are only going to visit the two theaters that Flora had playbills for and inquire about her there." Robert stood up. "If we're lucky, we might find Polly Carter as well."

"Somehow I doubt that. Tomorrow I intend to call on Polly's mother."

"I will come with you."

"You are more than welcome to accompany me, but if you find out something important at the theater tonight, you might wish to make the best use of our time here and investigate that."

Robert paused as he buttoned his coat. "If I do have to go elsewhere, you will take Silas with you."

"Of course, I will. I'm not unintelligent."

He went over to kiss her cheek. "I know. Now, don't stay up until I return. You need your rest."

"I fear you are right." She sighed and placed a hand over her stomach. "I have no notion why sitting in a carriage is so tiring."

"Perhaps Mrs. Fletcher is the cause of your symptoms rather than the carriage ride."

"And yet you allowed her to come on this journey with us."

"I didn't have a choice." He kissed her cheek again. "I do apologize."

She waved an irritable hand at him, and he retreated to the door. As Silas left, Robert asked him to make sure that Dr. Fletcher was ready to leave, and to send up Betty, Lucy's maid, to help Lucy get ready for bed.

He went down the main staircase into the grand entrance hall and immediately encountered the butler, who had more gravitas than the earl himself.

"Are you going out, Sir Robert?"

"Yes, I am."

The butler inclined his head. "Then I will make sure that someone is up and alert for your return."

"There's no need," Robert said. "We can enter through the kitchen."

"That would hardly be fitting, now, would it, sir?"

"It will be a lot easier." Robert held his gaze. "Thank you for your concern, but I don't wish to cause additional work for any member of the earl's staff."

The butler gave a slight sigh. "As you wish, sir. I will make sure that the kitchen door is left unlocked."

"Thank you."

Patrick came down the stairs just as the butler glided off into the nether regions of the house.

"Is everything all right?"

Robert grimaced. "I forget how restrictive London society is sometimes."

"Which is why we both prefer to live in the countryside." Patrick headed for the door. "Shall we go? I expect it will be easy to pick up a hackney cab if we walk down to the main thoroughfare."

In the rarified air of Portland Square, the lamps were lit, and there were no loiterers in the cobbled street or in the garden center. Robert carried his walking cane, but that was more as a precaution and a potential weapon than because he needed it. Since Patrick had opened up his leg again and he'd enjoyed the spa waters in Bath, he'd been in remarkably good health.

"Where first?" Patrick asked as they approached the much busier main road.

"Covent Garden. The Corinthian is just behind the church."

Patrick hailed a hackney cab, and they were soon delivered to the front of a small theater huddled between a bank and a church. It was an insignificant place and quite unlike the more fashionable theaters where Robert squired Lucy. It was, however, exactly the sort of place he had frequented as a young officer of the Hussars.

"Let's go around to the back." Robert indicated an alley to the right of the building. "But be on your guard."

It had never occurred to him as a young man convinced of his own invincibility to worry about such things. He and his companions had roamed around the city, oblivious to the dangers in a reckless fashion that made him shudder now. The thought of Ned behaving in such a way made him feel quite unwell . . .

A single lantern illuminated the shabby stage door. Robert knocked, and a burly individual who looked remarkably like an English bulldog opened the door.

"What do you want?" he asked, his gaze sweeping over Robert and his companion.

"Good evening," Robert said. "I wish speak to the manager of the theater for a few moments."

"Do you now?" The man held out his hand. "I might see about making that happen for a small fee, if you gets my meaning."

"Indeed." Robert placed half a crown in the man's palm and waited until he was invited in over the threshold.

"Come this way, sir."

Despite their giggles and calls, Robert averted his gaze from the skimpily attired females who were changing their garb behind the stage and focused on his destination.

"Gentleman to see you, Mr. Bourne."

"Thank you, Will."

Robert waited until Will left him and Patrick alone with the man in front of them, and then focused his attention on him. Mr. Bourne was a large man with an even larger moustache and very bushy eyebrows.

"What can I do for you?"

"I'm wondering if you currently have a Flora Rosa in your employ?"

Mr. Bourne's welcoming smile died. "Did the little bugger ditch you, too?"

"I'm not quite sure I understand you."

"She was working here, all right, and then suddenly, she says she's gotten a better offer, and off she goes without a word of thanks." Mr. Bourne shook his head. "I was foolish enough to employ her when she was just a child, and that's how she repaid me. With all due respect, sir, did she leave you for that toff?"

"Leave me?" Robert suddenly realized Mr. Bourne's meaning and almost recoiled. "Her family are concerned for her safety, and as one of her cousins works for me, I offered to inquire for her when I was next in London."

Mr. Bourne didn't look particularly convinced by Robert's hastily contrived explanation but didn't seem inclined to argue about it, either, which suited Robert perfectly.

"Just to make sure that we are talking about the same woman, was Flora Rosa blond-haired and very pretty?" Robert asked.

"Yes, indeed. And she was a passable actress as well." Mr. Bourne nodded. "Much better than I realized after all her bamboozling, promising to stay here forever, to elevate my theater with her talent . . ." He sighed. "I heard she went to the Prince of Wales on the Strand, but I haven't bothered to go and see her perform. What's the point?"

"I will certainly ask for her there," Robert said. "Did you ever employ a woman called Polly Carter?"

Mr. Bourne shook his head. "The name's not familiar to me, but you might care to ask Will on your way out. He knows everyone who has been employed here for the last ten years."

"Thank you for your assistance, sir." Robert handed over his card. "If you do see Flora or Polly Carter, I would appreciate it if you would let me know. I am currently residing at number nine Portland Square if you need to reach me."

"Fancy address, eh?" Mr. Bourne's shrewd gaze reassessed Robert's worth.

"My wife's family."

"Married up, did you?" The manager gave him an approving nod.

"Not that it is any of your business, but yes," Robert replied. "Thank you again."

He turned and followed Patrick out, down the corridor and through the green room. The dancers were now onstage, so there was no one to impede their departure or offer unsolicited advice. Patrick paused at the door to ask Will something, and then they were both out in the rapidly cooling night air.

"He doesn't remember Polly Carter," Patrick remarked as they made their way back down the alley to James Street. "We can walk down to the Strand from here if you like."

"Yes, let's walk."

It wasn't very busy, which was a blessing, and there was no rain, which made the cobbled streets much easier to walk on. Keeping a close eye on his pockets, Robert skirted the delights of Covent Garden proper and headed down Southampton Street. The unpleasant stench of the River

155

Thames wafted up to them, making Robert catch his breath.

"I am not the sort of man to inquire too deeply into your private life, Major, but perhaps you might enlighten me as to why we are searching for two women, one of whom is currently dead and awaiting burial in Kurland St. Mary?"

"Lady Kurland and I believe that the woman we knew as Polly Carter was actually an actress called Flora Rosa."

"Ah." Patrick walked another few steps. "Why was an actress impersonating your nurse-maid?"

"That is the question I am attempting to answer. As far as I understand it, Polly Carter sent Flora down to Kurland St. Mary to avoid some trouble in London."

"I doubt Mr. Bourne would've come all that way to find her."

"I agree, but you never know." Robert paused on the corner of the Strand, which was a much busier road and looked both ways. "I hope we will find out more at the Prince of Wales."

"Did someone murder Flora thinking she was Polly, or was Flora murdered for herself?" Patrick asked.

"I hadn't thought of it like that." Robert stopped to look at his friend with grudging admiration. "I assumed Flora failed to escape whatever or whoever was pursuing her in London. If we find no trace of Polly Carter, either, I might have to reconsider."

The Prince of Wales was a better class of establishment than the Corinthian and probably twice the size. Robert noted several private carriages dropping off their occupants, which indicated that the audience was probably of a higher social class.

There was no obvious entrance to the rear of the theater, so Robert stepped inside to ask for directions from one of the footmen.

He was directed down a narrow lane to the left, which, after a right turn, eventually led around and past two other buildings to the rear of the theater. The stage door was brightly lit, and there was a man on guard outside it.

"Good evening. I wish to speak to the manager of the theater," Robert said.

"Then you'll have to call back tomorrow, sir. Mr. Frobisher doesn't allow visitors in while the performance is on. He likes to direct his full attention on the show."

"Which is admirable, but what about during the interval or between acts?" Robert asked. "I need only a few moments of his time."

"He will not see you, sir." The man was respectful but firm. "He will be here tomorrow afternoon, working on the new production, if you wish to speak to him then."

Unwilling to draw too much attention to himself by getting into a pointless argument, Robert nodded. "Thank you. I will come back."

"Is there a message you wish to leave for Mr. Frobisher, sir?"

"No. I'll speak to him tomorrow. Thank you."

Robert retreated, Patrick at his side.

"Why didn't you leave a message?" Patrick asked as they walked away.

"Because I'd rather see his face when I ask my questions than give him the opportunity to think up a story."

Patrick chuckled. "Which is exactly why all the men under your command were so afraid of you." He paused to read the playbill at the front of the theater. "Shakespeare, followed by dancers and a contemporary farce."

"As the theater appears to be prospering, I have to assume he knows his audience," Robert commented.

A hackney cab pulled up behind Robert, and he stepped aside to avoid being knocked down by the gaggle of gentlemen who were descending, intent on rushing into the theater. None of them thanked him for his efforts or excused themselves, which irritated Robert, and then made him realize he was getting old.

One of the men turned to shout back at a companion, his face illuminated in the theater lights before he went into the theater proper.

"Interesting," Robert murmured.

"What is?"

"I just saw Lord Northam, my cousin Henrietta's husband."

Patrick shrugged. "Maybe he enjoys Shakespeare."

"Somehow I doubt it. The man barely knows how to read." Robert stared into the theater. "According to my aunt Rose, who does not like him at all, he does have a fine appreciation of the female form. At her daughter's behest, she once paid off one of his mistresses who was with child. Northam refused to accept any responsibility in the matter."

Patrick snorted. "Typical."

"I wonder if he comes to this place often." Robert turned away from the theater. "It might be worth the attempt to find him at his club and ask him if he has any memory of Flora Rosa."

Robert looked up to find that Patrick's attention had wandered down the street.

"Is there something the matter?"

"Not at all." Patrick grinned at him. "Seeing as our investigations have ended for the night, maybe we might stop for a tankard of ale at the Crown and Anchor?"

"I think that is an excellent notion," Robert agreed and clapped his friend on the shoulder. "Let's go."

Chapter 10

❧

"It is very kind of you to see me, Mrs. Carter."

Lucy smiled reassuringly at the pinched face of Polly Carter's mother, who had only very reluctantly allowed Lucy through her front door. It was almost midday, but very little light filtered through the lace curtains and dirty front window of the terraced house in St. Giles where the Carter family resided. Silas, who had accompanied her when Robert had decided to go and speak to his cousin's husband, remained outside the front door, his billy club prominently displayed and his expression menacing.

"I apologize for not apprising you of my intended visit sooner."

Mrs. Carter's gaze fixed on the unlit fire in the grate, and she ducked her head low. She wore a gray dress with a high neckline and very little ornamentation that made Lucy's choice of a fashionable blue ensemble positively garish by comparison. They were sitting in the cramped parlor at the front of the house on the two chairs that faced each other across the fireplace.

"Did you receive my letter about Polly?" Lucy asked.

"I don't read too well, my lady."

"Ah, was one of your family able to read the letter to you?"

"Mr. Carter did. He told me not to bother my head about one of Polly's friends getting herself into trouble."

"So Polly did know Flora Rosa?"

"Polly works as a seamstress at the theater, my lady. That's probably where she met the woman."

"Which theater?" Lucy asked.

"The Prince of Wales on the Strand."

Lucy nodded. That information certainly established a connection between the two women. "Did you ever meet Flora?"

"Oh, no, my lady." Mrs. Carter pursed her lips. "Mr. Carter doesn't approve of such goings-on. He didn't want Polly working there, either, but she wouldn't listen to him."

"Mr. Carter doesn't approve of the theater?"

"He believes it is ungodly and sinful, ma'am." Mrs. Carter glanced at the table beside Lucy, where a large family Bible was prominently displayed. "And when we received your letter asking whether we knew this Flora, he was rightfully angry with Polly for dragging us into a scandal."

"Did he and Polly argue about it?"

"Yes, my lady." Mrs. Carter sighed. "Polly hasn't been back to see us since."

"She doesn't live here with you?"

"She has her own place near Covent Garden with some friends."

"Could you give me that address?" Lucy asked. "It is imperative that I speak to Polly as soon as possible."

Mrs. Carter reluctantly obliged, and Lucy stored the information in her memory.

"How often do you see Polly, Mrs. Carter?"

"She usually comes during the day when her father is out and helps with the younger ones. She does a lot of her work at night—repairing costumes after the performances, refitting under-studies, and generally making sure the props are still usable. So once she's had a sleep, she comes to see me."

"You must be proud to have brought up such a helpful daughter."

Mrs. Carter's expression didn't reflect much pride. "She is not good at obeying her father, and she causes many disruptions to the peace of this household."

"Did Polly read my letter herself?"

"Yes, indeed," Mrs. Carter nodded vigorously. "Mr. Carter *made* her read it before he expressed his disapproval about her immoral friends."

"And that caused an argument and Polly left?"

"Yes, my lady." Mrs. Carter hesitated. "Usually after one of their rows, Polly still comes to see me, but she hasn't been in for over a week."

"Did Polly say anything to you about the letter, or about what happened to Flora Rosa?" Lucy asked.

"She seemed . . . shocked and became tearful, which was when Mr. Carter lost his temper with her for caring about an immoral woman who had probably met her just end."

Lucy rose to her feet. "I don't wish to disturb you for too long, Mrs. Carter, so I will take my leave. Thank you for your help in this matter." She took her aunt's calling card out of her reticule and placed it in Mrs. Carter's lace-mittened hand.

"If Polly does return, I would appreciate it if you could let me know. I'm staying with my aunt and uncle at this address, and I would very much like to speak with her. I had hoped to deliver a letter for her from her cousin, Agnes."

Mrs. Carter glanced down at the card but didn't seem inclined or able to read it. "If you see Polly yourself, my lady, would you tell her to come home?" For the first time, she looked worried. "I would very much like to see her myself."

"Of course, Mrs. Carter." Lucy closed her bag and made sure she had her umbrella with her. "I will certainly do that."

She went back out to the front of the house, where despite his menacing demeanor, Silas had gathered a small crowd of youthful admirers. Compared to a lot of streets in St. Giles, the Carters' road was remarkably clean, with a drain down the center of the cobbles containing only water and no refuse, human or otherwise. Lucy abhorred the poverty in the countryside but found the scale of misery in the capital far more harrowing.

"Are we going back to Portland Square now, my lady?" Silas asked as he followed her to the end of the road.

"No, we have one more visit to make." Lucy looked up and down the street. "Which is the best way to reach Covent Garden?"

Silas frowned. "It isn't far from here, my lady, but I suggest we find a hackney cab." He, too, scanned the street. "We will probably need to walk down to the main road. I doubt many drivers venture in here for fear of being robbed."

"I suspect you are right." Lucy was glad that she'd put on her stout walking boots. It started to rain, and she handed Silas her umbrella to protect them both.

"I don't suppose any of the children you were talking to mentioned Polly or the Carter family?" Lucy asked.

"They said that the old man was a miserable sod—begging your pardon, my lady—and that no one liked him much."

"He didn't sound very likable," Lucy commented, and she increased her pace as the rain came down faster.

"Mr. Carter works as a clerk down at the docks

and preaches at one of the local religious halls when he has the time."

Lucy cast Silas an approving glance. He'd gleaned almost as much information from the doorway as she had from inside the house.

"Are you sure that you don't want to return, my lady?" Silas asked again. "Sir Robert told me to make sure you didn't wear yourself out."

"I am feeling quite well, Silas." Lucy spotted a hackney and waved energetically at the driver. "I assure you that after we visit this last address, I will be more than happy to return to my uncle's."

Robert signed into his cousin's club and was welcomed into the dining room by a waiter who led him directly over to where his cousin's husband was sitting.

"Good afternoon, Northam." Robert bowed.

"Kurland." Lord Northam offered Robert a seat opposite him. "Would you like a brandy before we eat?"

"No, thank you." Robert nodded at the waiter, who disappeared as silently as he had arrived. "How is my cousin?"

"Henrietta is in good health and is currently visiting my mother up in Northamptonshire."

"That is a shame. I was hoping to pay my respects to her in person," Robert said. "I have a letter from her mother."

"Give it to me." Robert passed it over, and Lord

Northam made a face as he stowed it in his coat pocket. "I doubt she'll want to read it. She hasn't forgiven Rose for marrying that rector fellow yet."

"That 'rector fellow' is the younger son of an earl and seems very fond of her," Robert commented.

"Well, you would say that, seeing as he's your wife's father, isn't he?"

"I'd say that anyway." Robert held Northam's gaze. "Henrietta should have no fears on her mother's account. Mr. Harrington is a true gentleman."

"Henrietta doesn't care how Mr. Harrington treats her mother." Northam waved a dismissive hand. "She's worried about her inheritance, and quite frankly, so am I."

"Mr. Harrington certainly didn't marry Rose for her money." Robert had never imagined he'd end up defending his father-in-law, but something about Northam's attitude toward Rose had always set his hackles rising.

"But what if she dies first? Will he inherit everything?" Northam complained. "From what I understand, he has three sons and a daughter from his previous marriage left to provide for. Rose's money would certainly help with that."

"I have no idea who she has left her money to. Surely, that is between her and her solicitor?" Robert asked.

"Not according to Henrietta. She's deliberating writing to her mother and demanding a substantial sum up front."

Robert pretended to look puzzled. "Didn't Aunt Rose settle a large sum on Henrietta when she married you?"

"That *pittance* is all gone." Lord Northam looked up as the waiter appeared, ordered himself another brandy, and took the suggestion to have the game pie for his dinner, as did Robert.

Robert had helped his aunt set up the marriage settlement, and he knew that was an outright lie. His cousin and her husband had always treated Rose like their own personal bank, while conveniently looking down on her for being not the "right class."

It was hard to bite his tongue and continue listening to Northam's complaints while he waited for the opportunity to ask some questions of his own. But after Northam's fourth brandy, and well into his dinner, Robert broached the subject of his cousin's theater-going habits.

"I saw you going into the Prince of Wales Theater on the Strand last night," Robert said.

"Did you now?" Northam winked. "Good thing my wife is away then, isn't it?"

"Was it a good show?" Robert asked.

"Didn't see it. I had a more . . . personal quarry in mind in the green room."

"Did you ever meet an actress called Flora Rosa there?"

Northam set down his glass and stared at Robert. "That's a very specific question, Kurland. Has someone been singing her praises, so you thought you'd go and have a gander for yourself?"

"Her cousin works in my house. She asked me to deliver a letter to Flora while I was in London."

"I can't imagine any cousin of Flora's working in a country house, but I'm not going to argue with you." Northam leaned in closer and whispered, "Lady Kurland not with you on this trip, eh?"

"Lady Kurland accompanied me," Robert said as pleasantly as he could. "Our nurse entrusted the letter to her, and I am merely attempting to deliver it."

"If you say so." Northam winked again, and Robert barely managed not to plant him a facer.

"Anyway, if you want Flora, you're too late. She's already found a protector, and seeing as he's as rich as Croesus, he's set her up in a nice little house in Maida Vale, and she's retired from the stage."

"Do you have a name for this man?" Robert asked.

"Viscount Gravely. Do you know him?"

"I can't say that I do."

"He's a widower with two sons. He made his fortune in India and came back to England about three years ago."

Robert might not know him, but he was fairly certain Lucy's aunt Jane would. As a society hostess, she knew every aristocrat in the country, and all their secrets.

"I doubt he'll be open to offers for her, seeing as he only just persuaded her to accept his protection." Northam chewed noisily and finished his wine before wiping his chin.

"I have no intention of 'bidding' on a woman. I am simply attempting to deliver a letter." Robert also finished his wine and sat back. "Well, this has been delightful, but I have to be going. Lucy's aunt and uncle are having a dinner party for us tonight, and I need to try on the new coat from my tailor."

He was, in fact, heading back to meet with the manager of the Prince of Wales, but that was the last thing he intended to let slip to Northam.

His companion held up his brandy glass to the waiter. "I know where you're off to, Kurland, you can't fool me. But rest assured, I'll keep mum if I see Lady Kurland."

Robert pushed in his chair and fought to keep the loathing from his voice.

"Thank you for dinner, and give my best to Henrietta."

"Right, ho, I will."

• • •

Robert was still seething when he arrived at the theater and was ushered inside the empty building to meet Mr. Frobisher. The manager sat in the front row of the empty stalls, watching what was obviously a rehearsal for his next production. In the daylight, the theater looked as shabby and threadbare as an actor without his stage paint and costume.

Robert introduced himself and settled into the seat beside Mr. Frobisher, who had the alert face of a terrier and red, bushy whiskers to make the likeness even more applicable. He sent his cast off for a break and gave his full attention to Robert.

"How can I help you, sir?"

"I am inquiring about a woman called Flora Rosa."

"Not another one." Mr. Frobisher sighed. "I regret to tell you that she has decided not to continue her career on the stage and has gone off to be a kept woman. Which in my opinion is a waste of her talent and beauty."

"So she did work for you, then?"

"Indeed. I persuaded her to abandon the abominable Corinthian and offered her a chance to shine here instead." He snorted. "Unfortunately, she shone rather *too* brightly and caught the eye of an aristocrat, and that was that."

"The man who persuaded her to leave was Viscount Gravely?"

"Yes." Mr. Frobisher met Robert's gaze. "Why are you asking all these questions? Is Flora in trouble? Are you a Bow Street Runner?"

"I am merely trying to establish her identity. Did she have any family?"

"Not that I know of. She grew up in an orphanage, was placed as a kitchen maid, and swiftly decided her beautiful face and figure would provide her a far more lucrative career on the stage. She was correct about that. If she'd stayed, she could've gone on to become one of the greats." Mr. Frobisher paused. "Has something happened to her?"

Robert made a quick decision. "May I ask you one more question? And then if you are willing, I will attempt to explain myself."

"If you wish."

"Do you have a Polly Carter working here?"

"I did until about a week ago. She hasn't come in for a while."

Robert slowly exhaled. "This is going to sound as fantastic as one of your more lurid plays, but I have reason to believe that Flora Rosa, who was masquerading as Polly Carter, is now lying dead in the cellar of the Kurland St. Mary undertaker."

Mr. Frobisher blinked slowly and leaned in. "Please, *do* go on."

• • •

Robert returned to the Harringtons'. He had just enough time to try on his new coat and to proclaim that the fit was perfectly adequate before it was time to dress for the dinner party. He met up with his wife in their dressing room. For a while, there was no chance for conversing as Betty and Silas helped them into their best clothes.

"Thank you, Silas. You may go now, and please, don't wait up for me," Robert said.

"Thank you, sir." Silas gave Robert's sleeve a last brush and went out.

Robert studied his new blue coat in the mirror and considered the gray waistcoat his tailor had persuaded him to wear under it. Did he look too flashy?

Lucy glanced over from her dressing table. Betty had just finished arranging her hair and was sliding in some jeweled pins to keep everything secure.

"You look very nice, my dear."

He frowned at his reflection. "Is the color perhaps a little bright?" He fingered the cuffs. "And these silver buttons?"

His wife's quiet chuckle made him turn to face her.

"From a man who used to dress up in a uniform created by the Prince of Wales that included fur, gold buttons, and silver lace."

"I suppose you do have a point," he acknowledged. "Now that I think of it, the colors are rather similar."

"You always choose blue." Lucy rose from her seat and shook out the satin skirts of her green gown. "I think you feel most comfortable wearing it."

"After twelve years in uniform, I suspect you are right." He went over to take her hand. "You look beautiful."

"Hardly that." She made a face. "But I do at least look *presentable,* and considering the caliber of Aunt Jane's guests, that will have to do."

"You are the granddaughter of an earl and the wife of a baronet, and can hold your head high in any company." Robert kissed her nose. "I have no doubt that you will enjoy the evening far more than I shall."

"Did you find out anything interesting from Lord Northam?"

"Only that he is a wastrel and doesn't deserve a penny of my aunt's money."

"I believe we already knew that. What about his connections at the theater?"

"He knew who Flora was. He said that she recently took up with a 'protector' and left the theater."

"Did he know who it was?"

"Yes, a Viscount Gravely. As far as Northam knows, Flora Rosa is living a life of luxury in a house bought for her in Maida Vale."

Lucy grabbed his sleeve. "Perhaps Polly is there!"

"Was she not at home?" Robert asked. "Silas said that you spoke to her mother."

"She doesn't live there anymore, and I can quite see why. Her father is very religious and doesn't approve of her working in a theater, and her mother seems too afraid of her husband to do anything but agree with him."

"Then where *does* Polly live?"

"In a house near Covent Garden." Lucy went over to pick up her gloves, the emerald necklace Robert had given her for Christmas shining in the candlelight. "I went there as well, but no one has seen her for over a week." She looked back at Robert. "Her mother hasn't seen her since she got my letter. Polly and her father had an argument over it."

"This is somewhat of a hindrance to our plans to speak to her." Robert frowned. "One can only hope that she, too, has not been a victim of this murderer."

"Bert Speers came back to London for three days after Flora disappeared," Lucy said slowly. "Perhaps he came back to find Polly and make certain she could never share her story with anyone."

"It does seem all too likely, but I will continue to hope we can find Polly."

"I asked her mother to let us know if she

174

returned home." Lucy arranged a shawl over her elbows and checked her reflection in the mirror.

"And I asked Mr. Frobisher to do the same thing if she returned to her job at the theater." Robert reached for his wife's gloved hand. "Unfortunately, for the moment—until I get the opportunity to speak to Viscount Gravely—all we can do is wait."

Chapter 11

Robert paused in front of the steps leading up to Viscount Gravely's house and briefly considered how much money the man had made in trade to be able to afford such a place. Not that he had any issue with how a man created his wealth, unless it was through the slave trade. His mother's family wealth gained in the industrial north ably propped up his own finances.

He'd asked Lucy's aunt if she could introduce him to Viscount Gravely, and as she had already met the man, she had agreed to write a note suggesting he might allow Robert to meet him on a matter of some urgency. An invitation to visit had arrived promptly, and Robert had immediately set out before his wife had returned from her shopping expedition with Penelope.

Patrick was busy visiting the London hospitals, reconnecting with his peers, and attending lectures about new scientific discoveries, while Penelope was reveling in the social interactions of the very well-connected Harrington family. Robert was rather keen to get back to Kurland St. Mary and could only hope that the viscount would help him reach some conclusions as to the mystery surrounding Flora Rosa.

He went up the steps and knocked on the front door, which was opened by a butler with a turban wearing a distinctly un-English embroidered coat.

"Welcome, Sir Robert. Lord Gravely will see you in his study. Please follow me."

"Thank you." Robert followed the softly spoken man into the depths of the house until he paused and knocked on a door.

"Your visitor, my lord."

Robert stepped into the room and immediately went still. It was crammed full of souvenirs from a life spent overseas and smelled like the interior of a spice cabinet.

"Sir Robert?" A frail, wizened man with a somewhat yellowish skin gestured at the chair in front of him. "Please."

"Viscount Gravely." Robert bowed and took the seat, his nose twitching at the trail of smoke coming from some burning sticks on the desk.

"I appreciate you seeing me on this somewhat delicate matter." Robert wasn't one to waste time on pleasantries. "I understand that you recently took a young actress under your protection?"

"That is correct, although what it has to do with you is beyond me."

"Was her name Flora Rosa?"

His host simply nodded, his distaste for the

nature of the conversation more evident with every second.

"You installed her in a house in Maida Vale."

Again, there was no answer, and Robert sat forward. "I do not ask these questions with any pleasure, my lord, but I do wish to know the answers."

"I am not aware that I am obliged to tell you anything, sir. This is not a court of law."

"I am merely trying to establish that you knew Flora Rosa," Robert persevered. "When did she leave her house in Maida Vale?"

"Whoever told you that she did?"

"You are suggesting that she is still there?" Robert raised an incredulous eyebrow. "Then, if that is the case, perhaps you would furnish me with her address so that I can go and pay my respects to her and clear up the current confusion."

Lord Gravely looked down at his joined hands. "You suggested that you had important information to share with me about this matter. If this is not merely a fishing expedition to see if you can persuade her to become your mistress rather than mine, then I wish you would get to the point!"

Robert gave up all pretense of trying to be reasonable. "I am looking for someone to identify the body of a woman who I suspect is Flora Rosa and who was murdered in my home village of Kurland St. Mary."

Because he was looking carefully at the viscount, Robert clearly saw the man's shock at his deliberately harsh words. He rose to his feet.

"If you wish to discuss the matter or offer me your assistance, please be advised that I am staying with the Harrington family in Portland Square for the next two days before returning to Kurland St. Mary. If you still insist that your mistress is alive and well, and happily residing in Maida Vale, I would ask that I might speak to her, and offer both her and you my apologies."

The viscount looked up. "I have nothing further to say to you."

"As you wish." Robert inclined his head an icy inch. "I appreciate your time and consideration."

He turned on his heel and walked out, keeping a very tight rein on his temper. He should have brought his wife with him. She was far better at extracting information from people than he was.

He looked ahead and saw two men in the hallway. They appeared to be arguing about something. Both of them turned as Robert approached.

"Are you Sir Robert Kurland?" the taller one asked.

"Yes."

"I'm Trevor Gravely, and this is my brother Neville. We understand that you have just been speaking to our father." Trevor glanced at his brother, who frowned at him. "Would you mind very much if we asked you if this was about his mistress?"

Robert studied the two young men, who looked nothing like their father, both being tall and fair. He wondered whether they had stayed in England with their mother while the viscount had been occupied in India.

"Why do you want to know?"

"Because I have information that I think might help you," Trevor Gravely said. "Would you be willing to accompany us to a coffee shop so we can discuss the matter further?"

Robert retrieved his hat and cane from the silent butler and came to a decision.

"Yes, indeed. I would appreciate your thoughts on the matter."

He followed the two men out into the square and down toward the river where there were more people around. The fragrant smell of coffee caught his nose as the brothers turned down a side alley and approached the small shop.

They found a table in the corner and ordered their drinks. Around them, other men discussed business issues and politics, sometimes quite loudly, while smoking clay pipes and eating the meat pies the shop also offered.

"Before we start, you should be aware that your father refused to divulge any information about his mistress to me," Robert volunteered. "In truth, he claimed that all was well, and that she was still living happily in Maida Vale."

Neville grimaced. "She's not there. She ran off over a month ago, taking a substantial sum of cash and all the jewelry my father foolishly bestowed on her."

"You did not approve of the liaison?"

"Why would we?" Trevor answered him. "She is younger than us, and hardly the kind of woman a man of our father's class should be associating with."

"It is not uncommon for elderly men to take young mistresses," Robert pointed out. "Perhaps he was lonely."

Trevor snorted. "Or he was beguiled by a pretty face and an avaricious mind."

"I thought your father was a renowned businessman? I doubt he would allow himself to be 'beguiled,' " Robert continued. "Does your father realize that Flora Rosa is missing?"

"Of course, he does," Trevor said.

"Then why did he deny it?"

Neville sighed. "I think he is feeling ashamed for being bamboozled, and the thought of anyone outside the family knowing what happened is embarrassing for him."

Robert sat back as the waiter placed his pot of coffee in front of him. "Thank you. Where do you believe Flora Rosa is now?"

Neville cleared his throat, his anxious gaze on

his brother. "I assumed—we *both* assumed—that she had taken up with another man."

"Why would you assume that?" Robert asked.

"Why would we not?" Neville raised his eyebrows. "Flora is well known as an actress and an ambitious woman. There are many gentlemen who would be happy to become her protector."

Robert considered his options and decided to be blunt. He had an awful sensation that he was running out of time to solve Flora's murder.

"Then I regret to inform you that she is dead."

"God, *no!*" Neville blurted out, his voice shaking with emotion.

"I . . . I beg your pardon?" Trevor croaked. "Did you say *dead?*"

"Murdered, actually," Robert said. "That's what I came to tell your father today. I need someone to come down to Kurland St. Mary to identify her body."

The brothers glanced at each other.

"We both met her. We could identify her," Trevor said hesitantly. "We had no *idea* . . . we thought she'd just moved on to another man."

"It's certainly complicated," Robert said diplomatically. "But if one of you were willing to come down to Kurland St. Mary and make sure that we have the right woman, we could get on with the business of giving her a proper burial."

Trevor patted his brother's arm as Neville

struggled to speak. "It's all right. I can go. I wouldn't ask that of you."

"No, you *can't*—I mean, I must—" Neville shot to his feet, his face pale. "If you will excuse me for a moment, Sir Robert?"

Trevor waited until Neville was out of earshot before turning back to Robert. "I do apologize for my brother's behavior. He's terribly upset. He was the first person to meet Flora Rosa, and he was vastly taken with her. He made the mistake of introducing her to our father, and that was that." He grimaced. "The little bitch changed her allegiance in a flash."

"I'm sorry to hear that, but perhaps, as things stand, your brother was well rid of her."

Trevor sipped his coffee. "I hate to speak ill of the dead, but I think we're all well rid of her. Hopefully, next time, my father will form a liaison with someone more suitable."

"Would you object if I went to visit Flora's house in Maida Vale?" Robert asked.

"Not at all." Trevor produced one of his cards and wrote the address on the back of it. "Just give this to Mrs. Pell, tell her I sent you, and she'll be happy to let you in."

As they traveled away from the center of the city, Lucy glanced out of the carriage window, watching the houses gradually become less grand and the vistas less opulent. When Robert had returned from meeting Viscount Gravely and his two sons, she had been hard pressed to hide her frustration at the way the discussion had gone. She couldn't fault Robert for his direct attempt to alert the Gravelys to the fate of Flora Rosa, but she wished she'd been there to aid him.

"What if Dr. Fletcher is right?" Robert suddenly spoke after sitting in frowning contemplation for the past half an hour.

"Right about what?" Lucy asked.

"That the murderer came to kill Polly Carter and accidentally killed Flora instead?"

"I suppose it is possible," Lucy allowed. "But my inclination is to believe that Flora Rosa was killed for herself. She certainly stirred up something of a hornet's nest in her life, didn't she? I can't imagine what it would be like to have men fighting over *me*."

"I'd fight for you," Robert observed.

"Of course, you would, my dear." She smiled fondly at him. "But we are speaking of Polly Carter, who appears to have been working as a seamstress at the theater while Flora Rosa acted on the stage and acquired a large crowd of admirers."

"But what if Flora saw Polly being killed and fled to Kurland St. Mary to avoid the same fate?" Robert speculated.

"Flora had the protection of a peer of the realm. Do you not think she would've asked him to direct the authorities to investigate Polly's murderer?"

"I suppose that would've been the sensible thing to do." Robert pondered the matter for a moment. "What do you make of the two sons being involved in the matter?"

"It sounds remarkably embarrassing to me." Lucy shuddered. "Why on earth would an older man take his son's mistress away from him?"

"Because he could? And because Flora realized that the father would be more able to support her financially? We don't know for certain that Flora was Neville's mistress, just that he met her first. Needless to say, neither of the Gravely sons have much love for Flora Rosa any longer."

Lucy held onto the strap as the carriage turned a sharp corner into a tree-lined street of modest terraced houses with small front gardens.

"Were they really shocked to hear that she was dead?"

"I'd say so." Robert paused. "Although neither of them seemed particularly surprised. The only person who showed any real emotion was Neville, the younger son. He was so devastated he could barely speak." Robert sighed. "In truth, the sons seemed relieved that Flora was no longer around to bother their father."

Lucy had no answer for that. The carriage, which they had rented at the local mews, slowed down and eventually stopped opposite one of the identical yellow-bricked houses.

Robert looked out of the window and checked the number on the door. "This must be the place." He got out from the carriage, spoke to the driver, and then came around to help Lucy down. "I told him to come back in two hours. That should give us sufficient time to search the place and interview the remaining staff."

Lucy went ahead of him, opened the cast-iron gate, and went up the central path to the square-set house. It was modest in size, consisting of a bow-fronted window on either side of the front door with two identical stories above it.

Robert knocked on the door, which was opened by a middle-aged woman who didn't look particularly pleased to see them.

"Are you Mrs. Pell?" Robert asked. "I have a note for you from Mr. Trevor Gravely."

Mrs. Pell insisted on inspecting Trevor Gravely's card very carefully before she allowed Lucy and Robert inside the door.

"I'll be in the kitchen if you need me." She stomped off to the back of the house, leaving Lucy and Robert alone in the narrow hall.

"Charming," Robert murmured.

"Where shall we begin?" Lucy asked.

"How about we start at the top and work our way down on either side of the house?" Robert suggested. "I doubt we will find much to interest us, but we should be as thorough as possible."

"Agreed." Lucy raised the hem of her skirt and

186

went up the stairs. "And when I am finished, I will go and speak to Mrs. Pell in the kitchen."

"You think you will finish more quickly than I will?" Robert asked.

"Naturally." Lucy raised her chin.

"You are probably right. And when I am done, I will question any male staff still in residence."

Neither of them spent much time in the attics because it appeared that most of the staff that had tended Flora Rosa either lived out or had already left. Lucy was more certain of success when she opened a door on the first floor and was engulfed in a wave of stale perfume.

Robert disappeared into the opposite room, which smelled of cigar smoke and which had probably been occupied by Viscount Gravely.

Lucy stood with her back against the door and surveyed the bedchamber. There was a large four-poster bed made up with pink and lace linen, two comfortable chairs by the fire, and a chest of drawers. An ornate dressing table took advantage of the light pouring through the front window of the house. To Lucy's disappointment, it was remarkably devoid of substance or character. Flora's room at Kurland Hall had displayed more of her tastes and personality than this blank space.

It was fairly obvious that someone must have been in and tidied up everything after Flora's departure. Was it Mrs. Pell? Or had Polly Carter come to the house and removed all traces of the woman she was trying to help?

Refusing to be thwarted, Lucy set about opening drawers, peering into cupboards, and checking under the bed. The dressing table held no hairbrushes or cosmetics, and the perfume that still lingered in the air had long been packed away. From all accounts, Flora had not arrived at Kurland Hall with much luggage, so where had everything gone? Where were her London gowns, hats, and outdoor wear?

Robert said the Gravely sons had suggested that Flora had been given a lot of jewelry, yet Lucy had found only one necklace and a couple of rings among Flora's possessions. The more Lucy thought about it, the more she was convinced that the rest of Flora's things must be somewhere else.

In the back of one of the dresser drawers, Lucy discovered a note that had half-slipped under the back of the drawer, leaving a ripped piece behind. She carefully drew it out and considered the words.

Meet me after the performance, or else I'll tell him—

She didn't recognize the handwriting but did wonder at the implied threat. Was this simply another note from an unwanted admirer that Flora had stuffed in the drawer? Or had she kept it for a reason? Lucy was beginning to believe that the life of a beautiful actress involved far more hazards than she had ever imagined. Perhaps it was better to lack talent and looks, and be loved just for yourself.

There was an interior door leading into a shared dressing room that reached across the front of the house to the room next door. Lucy walked into it and noticed that none of the cupboards had clothes in them. She went to open the door into the other side and found it locked.

"Robert? Are you still in there?" Lucy knocked on the wooden panel.

Her husband opened the door and regarded her keenly. "Did you find anything interesting?"

"Not really. I suspect that someone has cleaned up very carefully." She looked up at him. "But where are all Flora's things? She certainly didn't take them to Kurland St. Mary."

"Maybe she pawned them to afford her ticket on the mail coach, or perhaps the servants here disposed of everything on Viscount Gravely's orders."

"Was there anything of interest in his room?" Lucy asked in return.

"Nothing—except the man obviously likes cramming his personal rooms with as many artifacts as a museum." He pointed at the far wall. "I wonder if he personally shot all those stuffed animals?"

"I thought you said that he was sickly?"

"He is now." Robert grimaced. "Perhaps he is trying to recapture the glories of his youth—which would also explain his desire to set up a woman young enough to be his granddaughter as his mistress."

She showed him the scrap of note, and he sighed.

"Poor Flora. I am beginning to feel that most of the men in her life were not very kind to her."

"I suspect you are right." Lucy eased a hand onto the small of her back as the baby kicked hard. "Do you think you could deal with the two downstairs rooms while I go and speak to Mrs. Pell?"

Robert's keen gaze searched her face. "Are you overdoing it?"

"I would certainly like to sit down for a while, but other than that, I am feeling quite well," Lucy retorted.

"Then go." He offered her an elaborate bow. "And good luck getting Mrs. Pell to reveal anything at all."

Lucy went down the stairs and made her way to the back of the house, where Mrs. Pell was sitting at the kitchen table with a cup of tea beside her. The housekeeper didn't bother to get up or even offer Lucy a greeting, which didn't really surprise her. Having dealt with the awfulness of Mrs. Fielding, who had been both her father's cook and bed warmer in the rectory for years, Lucy wasn't easily cowed.

Lucy rubbed a hand over her rounded stomach. "Do you have another cup somewhere? I would love some tea."

"Third cupboard on the right of the stove. Help yourself."

"Thank you, I will." Lucy found a cup and took it to the table. She sat directly opposite Mrs. Pell and helped herself to the contents of the teapot and the plate of shortbread that sat beside it.

"What wonderful shortbread, Mrs. Pell. Did you make it?"

"I did."

"Then Flora Rosa was a lucky woman to have you as her cook and housekeeper." Lucy munched determinedly on the dry biscuit. "And the house is kept so well. I wish my housekeeper was as dedicated as you are, Mrs. Pell."

"Thank you, ma'am." Mrs. Pell offered her the plate again. "Have another piece."

"Thank you." Lucy smiled at the woman. "Do you have a family, Mrs. Pell?"

"I have three of my own, and two grandchildren; one boy is three and the other five."

Lucy undid her coat to show her rounded stomach. "I have a two-year-old son and another child due at Christmas. Which is why I am appreciating your shortbread, as I find I get tired and hungry during the day."

"My daughter was the same way," Mrs. Pell said grudgingly. "Like a little rabbit, always nibbling on something."

Lucy chuckled. Mrs. Pell's expression softened fractionally as Lucy asked her a thousand questions about her grandchildren and family. Growing up in a rectory and having to take her mother's place in coping with the parishioners had given Lucy the perfect set of skills to converse with anyone. After a while, she guided the conversation back to her original purpose.

"I suspect you are wondering why Sir Robert and I are invading your house while your mistress is missing." Lucy sipped her strong tea.

"You're not the first to come barging in here, my lady, and I doubt you will be the last."

"Oh? Who else has come?"

Mrs. Pell crossed her arms over her chest.

"Did a woman named Polly Carter ever come here?" Lucy asked. "Her cousin Agnes works in my nursery. I *had* hoped to deliver a letter to Polly from Agnes while I was in London."

Mrs. Pell stared at her for a long time before she reluctantly opened her mouth again. Perhaps it was not going to be as easy as Lucy had anticipated. "Polly *did* mention she had a cousin called Agnes."

Lucy fought to conceal a spurt of triumph as another piece of the puzzle slid into place.

"Agnes is very good at her job. I believe she

was attempting to persuade Polly to forgo her work at the theater and come and work for me." Lucy patted her stomach. "As I am expecting again, I am eager to add to my nursery staff."

"Polly was a good girl," Mrs. Pell commented.

"I spoke with her mother recently. She hadn't seen Polly for a while." Lucy ventured into more problematical territory. "Has she been to see you since your mistress left?"

Mrs. Pell made a great show of pouring herself more tea and pursed her lips in thought. "I don't rightly know when I last saw Polly."

"She didn't help Flora Rosa leave here?"

"That dratted girl left in the middle of the night without telling anyone where she was going," Mrs. Pell said. "And the mess she left you wouldn't believe!"

"How horrible for you," Lucy said sympathetically. "Did you have to clean everything yourself, or did you have help?"

"We had a maid back then—Marjory, who also works next door—and she helped me set things to rights." Mrs. Pell shook her head. "I had to send young Paul, the boot boy, to tell Viscount Gravely that she'd gone and to send the stable hands out looking for her." She sighed. "No one could find a trace of the stupid girl."

"Well, leaving in the middle of the night is never very wise," Lucy agreed. "How awfully trying for you and your staff."

"Viscount Gravely didn't come himself, but he sent Mr. Neville and Mr. Trevor, and they did their best to help. Mr. Neville was beside himself."

"Where do you think Flora went?" Lucy asked.

"To another man?" Mrs. Pell sniffed. "We all know that actresses are just better-dressed whores, don't we?"

"Has anyone seen her with another man since she left?"

"Not that I know of. She's probably staying indoors until the fuss dies down and her new protector can come to some kind of financial arrangement with Viscount Gravely."

"Was she hard to work for, then?" Lucy added more tea to Mrs. Pell's cup.

"To be fair, she wasn't much trouble, and she was always very pleasant to me. She didn't hold parties here, and she kept very much to herself, entertaining only the viscount when he turned up, which wasn't often, and going to work at the Prince of Wales."

"When you decided she was unlikely to come back, did you box up her clothes to send them on to her?"

"No need. She stripped the place bare when she left." Mrs. Pell's truculent tone emerged again. "It was my day off. I'd been down to Southend to see my sister. When I returned, she'd up and gone during the night."

"But how did she carry everything?" Lucy wondered.

"I suspect she must have had help, which goes to show that she'd found a new man."

"That would make perfect sense," Lucy agreed. "I do hope Viscount Gravely didn't blame you for anything?"

"He's not been here since she left, my lady, so I haven't seen him. But he's kept me on to keep the place nice while he decides what to do with it."

"He is lucky that you chose to stay on and do your job so competently," Lucy said admiringly.

"It's much easier to look after a house than its occupants." Mrs. Pell shrugged. "I'm the only one who lives here full-time now."

"How many staff did you have before Flora left?"

"Marjory, the kitchen maid, and the boot boy." Mrs. Pell ticked them off on her fingers. "And Mr. Biggins, the man who took care of the horses, but he lives at the livery at the end of the street. I'd send Paul down when she needed the carriage."

"Did you hire your own staff, Mrs. Pell?"

"No, they all came from Viscount Gravely's various establishments."

"And that's where they have probably returned," Lucy guessed. "At least they weren't all out of a job when this unfortunate event happened."

The kitchen door opened, and Robert came in. Mrs. Pell immediately stiffened as Lucy offered him a warm smile.

"Ah, there you are, my dear. You will be pleased to hear that Mrs. Pell remembers Polly Carter but hasn't seen her for a while." She held her husband's gaze. "I told her that we'd originally been seeking Polly to deliver a letter to her from Agnes and only learned about Flora Rosa because of that."

Robert placed two calling cards on the table. "I am glad that you have seen Polly, Mrs. Pell. If she turns up here again, will you please let us know? We would like to speak to her before we leave London."

Chapter 12

❧

They exited the house together, and Lucy waited until Mrs. Pell had shut the door before turning to Robert.

"I didn't mention that Flora Rosa was dead."

"So I gathered." He paused by the carriage. "What do you want to do now?"

"I suggest we go and speak to the parlor maid next door, and then to Mr. Biggins at the mews."

"You have been busy." Robert smiled at her. "What if I go and find Mr. Biggins, and you concentrate on the maid?"

"You had better take me up in the carriage first in case Mrs. Pell is watching us through the curtains," Lucy suggested. "You can drop me off at the alley between the mews and the livery stables. I can walk back to the house next door."

"As you wish." He opened the door for her with a flourish. "And then we will return to the Harringtons, and you will rest until dinnertime."

"I'm not going to argue with you," Lucy said as he handed her up the steps. "I am quite fatigued."

"Then perhaps we should postpone our visits until tomorrow?"

She turned and placed a hand on his shoulder. "I'd much rather we didn't. I want to go home. The longer we stay in London, the more I miss my dearest Ned."

He met her gaze and nodded. "Although your aunt and uncle have been most hospitable, I am more than happy to leave this place myself."

He walked around the carriage, had a word with the driver, and got in the other side.

"What exactly am I supposed to be asking Mr. Biggins?"

"Ask him about Flora Rosa and whether he remembers Polly, and try to confirm that he is employed by the Gravely family."

Robert snapped a salute. "Yes, my lady."

They moved off and stopped again after the carriage had executed the turn onto the next street.

"Everything is arranged, my dear," Robert said. "Shall I wait for you at the livery stables?"

"Yes, please." She offered him an encouraging smile, straightened her bonnet, and descended from the vehicle without waiting for his assistance. He watched her walk off down the cobbled alley, her head high and her step firm. Despite his steady belief in her abilities, he still worried when she set off anywhere by herself. She did have a tendency to end up in trouble, and as she was currently with child, his concerns were higher than usual.

At the livery stables, he asked for Mr. Biggins

and was directed into the office at the rear of the building. A wiry, dark-haired man who had the look of a jockey stood up as Robert approached.

"What can I do for you, sir?"

"Are you Mr. Biggins?" Robert asked.

"Indeed I am."

"Did you work for the lady who lived at number seventeen Gloucester Street?"

"I did, sir. A pretty lass and a rising star of the theater." He grimaced. "She's gone now, though. Took my sunshine away with her, didn't she?"

"When did you last see her?" Robert asked.

Mr. Biggins gave him the eye. "Who's asking, and why?"

"I'm Sir Robert Kurland. I've been trying to trace the cousin of our nursery maid, who was supposed to come and work for us, but she seems to have disappeared. She apparently worked with Flora Rosa. I was hoping that the lady might help me discover Polly's whereabouts."

"Polly Carter?"

"Yes." Robert looked searchingly at Mr. Biggins. "Do you know her?"

"I sometimes took her up with Miss Flora to the theater. She was a nice girl. Not a beauty like Miss Flo, but a pleasant and respectable young woman." Mr. Biggins got out his pipe. "I can't say I've seen her recently. Viscount Gravely closed the account with the livery about a month ago, after Miss Flora left."

"Did he come here personally to deal with you?"

"No, his son summoned me to his big house on Grosvenor Square and paid me off. He did offer me my old job back in the stables, but I told him I'd decided to stay here and manage this place."

"Why was that? Were you unhappy at the Gravelys'?" Robert asked.

"The pay is better here, and I can arrange my own time, which I appreciate after getting up at the crack of dawn every day just in case one of the Gravelys wanted to ride or needed a carriage." Mr. Biggins got out his tobacco pouch and filled the bowl of his pipe. "And there's no chance of being promoted there because the bloke who held this job before me went back to work for the Gravelys, and he's been with them since he was a lad."

"Why did he leave this position?" Robert asked.

"Miss Flora didn't like him. I thought the viscount would kick him out on his ear, but apparently he took him back."

"Why didn't Miss Flora like him?"

"She resented him 'spying' on her." Mr. Biggins lit his clay pipe and sucked on the stem to draw the air through. "Now, I was asked to keep an eye on her myself, but I did it a lot more discreetly than Bert, and she never complained or realized I was reporting back to the Gravelys."

"And Bert went back to work for the Gravelys?" Robert asked slowly.

Mr. Biggins shrugged. "As I said, he was a good worker and never caused any trouble before he met Miss Flora."

"Did you help Miss Flora move her baggage to a new residence?" Robert decided he had nothing to lose in simply asking the question.

Mr. Biggins looked around and then lowered his voice. "I *might* have helped her out with that, sir, but that's only between you and me."

"Where did you take her belongings?"

Mr. Biggins looked Robert up and down expectantly, and with a sigh, Robert produced a gold crown. "Will this help jog your memory?"

"Well, thank you, sir." Mr. Biggins pocketed the coin. "If you'll give me a moment, I'll write the address down for you."

After knocking on the kitchen door of the house next to Flora Rosa's, Lucy was let into the kitchen by the very woman she'd wanted to see. Marjory Wallis was a chatty girl who explained that she was alone in the house because her mistress was shopping in town and Cook had taken the day off.

"She'll return to cook dinner in the evening, if it's wanted, but knowing Miss Eileen, she won't be coming home until the small hours, anyway." Marjory winked at Lucy and patted the bench seat of the kitchen table. "She's an actress, and she goes to grand parties, and all kinds of dinners, and balls . . ."

Marjory paused to breathe. "Now would you like a cuppa? I bet that Mrs. Pell didn't offer you one. She's a mean old biddy. I don't miss working there at all—except for the extra pay, and that Miss Flora was so kind and sweet to everyone."

She filled the kettle and set it on the stove. Lucy resigned herself to drinking more tea, which in her current condition was somewhat burdensome.

"I want to be an actress one day," Marjory confessed. "Although I'm not beautiful like Miss Flora and Miss Eileen, I do have a good singing voice, and I can dance."

Lucy swallowed back her desire to advise Marjory to stay in her current position and merely smiled.

"Were you surprised when Miss Flora left so suddenly?"

"Well, yes, seeing as she'd only just settled in with Viscount Gravely, and she seemed so happy and grateful to be under his protection." Marjory paused to place a jug of milk on the table. "She told me once that she felt safe for the first time in ages."

"And then she just left?" Lucy waited as Marjory half-filled the teapot that sat next to the kettle and brought it over. "Did she seem upset before that?"

Marjory sat opposite, her expression worried.

"She was certainly upset about something. I found her crying in the parlor one day." She grimaced. "I couldn't help but hear there had been an argument going on earlier."

"Between her and Viscount Gravely?"

"It was hard to tell from the kitchen, but it did sound like him." Marjory poured the tea. "He was telling her she was stupid, and that she was imagining things. *Mr.* Gravely came around to see her later, and she said he was very kind to her indeed." Marjory laughed. "In truth, I think she saw more of the Gravely brothers than she did their father."

"Oh dear." Lucy added lots of milk to her tea and sipped politely. "Perhaps things had soured between her and the viscount, and she was thinking of moving on."

"That's what everyone thinks, but . . ." Marjory gripped her hands together on the table. "Where is she? If she had a new man to flaunt, why isn't she back at work in the theater?"

"Perhaps she feels it is too soon to show she has changed . . . allegiances?" Lucy suggested.

"But for an actress, such notoriety would bring the public to see her in droves," Marjory replied. "She'd be even more in demand and more famous than ever."

"I hadn't thought of that," Lucy admitted.

"I'm worried about her, ma'am." Marjory met Lucy's gaze straight on. "She always said that if she ever did leave Viscount Gravely, she would take me with her, and I haven't heard a word." She paused. "I *did* wonder whether she'd gone back to *Mr.* Gravely, and that's why she'd gone to ground, but I doubt the viscount would've put up with that!"

Lucy considered what to say next. Should she tell Marjory the truth or leave things as they were? As the maid obviously liked to chat, telling her that Flora was dead might spread the news back to Mrs. Pell and complicate matters even further.

"Did you ever meet a woman called Polly Carter at Miss Flora's?" Lucy asked.

Marjory sipped her tea, her gaze sliding past Lucy's toward the kitchen door as if she was imagining someone entering. "Yes, she sometimes came back with Miss Flora from the theater to fit her costumes. Do you know her?"

"In truth, I am looking for her. I have a letter from her cousin Agnes that I am attempting to deliver. I had hoped that Polly was staying with Miss Flora, as she has not been home to see her mother recently." Lucy paused. "I don't suppose you know where Polly might be staying?"

"I don't, ma'am, but if I see her, I'll be sure to tell her that someone is looking for her."

"I would appreciate that." Lucy offered Marjory her card. "I will be returning home in a day or so and would hate to miss her."

Lucy took her leave of Marjory and walked back down the quiet alleyway in deep thought. Flora had been arguing with someone just before she'd left and had confessed to being worried about something. Apparently, Viscount Gravely had just gone along with the general impression that she'd left him for another man.

Had he really not known that his mistress had disappeared completely? Robert had met the viscount and his family and hadn't been convinced that they were ignorant of Flora's death. But how would they have known about a murder in Kurland St. Mary unless someone from their household had been present when it occurred?

"Ah, there you are, my dear." Robert hailed her from the entrance to the livery. "Are you ready to leave? I have a lot to tell you."

He helped her up into the carriage and shut the door, leaving them in relative privacy. Lucy sank back into the seat, aware that her feet were hurting and that she really did need to sleep . . .

The next thing she knew, a burly footman was carrying her up to her room while Betty drew the curtains and pulled back the bedclothes. Robert appeared briefly at her side.

"I'll see you at dinner, my love."

She grabbed his hand. "But I have so much to share with you!"

He smiled and kissed her fingers. "It will keep. I have a lot to tell you, too."

● ● ●

Dinner at the Harringtons proceeded in its usual fashion, with excellent food and clever conversation—something Robert enjoyed participating in but didn't miss in his own home on a daily basis. He planned to visit the address Mr. Biggins had given to him on the following morning, speak to the Gravelys again, and leave for Kurland St. Mary the day after. Like Lucy, he was missing his son and his home too much to stay away for much longer. He also had a sense that the mystery behind Flora's death was rapidly becoming clearer.

He pictured her beautiful face as he sipped his port. From all appearances, she had done little to deserve her fate, and the person who had ended her life ought to suffer for it. Jealousy was rarely becoming in anyone, and killing the object of your supposed love? Something he could never fathom at all . . .

He looked down the long table toward his wife, who was conversing amiably with her dinner partner. She did look well, and his fears about her current condition receded somewhat. He might admit to being slightly overprotective of Lucy, but she did have a remarkable ability to find herself in dangerous situations.

Penelope Fletcher appeared to be enjoying herself immensely at the dinner party. She had gathered a small circle of respectful admirers around her since renewing her acquaintance with the ton, something his friend Patrick appeared to find amusing rather than worrying. Like Flora, she was a beautiful woman. Robert was glad she'd decided he wasn't good enough to marry her, but he was still rather perplexed as to why Patrick seemed so happy with her.

In fairness, Penelope had chosen to give up her dreams of London society and live in a small village with an Irish doctor who was unlikely to ever make more than a comfortable living. Idly, Robert wondered what would've happened if Flora and Penelope's lives had been reversed. Would Flora have succeeded in marrying a duke, and would Penelope have allowed herself to become a man's mistress or striven to be the best actress in London? He suspected they would both have found a way to succeed on their own terms, as did most resourceful women.

He reminded himself that Flora had reached high and was now dead. Perhaps Penelope's decision to embrace love instead of status had been a wiser choice after all . . .

Robert sipped his wine and helped himself to more fish. The earl of Harrington had approached him earlier in the evening about a potential opening for a seat he controlled in parliament. He'd offered it to Robert with the assurance that he would not dictate matters of policy on most matters, as he believed their interests were already well aligned. Lucy could have told her uncle that was not the case, as Robert truly wished to address the inequalities in the current voting system and would, if given the chance, probably vote to abolish his own seat.

But it was something to think about and discuss with Lucy when they returned home. At the moment, all he wanted was for Flora's murderer to be brought to justice. And in his opinion, returning to Kurland St. Mary would help greatly with that matter.

At a signal from the countess, the ladies rose from their seats and left the dining room, leaving the men to their port and conversation. Robert extracted a cigarillo from his case and prepared to sit back and listen to the latest political scandal while his wife enjoyed her tea. If he did intend to take up a seat in the House of Commons, he should, perhaps, pay better attention to current affairs.

He got up to find a light for his cigarillo. A commotion in the entrance hall caught his attention, and he walked over to the door to observe what was going on. There was an older man dressed in an ill-fitting coat, tricorn hat, and white stock tie waving a book in the face of the usually unflappable Harrington butler.

"I demand to see that woman now!"

"Lady Kurland is not at home to the likes of you, sir!" the butler raised his voice to match his opponents. "Now, if you won't leave, I will call the Watch."

Robert quietly closed the door into the dining room behind him and advanced into the hall.

"Is something the matter?"

The butler turned to him. "Not at all, sir. This . . . gentleman is just leaving."

Robert regarded the red-faced man. "What do you want with Lady Kurland?"

"She's here, isn't she?" The man shoved a card under Robert's nose. "She gave this to my wife."

Robert raised his gaze to the man's angry face. "Who are you, exactly, sir?"

"I'm Mr. Carter. Polly's father."

"Ah." Robert turned to the butler. "Would you find somewhere for me to speak to Mr. Carter, and ask my wife to join us?"

"Are you quite sure about this, Sir Robert?" the butler asked. "Because—"

"Quite sure," Robert said firmly. "Please lead the way."

He followed the stiff-backed butler down one of the corridors that led toward the servants' stairs until he opened a door into a cramped office that belonged to the earl of Harrington's secretary.

"I will fetch Lady Kurland, sir, and if you permit, I will ask one of my footmen to wait outside this door in case you need anything." The butler bowed.

"As you wish." Robert lit one of the candles

from the embers of the fire, banked up the coals, and lit the remaining candles in the candelabra.

"Please make yourself comfortable, Mr. Carter."

"There's no comfort on this earth, Mr. Kurland, that will cover the stench of sin."

"I beg to differ, sir, but please remain standing if you wish."

Mr. Carter glared at him, one hand pressing the leather-clad book to his chest as they waited for Lucy to join them. Robert didn't bother to fill the silence with polite chatter. He had a sense that Mr. Carter would not respond well, and he had no desire to enrage the man further before he knew why he'd turned up at the Harringtons'.

Lucy came in, her gaze moving instantly from Robert to Mr. Carter, who scowled at her.

"You must be Mr. Carter, Agnes's uncle. She is such a credit to your family." Lucy said pleasantly. "I will make sure to tell her that we saw you while we were in town. Do you have any message you wish me to pass onto her?"

"I didn't come here to talk about Agnes."

"Then why did you come?" Robert asked.

"Because she," Mr. Carter pointed at Lucy, "has been upsetting my wife."

"How so?"

"By coming around, asking questions, stirring things up that don't need to see the light of day." He frowned at Robert. "You, sir, should have your wife under better control."

Robert's lips twitched, but he didn't reply. He was fairly certain Lucy was perfectly capable of defending herself.

"All I did, Mr. Carter, was ask your wife if she had seen her own daughter," Lucy stated.

"Well, she ain't," Mr. Carter still addressed his remarks to Robert. "And she isn't going to be seeing her for a long time."

Lucy stiffened, and Robert leaned forward, took her fisted hand in his, and gently drew her back to stand in front of him.

"Why is that, Mr. Carter?"

"Because Polly came around today to see her and said she's leaving London for good because of you lot."

"Because of us?" Robert frowned. "I hardly see the logic of such a statement when we have never even met her."

"She's leaving because you have been going around town asking after her and making her afraid."

"Afraid of what?" Robert persisted. "We merely wish to deliver a letter to her from her cousin Agnes and ascertain that she is well. What's the harm in that?"

"Because Polly does not need your attention or that of any aristocrat!" Mr. Carter snapped. "I knew allowing her to work with those whores and posturers at the theater would turn out badly. And I was right. Her reputation is ruined."

"Simply because she worked at a theater? How small-minded of you, sir," Robert replied.

"I know my Bible, Sir Robert. She has consorted with sinners and now must pay the price by being separated from her family."

"I thought she already was," Robert said, and continued by asking, "Didn't you make her leave because she was friendly with Flora Rosa?"

Mr. Carter's color grew noticeably redder. "Polly was brought up in a godly home! She only needed to repent of her wickedness, and she would've been allowed back into the fold."

"Then seeing as she obviously hasn't repented and would rather leave London than come back to live at home, I hardly see what this has to do with me or my wife." Robert glared at Mr. Carter. "You are at fault, and you chose to come here merely to vent your spleen on an innocent party, my wife, because you are angry that your daughter disobeyed *you*."

He stalked over to the door. "We have nothing to apologize for." He opened it wide. "I bid you good night, sir."

For a moment, Mr. Carter locked gazes with Robert, and then, with a last indignant sniff, he turned and walked away, his nose in the air. Robert beckoned to the footman stationed outside door.

"Escort Mr. Carter to the front door, please. And make sure he leaves."

"Yes, Sir Robert."

He turned to see his wife sink down into one of the chairs and regarded her from the doorway.

"Are you all right?"

"Yes, but what on earth was that all about?" Lucy asked.

"I'm not quite sure, but we did learn one important thing." He sauntered back toward her. "Polly Carter isn't dead, and that, my dear, was well worth hearing."

Chapter 13

Lucy plaited her hair into a single braid and climbed into bed to wait for Robert to emerge from the dressing room. After dealing with Mr. Carter, they had parted company again and gone to complete their social duties. It was now almost midnight, and Lucy, who was not used to keeping town hours, was almost ready to fall asleep again.

Robert emerged from the dressing room wrapped in his silk banyan and got into bed beside her.

"Did you know your uncle was going to offer me the opportunity to represent his interests in parliament?"

"He did mention it, but I thought it would be best for him to approach you directly," Lucy said.

"How very diplomatic of you."

She smiled at him. "What did you say?"

"I said I would consider my options." Robert settled back against the headboard. "The thought of having to live in London while the House is in session doesn't appeal to me much."

"It's not a place I would choose to raise our children, either," Lucy said. "Until they are older, I would probably not accompany you."

"Which would make for a very lonely existence." Robert kissed her cheek. "I miss my son more than I anticipated."

Lucy savored his unguarded response. He was not a man who expressed his emotions easily, and the fact that he was even admitting that he missed Ned was worthy of note. She yawned again and hastily covered her mouth.

"Do you want me to blow the candles out?" Robert inquired.

"Not yet. I'd like to tell you what happened today with Marjory, the parlor maid, and review the possibilities about Flora's murderer."

"Please go ahead."

His somewhat smug smile was unexpected, as was the way he leaned back on the pillows and invited her with an extravagant gesture to continue.

"Marjory was the chatty sort and told me quite a lot about the goings-on in Flora Rosa's house. She also raised an interesting question. If Flora had found a new protector, why wasn't she flaunting him at the theater to enhance her reputation?"

"Because someone had murdered her and left her body in a ditch in Kurland St. Mary?"

Lucy ignored her husband's attempt at sarcasm.

"Marjory also said that Flora was still close to Viscount Gravely's sons."

For the first time, Robert looked thoughtful. "Which disputes their account of hating her somewhat."

"Exactly." Lucy nodded. "Marjory wondered whether Flora had gone back to Neville, and *that* was why Viscount Gravely was so angry about what had happened."

"I definitely don't think Viscount Gravely would've approved of her taking up with his son again after he'd spent all that money on her."

"Perhaps he didn't approve?" Lucy faced Robert. "Perhaps he decided to teach Flora a lesson?"

"And pop down to Kurland St. Mary and kill her? I think Mr. Jarvis or one of the village gossips might have noticed if a viscount had appeared in their midst," Robert countered.

"But *what* other man?" Lucy frowned. "I agree with Marjory. If there was someone else, I'm fairly sure we would have found him by now. Don't you think he might be wondering where she's gone as well?"

"You're also assuming that Viscount Gravely somehow knew Flora had switched places with Polly Carter and taken her job at Kurland Hall. How do you think he would know that?" Robert asked.

"Seeing as Polly is doing everything she can to

stay away from us, maybe, she told him." Lucy suggested.

She searched his face, but he seemed remarkably unperturbed by all her suggestions.

"What is it?" she demanded. "What aren't you telling me?"

"These are all very interesting theories, my dear, but I have an even better one." He grinned infuriatingly at her.

Lucy raised her eyebrows and sat back. "Then do, pray, tell."

"Mr. Biggins wasn't the first Gravely employee to drive Flora Rosa around."

"So?"

"The original driver was a man named Bert, who quarreled with Flora and was replaced when she complained about him to Viscount Gravely."

"*Our* Bert?"

"Apparently so." Robert's smile disappeared. "One might begin to come to the conclusion that our journey to London was wasted, and that we had the culprit safely locked up in Mr. Jarvis's cellar all along."

Lucy stared at him. "Are you quite certain it is Bert Speers who worked for Viscount Gravely?"

"I believe so. Mr. Biggins described him to me quite accurately. I'll attempt to confirm it tomorrow when I speak to Viscount Gravely."

"But what if Viscount Gravely sent Bert to murder Flora?"

"I suppose that is possible." To her annoyance, he didn't sound in the least bit convinced. "But surely Bert has already half-convicted himself. He was seen with Flora, and he admits to man-handling her. Maybe, for once, this is far more straightforward than we realized. Bert falls in love with Flora, he oversteps his place, and she complains about him to Viscount Gravely, who removes him from his position. Angry that he has been denied access to his 'one true love,' Bert decides to follow her down to Kurland St. Mary and kill her."

"But—"

Robert held up a finger. "Will you at least concede that I might be right? You do tend to overcomplicate things."

She regarded him in silence, her arms folded over her chest. "I just like to make sure that I ask all the questions, even the silly ones."

"You certainly do."

"And sometimes I am right to do so." She raised her chin.

"I can't argue with that." Robert agreed, mollifying her slightly, and then ruined it by patting her cheek. "I promise that I will speak to Viscount Gravely tomorrow and make sure that Bert Speers was employed by him. Will that suffice to make you believe the matter is settled?"

"What about Polly?"

He frowned. "What about her?"

"Aren't you worried about what has become of her?"

"I assume that after we leave London and stop attempting to speak to her, she will resume her life as usual."

Lucy sniffed. "I think you are wrong."

"And I think you are making mountains out of molehills." He kissed her nose. "Shall we agree to disagree and go to sleep? We will have a busy day tomorrow. Not only must I speak to Viscount Gravely, but Mr. Biggins gave me the address of a place where he took Flora's possessions when she left."

"What?" Lucy sat bolt upright again. "Why didn't you mention this earlier?"

"Because I didn't want you to get all excited about something that has no bearing on our investigation."

"Only if your scenario is correct," Lucy reminded him.

He started to blow out the candles beside the bed. "I'm not saying we can't go and look, so don't get too cross with me."

Lucy lay down on her side and allowed Robert to put her arm around her. She feared her mind was wrestling with too many possibilities for her to sleep.

"Ouch," Robert murmured against her ear. "The little blighter just kicked me."

"Serves you right," she whispered back. He chuckled, and his arm tightened around her

Her eyes closed despite her worries, and she smiled her way into sleep.

After instructing Betty to let Lucy sleep for as long as she needed, Robert tiptoed out of the bedchamber, ate a hurried breakfast, and walked around the back of the house to the Harrington mews to borrow a horse. He'd willingly take Lucy to Flora's other address, but he saw no reason to inflict Viscount Gravely on her. He also hated riding so much that the mere thought of getting on the back of a horse was making him feel physically sick.

He reminded himself that it was only a short distance to Grosvenor Square, and he needed an excuse to visit the Gravely stables before he confronted the master of the house. The Harrington groom was rather surprised when he asked for the oldest, most docile horse in the stables, but he was far too well trained to ask awkward questions.

After two minutes of contemplating getting up on the back of the horse and failing to execute his plan, Robert decided he was bloody well going to walk his steed the quarter mile to the Gravely House and be damned to anyone who saw him. He could always claim that the horse had gone lame.

When Robert arrived at the Gravely House mews, he waited while his horse was led away and asked to speak to the head coachman.

Five minutes later, he was on his way up to the house. He hadn't sent notice of his arrival and hoped to catch the viscount before he left home. From his quick survey of the stables, none of the carriages or horses had been absent, which he assumed meant that all the Gravely men were present.

He knocked on the front door, and the Indian butler let him into the hall before asking his business.

"Good morning. I'd like to speak to Viscount Gravely."

"He is not available to callers yet, Sir Robert. Would you like to leave your card?"

"I'd prefer to see him immediately. Can you go and tell him I'm here?"

The butler frowned. "Viscount Gravely is not well, sir. He is still in bed."

"And I would still like to speak him." Robert held the butler's gaze. "I'm leaving town tomorrow, so it is imperative that I see him on a matter of great importance."

"What's going on?"

Robert turned as Trevor Gravely came down the staircase dressed for a morning ride, a whip dangling from one of his hands.

"Good morning, Mr. Trevor." The butler bowed.

"This gentleman wishes to see your father, sir. I am trying to explain that the viscount is not well enough to receive visitors."

Trevor stared at Robert. "Is this about that woman?"

"Yes, I just need to clarify a couple of points with your father, and then I promise I will leave him in peace."

"I'll take him up," Trevor announced to the butler. "Don't worry, Ahuja. I'll take complete responsibility for this."

Robert handed over his hat and cane to the reluctant butler, and followed Trevor up the stairs.

"My father is awake and eating his breakfast. I spoke to him just before I came down. I'm not sure why Ahuja didn't want you to see him."

Robert was fairly certain that Viscount Gravely wouldn't want to see him but said nothing as Trevor knocked on the door and went in.

"Father? Sir Robert Kurland is here to see you."

Trevor stepped aside, allowing Robert to see that the viscount was propped up on his pillows in his large bed, reading the paper. His expression when he saw Robert was not encouraging,

"I thought we had agreed to part company on this matter, Sir Robert."

Robert shrugged. "I don't remember agreeing to that. I asked you to let me know if you had any further thoughts about the murder of your mistress."

"I don't." The viscount looked past Robert to his son, who was leaning against the door frame. "Tell Ahuja to escort Sir Robert out."

Trevor sighed. "Father, just let him speak, and then I promise I will escort him out myself. This attempt to pretend that everything is fine is ridiculous."

The viscount slammed his glass down on the tray with such force that the liquid inside spilled over the top. "If I am going to be subjected to Sir Robert's company, then you will leave us in peace!"

Trevor held up his hands. "As you wish."

He left the room, and Robert turned his attention to the man in the bed.

"Do you have a man named Bert Speers currently in your employ?"

There was a flicker of interest in the viscount's eyes. "No."

"Did you ever have such a man?"

"It's possible that he once worked in my stables. He left a while ago."

"Why was that?"

"I don't think that's any of your business, sir."

"It is when he has turned up in my village and is currently incarcerated in the cellars of my local inn. I am the local magistrate, and I can assure you that I take accusations of murder very seriously indeed."

The viscount put down his knife and carefully wiped his thin lips with his napkin.

"What an interesting coincidence that Speers turned up in Kurland St. Mary."

"Indeed." Robert tried to hold the viscount's gaze. "I understand that Bert drove Flora Rosa's carriage for a while."

"Did he?" The viscount raised an eyebrow. "I leave such piddling matters to my head coachman and butler to manage."

"I've already spoken to your coachman. He confirmed that Bert Speers worked for you, and that he drove Flora Rosa for a while before she asked for him to be replaced."

"If you know all this, why are you bothering me with this matter?"

Robert took a moment to gather his rapidly diminishing patience. "Do you not care that your mistress was found murdered?"

"She chose to leave me." The viscount looked up at Robert. "What happened to her after that is hardly my concern, is it?"

"From what I understand, she left because she was afraid of someone."

"Then perhaps she should have stayed and trusted that I would take care of her."

"Perhaps she felt you would not believe her concerns," Robert countered.

"She was an actress, Sir Robert; she often elaborated her misfortunes. Her whole life was based on dramatic notions and silly fantasies."

"I'll wager she *did* tell you she was afraid, and you chose not to believe her. She ran away to save herself and ended up dead in a ditch anyway."

His companion shrugged. "I suppose you might put it that way."

Robert was way past being pleasant now. "Or it might even be simpler. She was afraid of *you,* ran away, and you had her hunted down and killed."

The viscount gave a slow smile. "Now who is dealing in silly fantasies?" He nodded toward the door. "I suggest that as you have asked your impudent questions and heard my answers, then you will leave quietly before I call for assistance."

Robert studied the old man for a long moment before he took a step away from the bed.

"I see it was a mistake to assume you would be concerned about the fate of the woman you bought and paid for."

"Surely objects that allow themselves to be sold are hardly worth your anger or your attention, Sir Robert?" The viscount pushed the breakfast tray away from him. "Are you going to ask me for money to pay for her funeral next? The jewelry I lavished on her should easily pay for the most extravagant of funerals."

Robert inclined his head an icy inch. "I

wouldn't think to bother you with such niceties, my lord. Before her death, Flora worked in my house and is, therefore, my responsibility. Good day to you."

"And to you."

Robert had almost reached the door before the viscount spoke once more.

"If you appear on my doorstep again, Sir Robert, I will instruct my butler not to let you in the house."

Robert looked over his shoulder. "I doubt I will ever have reason to seek you out again, my lord. In truth, if I saw you in the street, I would probably cross it to avoid having to acknowledge your existence."

To his chagrin, the viscount smiled again. "As I am near death, your scorn does not bother me in the slightest. When you reach my age, sir, you too might be willing to close your eyes and do whatever is necessary to avoid such . . . a minor storm in your continued existence."

"As I would never consider the murder of anyone a 'minor inconvenience,' my lord, I'll beg to differ."

Robert yanked open the door with some force, startling Trevor Gravely, who was leaning against the wall in the corridor outside.

"Thank you for allowing me to speak to your father." Robert set off down the stairs, Trevor in pursuit. "You have my address. If you wish to come down to Kurland St. Mary to identify Flora Rosa's body, please let me know. You will be more than welcome to stay at Kurland Hall."

"Thank you, Sir Robert." Trevor managed to get ahead of Robert when he stopped to retrieve his hat and cane, and opened the front door. "Please forgive my father. He is not well."

"He—" Robert paused. There was no point in reviling the man to his own son. "It was good of him to see me when he was still abed."

"He was very worried when Neville became involved with Flora."

"Worried enough to ask her to be his mistress?"

Trevor grimaced. "I know it does sound rather odd, but Neville could be . . . rather intense when he imagined he was in love. I suspect Father thought he would save Neville a lot of unnecessary grief."

"Are you suggesting that Flora might have been afraid of your brother and asked your father to help out by offering her his protection?"

"Good Lord, no!" Trevor gaped at him. "I'd never even thought of that! I just mean that Neville tends to fall in love easily and can become rather obsessed, leading to . . . misunderstandings. My father might have believed it was his duty to step in and quash all his hopes. Neville was perfectly fine about it, by the way. He even *thanked* Father for stopping him from making a fool of himself."

"And instead allowed your father to be the fool?"

"You don't understand," Trevor said earnestly. "Father showed Neville what Flora was really like—a woman who wanted as much money as she could accumulate before her looks and mediocre talent faded."

"And Neville appreciated that."

Trevor grinned. "It took a while, but, eventually, yes, he did."

Trevor followed Robert all the way to the stables, his expression anxious as he attempted to apologize yet again for his father and brother. Robert didn't interrupt or offer his own opinion of the man. If Viscount Gravely truly were dying, his judgment would soon be in the hands of a far greater power than Robert's.

He finally managed to shake Trevor off as his horse was brought around. He thanked the groom and walked his own patient steed out of the stables and around the corner. As he walked back toward Portland Square, his hand tightly gripping the bridle, he wondered why Viscount Gravely had even bothered to find a mistress when he was so ill? Had he simply done it to spite his youngest son? Or had he tried to teach the lad a lesson, as Trevor thought? It seemed unlikely, but perhaps the viscount had no real relationship with either of his sons after having been abroad for most of their lives, and treated them accordingly.

Had he feared that Flora would extort too much money out of the seemingly gullible Neville, and put a stop to it by offering her more immediate gains? A man knowing he was near death might make such a decision to safeguard his son's inheritance, even if it made his son hate him. And if the viscount truly had nothing to fear except death, maybe he would have stooped low enough to order Flora's demise.

Robert firmly reeled in his imagination and reminded himself of Bert Speer's guilt. When he returned to Kurland St. Mary and sent Bert off to trial at the assizes, the truth would surely emerge.

He arrived back at Portland Square and went up the back stairs to his bedchamber to change into a less damp coat. There was no sign of Lucy, who had probably gone down to breakfast. He was eager to join her, his morning activities having made him hungrier than usual.

He put on his second-best coat, made sure his boots were presentable, and went down again, this time using the main staircase.

"Sir Robert?"

He was hailed from the hall by Penelope Fletcher and walked over to speak to her. She looked as beautiful as ever and, from a cursory glance of her fashionable clothes, was the happy recipient of a lot of Lucy's aunt's castoffs.

"Yes, Mrs. Fletcher?"

"Have you decided when you intend to return to Kurland St. Mary?"

"I intend to leave by the end of the week."

She frowned. "So quickly?"

"I didn't plan to stay this long, ma'am, but needs must."

"Is Lucy worn out with it all? She's never been entirely comfortable with the position she now holds, has she?"

"She seems in good spirits." Robert paused. "Why? Do you think otherwise?"

"Not at all, I was just wondering if that was the reason you wanted to leave so quickly."

"I am quite certain, if you wish to stay another week, ma'am, that the Harrington family would not object."

"Not *me*." She made a face. "Patrick is enjoying himself so much that I hate to tear him away. *I* want to go home and see my son."

Aware that he might have grossly misjudged the depth of her maternal affection, Robert hastened to reassure her.

"If your husband wishes to stay, I'm sure that it could be arranged."

She touched his sleeve. "If you could speak to the earl about the matter, I would *greatly* appreciate it. I do not think it is my place to do so."

"As soon as I have arranged my own travel plans, I will certainly ask the earl if Dr. Fletcher can continue to be his guest for a week."

"Thank you." She smiled at Robert. "I am already looking forward to spending the journey back to Kurland St. Mary in the company of you and Lucy."

Robert walked into the breakfast room. The thought of being cooped up in a carriage with Penelope for several hours a day without the buffer of her husband between them was not something he would ever wish for. His wife would not be very happy about it, either.

"Ah! There you are, Robert." Lucy looked over at him. She was alone in the vast room. "Have you eaten?"

"Not yet." He piled a plate high with victuals and came to sit beside her. Unlike many women she didn't immediately pepper him with questions about where he had been and allowed him to eat his fill before he started talking. "I went to see Viscount Gravely."

She studied him for a moment before she poured him some coffee. "From the expression on your face, I assume it didn't go well?"

"He's an awfully unpleasant man, Lucy." Robert sawed through a piece of gammon. "I cannot understand for the life of me why Flora decided to take him up on his offer."

"Money?"

"So everyone insists, but we both met Flora, and I don't know about you, my dear, but she didn't come across as the grasping sort to me."

231

"No, she didn't," Lucy said thoughtfully. "But one can't forget that she was apparently a very good actress. Maybe she fooled us both."

Robert sighed and swallowed a mouthful of ham. "Mayhap she did. She does seem to have meant many different things to different people."

"None of which justifies her murder," Lucy reminded him. "Do you still intend to visit the address Mr. Biggins gave you?"

"Yes, indeed." He ate an egg and another slice of gammon, and immediately started to feel better. "We can go as soon as you are ready."

Chapter 14

The address took them out of the east side of London toward Bethnal Green, which was not an area Lucy was familiar with. Dr. Fletcher had offered to accompany them as he had been there earlier in the week visiting a friend who worked in one of the hospitals established in that region.

"I'm not sure why Flora would have ended up here." Robert frowned as he looked out of the window at the rows of small houses and increasingly narrow streets.

"Perhaps her family came from here," Dr. Fletcher suggested.

"I don't think she ever knew her family," Robert said. "She grew up in an orphanage and was put into service when she reached the age of fourteen."

"There is a large orphanage right next to the hospital, and a workhouse," Dr. Fletcher said. "I have visited them all and struggle to believe that any child emerged from that unhealthy environment alive."

"If she grew up here, perhaps she still has

friends whom she trusts?" Lucy asked. "She told *me* that she came from a large family, but she told Mr. Frobisher something completely different. One has to wonder whether she picked up her skills with children helping to tend the smaller ones at the orphanage."

"That sounds logical." Robert nodded. "I expect she was more likely to lie to you about this particular matter because she wanted to be seen as competent with children than she was to lie to Mr. Frobisher at the Prince of Wales."

Lucy peered out of the carriage window as the natural lighting gradually disappeared, displaced by tall rows of houses with slate roofs and large front windows. It was not a pleasant area or somewhere Lucy would ever like to live, and she pitied anyone who was forced to endure it.

Dr. Fletcher noticed where she was looking.

"The Huguenot refugees who built these houses were often weavers and lace makers who needed as much light as possible for their work—hence the large windows."

"Are there still many of these weavers around here?"

"Not that many." Dr. Fetcher grimaced. "The new factories arising in the north can produce a much higher volume of lace than any single person these days. Most of these houses have been divided into smaller living accommodations, with whole families squeezed into two rooms. It is not ideal."

Lucy could only nod in agreement.

"Which street are we going to?" Dr. Fletcher asked.

Robert consulted the piece of paper Mr. Biggins had given him. "Paradise Row. Do you know of it?"

"Only for another reason." Dr. Fletcher chuckled. "Mendoza lived there."

"Good Lord!" Robert stared at his friend. "Is this where he established his academy?"

"Apparently so."

Lucy poked Robert in the side. "Who is Mendoza?"

He looked down at her as if she were witless. "Daniel Mendoza, the boxer."

"I believe I have heard my father mention him," Lucy said cautiously. "He wrote *The Art of Boxing*."

Both men were now staring at her approvingly. She allowed herself a small congratulatory smile.

"My brother Anthony was always quoting the text."

"Well, it appears that Flora once lived on the same street as the great man himself," Dr. Fletcher said. "Perhaps even in the same house."

"We shall see about that," Robert muttered as the carriage finally came to a stop. "From the look of the place, one would need to be handy with one's fists simply to survive."

"As long as we stay together and don't show off any valuables, we should be fine," Dr. Fletcher said encouragingly.

"Unless you wish to stay in the carriage, my dear." Robert turned to Lucy.

She considered her choices. "I think I'd rather come with you than be left out here by myself."

"Then stay close behind me," Robert advised. "We'll let Dr. Fletcher bring up the rear."

Lucy allowed him to help her out of the carriage and stared up at the blackened stone façade of the small terraced cottage. It was at the end of the row, and a dark passageway to the left of the house presumably led to the rear. The street was choked with debris and filth. There was no garden or cast-iron fencing, and the front step touched the pavement.

Lucy had a sense that she was being watched but was unable to work out from where, as it felt as if a hundred pairs of eyes were fixed on her. As they approached the front door, the curtains twitched. Robert knocked loudly, but there was no reply. Dr. Fletcher stepped back, his gaze fixed on the upstairs windows.

"There is definitely someone up there," Dr. Fletcher said. "Perhaps I should go around to the rear of the house while you stay here?"

"I'll go," Robert said firmly. "If anything

happens, make sure you get Lady Kurland to safety immediately."

"Robert—" Lucy reached out her hand, but it was too late. He was already moving away from her down the alley.

Robert opened the back gate of the small walled and cobbled yard, and went inside. The back door was ajar, and he went toward it, pausing to open it more widely, and then closed it behind him.

Someone clattered down the stairs toward him. "Is that you, Marj? I'm almost ready to go." There was a bumping sound of a case being dragged behind them. "There's someone at the front door. I don't like the look of this at all!"

As the woman came into the kitchen, Robert opened his mouth to speak and was met with a screeching sound.

"Bloody *hell!*"

A second later, he was engulfed in a load of clothing that temporarily blinded him, and he staggered against the table. By the time he'd unraveled himself from the stockings and petticoats, he was alone, and the back door was wide open again.

"Devil take it!" Robert growled as he stomped through to the front of the house to open the door.

His wife and doctor stared at him apprehensively as he invited them inside the house.

"What happened?" Lucy finally asked.

"Someone threw their clothing at me and escaped out the back."

"So I can see." Lucy stepped forward and removed a gauzy silk stocking that clung to his shoulder. Dr. Fletcher was openly chuckling now. "Did you see who it was?"

"Only for a second. It was a dark-haired woman. She barely entered the kitchen before she screamed and threw everything she was holding in my face." Robert rubbed a hand over his jaw. "She thought I was someone called Marj. When she realized her mistake, she reacted accordingly."

"Marj?" Lucy asked. "I'll wager that's the parlor maid who used to work for Mrs. Pell. She knew Polly, and she was very fond of Flora."

"She said she was ready to go, and I believe she had her bonnet on, which is why I don't have a particularly strong memory of her face." Robert frowned. "One has to suspect that I finally got to meet Polly Carter, my dear. She certainly looks more likc Agnes than Flora did."

"On the assumption that Polly won't be coming back, shall we take the opportunity to look around the house?" Lucy asked. She pointed at the corner of the kitchen, where there was an open trunk. "I assume this was where the clothing thrown at you was supposed to go."

Lucy went over to examine the contents of the trunk. "There is no carrier address, which

238

is a shame, because that might have helped us determine where Polly intended to fly away to next." She looked up at Robert. "Why don't you take Dr. Fletcher and search the rest of the house while I stay here in case Marjory does actually arrive?"

"As you wish," Robert said stiffly, aware that he still had his dignity after the mortification of being downed by an armful of clothes.

While Robert and Dr. Fletcher stomped off to deal with the rest of the house, Lucy took the opportunity to tidy the fallen clothes and place them in the trunk. Despite the seriousness of the occasion, the sight of her husband festooned in women's stockings would stay with her for a long time. She fought a smile as she closed the lid of the trunk and looked around the small kitchen.

The fire was out, and the whole place had a look of emptiness that didn't surprise Lucy. Polly knew that she was being searched for and that eventually someone would end up at the house and had already made plans to move on. But why? Why was she so afraid to meet with them?

"Afternoon, Polly! Sorry I'm a bit late, but—" Marjory came in through the back door and stopped with a gasp when she saw Lucy sitting at the table. "What the bloody hell are you doing here?"

"I might ask the same of you." Lucy rose from the table and went to shut the back door. "You didn't mention that you knew where Polly Carter was living all along."

"What have you done with her?" Marjory demanded, her hands on her hips.

"Nothing. She left before we could speak to her," Lucy said.

"I don't believe you." Marjory's gaze narrowed. "She said that if you found her, she'd be dead in a minute."

"What a peculiar thing to say." Lucy blinked at her. "I am hardly likely to kill the woman I wanted to take on in my nursery."

"Polly *lied* to you."

"I am well aware of that." Lucy remained with her back to the door, preventing Marjory from escaping. "I'm still not sure why all this subterfuge was necessary."

"Because Miss Flora needed somewhere safe to go, and Polly offered her the chance to take her job." Marjory's lip wobbled. "But Flora wasn't safe there, either, was she? Which means that you and the man she was fleeing were obviously in this together."

"Which man?"

Marjory glared at her. "You *know!*"

Lucy rubbed her temple with her fingers and prayed for patience. "If I knew who had killed Flora, I would immediately inform the authorities and have him apprehended. How do *you* know Flora is dead?"

Marjory opened and closed her mouth and then glared at Lucy. "Polly told me."

"And Polly immediately assumed that my family and the murderer were somehow in cahoots?" Lucy shook her head. "She couldn't be more mistaken. Sir Robert and I are only anxious to speak to Polly to discover who killed Flora so that we can get justice for her."

"Polly said—"

Lucy held up her hand. "Polly is mistaken. When you next see her, please tell her that she has nothing to fear from Sir Robert or me. If she had bothered to speak to us herself, she would've discovered that none of this ridiculousness was necessary."

"But—"

"Please stop arguing with me." It was Lucy's turn to interrupt Marjory. "I am tired. I wish to go home, see my son, and settle down to await the arrival of my new baby. Instead, I am traipsing around London trying to help someone who is convinced I wish to murder her!"

Marjory eased toward the table and pulled out a chair.

"You sound a little overwrought, ma'am. Why don't you sit down and put your feet up?"

Lucy was no longer in the mood to be placated. "I'll sit down when I return to my carriage, thank you. Has Polly been living here all the time?"

"When Flora moved her belongings from Viscount Gravely's house, Polly came here to take care of everything," Marjory said. "She expected Flora to come back to London quite quickly, but then she heard about what happened, and she was afraid."

"Of me, apparently," Lucy said. "Which is ridiculous, when she should have been afraid of whoever made Flora flee London. Who was that, by the way?"

Marjory grimaced. "If Polly knew, she certainly didn't tell me, and with everything that's been going on, I'm beginning to be glad about that."

"You should be," Lucy said severely. "Who owns this place?"

"The Gravely family own the land and the houses." Marjory seemed to have decided that Lucy was no longer a threat and was almost back to her chatty self. "Flora and Polly knew the bloke who rents this place. He let them stay here for as long as they wanted if they helped out with the rent."

"Have you met this man?"

"No, ma'am. Polly did say that Mr. Gravely came down the street once with the rent collector, and she and Flora hid upstairs until he left."

Marjory jumped as male voices echoed in the hall and glanced nervously up the stairs. Lucy hastened to reassure her.

"My husband and our family physician are here with me. You have nothing to fear."

Marjory didn't look convinced, her gaze moving between Lucy, the back door, and the corridor that led straight through to the front.

"If you want to go and find out what has happened to Polly, please do so," Lucy offered, stepping away from the door. "Tell her that we mean her no harm and only wish to help."

"Yes, ma'am." Marjory hurried toward the door as if afraid that Lucy would change her mind. "I'll tell her. I promise."

"Well, I still think you should have made the girl stay until I was able to question her." Robert repeated his point as he took off his coat.

They'd left Bethnal Green and arrived back in Portland Square with time to dress for dinner and very little else. As it was their last evening in London, neither of them had wanted to disappoint their hosts by retiring early. The earl had extended an invitation to the Fletchers to stay on for another week, and Dr. Fletcher had accepted, which meant that Penelope would be traveling back with Robert and Lucy.

His wife was lying on the bed with her feet propped up on a cushion and one hand cradling the small mound of her stomach. Despite her obvious tiredness, she was still managing to be remarkably obstinate.

"Marjory would not have told you anything new. She was quite terrified at the thought of even meeting you."

"I would've done my best to set her at ease!" Robert protested.

"There was nothing more to say. I was more interested in sending her after Polly to reassure the girl that neither of us had any intention of *murdering* her!"

"Polly sounds like a fool," Robert said. "Although why am I surprised? She is the one who thought up this ridiculous scheme to change places with an actress and foist that woman onto my household." He tore off his cravat and threw it onto the chair.

"We don't know who thought up the idea. It might have been Flora," Lucy objected. "Did you know that the house belongs to the Gravely family?"

"How could I if you didn't allow me to speak to Marjory?"

"Oh, Robert, will you please stop being difficult!" Lucy snapped. "It was far more useful for us to divide our time while we were at the house to gain as much information as possible."

Robert started on his cuff links. "The house was full of Flora's belongings. There were two bedrooms that had obviously been used by women, and one more masculine one. The man's room was still undisturbed."

"Were you able to find out anything about the man?"

"Only that he wasn't a gentleman. He had only one spare coat in the cupboard, and a single pair of good shoes." Robert wrapped his dressing gown around himself and sat on the chair facing Lucy on the bed. "Flora had an extensive wardrobe, but Polly's room was cleared out."

"Thank you." Lucy offered him a conciliatory smile. "One has to assume that Flora and Polly met this man through his connection with the Gravely family."

"I would agree with you, but one also has to ask why Flora fled from one Gravely-owned property to another."

"It doesn't make much sense, does it?" Lucy agreed. "Unless she thought Viscount Gravely would never imagine she'd stay that close."

"A double bluff?" He frowned. "Then I suppose it worked. We found Polly, not Viscount Gravely."

"Polly wasn't hiding from the viscount. She was hiding from *us*."

He registered the irritation in her voice.

"I find that as hard to believe as you do, my love." Getting up, he walked over and sat beside her on the bed. "You might be a little severe at times, but I've never considered you a murderer."

She reached for his hand. "I want to go home, Robert. I am sick and tired of this whole business." There was a catch in her voice that caught at his heart. "If the Gravelys and Polly do not wish to accept our help in solving this murder, we will do the right thing by Flora and bury her with dignity in Kurland St. Mary churchyard, and forget all about them."

"And let a murderer go free?" Robert asked.

She raised an eyebrow. "As you are convinced that we have the murderer locked up in the cellar of the Queen's Head, such matters will be resolved when he comes to trial."

Robert studied his wife's tired face. It was unlike her to admit defeat, and part of him was tempted to play devil's advocate, because the involvement of Viscount Gravely in the matter had begun to concern him, too. But he wanted to take her back to Kurland Hall, see her reunited with their son and happy in her own home.

"Then we shall leave tomorrow and put all this behind us." Robert kissed her cheek. "Why don't you go to bed while I finish undressing?"

Chapter 15

"N ed!"
Lucy took off her bonnet, knelt on the floor, and opened her arms wide to allow her son to run into them. As soon as the carriage set her down at the front door of Kurland Hall, she'd gone straight up the stairs to the nursery.

"Did you bring me a present?" Ned asked as he kissed her face.

Behind him Anna chuckled. "Are you not pleased to see your mama?"

"Yes." Ned kissed her again, his dark blue gaze fixed on hers. "But I like presents."

Lucy rose to her feet with some difficulty and patted her son on the head. "When Betty has finished unpacking, I'm sure there will be something there for you. Why don't you go down and see if you can find your papa?"

In truth, she'd spent more of her time in London purchasing presents for Ned than looking at the latest fashions, and she could only hope he'd appreciate what she'd chosen.

"I'll take Francis down to Mrs. Fletcher, ma'am." Agnes came into the room, her expression gloomy, holding Penelope's son by the hand. "I've packed his things."

"Thank you, Agnes," Lucy said.

Ned ran off down the stairs, and Agnes followed, leaving Lucy with her sister.

"How has everything been in the nursery?" Lucy asked.

"Ned has been very well behaved." Anna smiled as Lucy took a seat beside the fire. "He missed you quite a lot more than you might imagine from his greeting."

"Did Agnes behave herself?"

"She did her work, and she was never unkind to Ned, but she hasn't exactly been a pleasure to deal with."

"In what way?" Lucy asked.

Anna shrugged. "She's just rather miserable."

"As well she should be after inflicting an actress on us instead of her cousin," Lucy reminded her sister. "An actress who ended up dead in a ditch."

Anna winced. She had always been a more sensitive soul than Lucy. "Did you find out who she was in London?"

"Yes, and a lot more, but Robert is convinced that he's already found the culprit and that our trip was unnecessary."

Anna reached out to take Lucy's hand. "You sound upset. Are you not feeling well?"

Knowing her sister's fear of all things related to pregnancy, Lucy managed to smile.

"I'm just tired after having to put up with Penelope for two days in a closed carriage."

"Dear Lord, that would, as Father might say, try the patience of a saint."

"I forget how Dr. Fletcher manages to defuse the worst of her comments or laugh her out of the sullens." Lucy sighed. "He stayed in London for another week."

"It must be quite vexing when your husband's best friend marries the woman he was first engaged to and you have a duty to be nice to her," Anna remarked.

"It most certainly is," Lucy agreed. "But she does love Dr. Fletcher, and it was her idea that he stay on for another week."

Anna's face registered surprise. "There is no accounting for who one falls in love with, is there?"

"No. And Dr. Fletcher does bring out the best in Penelope." The sisters smiled at each other before Lucy reluctantly eased herself out of the chair. "I have to go back down, say good-bye to Penelope, and supervise the unpacking."

"Then I will come with you. I need to speak to Cook." Anna linked her arm through Lucy's. "I had a long letter from my new husband yesterday. He is already at sea and managed to send his missive from their first port of call in France."

"Is he well?"

"Very well, and happy to be at sea again—

although he tries to hide it." Anna's smile was a mixture of fondness and concern. "He does miss me, though."

"How could he not?" Lucy patted her sister's hand. "But he can be assured that you will be well looked after by your family, and by his own, while he is away at sea."

"He knows that. After you have the baby and are settled again, I will go and stay with his family for a while. It will eventually be *my* home, so I am looking forward to becoming better acquainted with his relatives and the people who live in the valley."

"They will love you," Lucy predicted.

"One can only hope."

Below them, the hall was still littered with boxes and trunks. Foley stood in the middle of the mess, directing the two footmen as to where to take each item. For a moment, Lucy wondered why it was taking so long, and then remembered the lack of another pair of hands.

"James is still locked in his room, I presume?" she asked Anna.

"As far as I am aware, he is," Anna confirmed. "And he isn't very happy about it. Mr. Fletcher has been remarkably quiet as well this last week."

"I'm sure Robert will speedily resolve this issue now that we are home again. He cannot like having a member of the staff sitting idle," Lucy commented.

Anna went off toward the kitchen. Lucy continued down the stairs, avoiding the baggage, and went into her husband's study, where she found Ned sitting on his father's lap playing with the buttons of his greatcoat.

She paused in the doorway to appreciate the two dark heads bent close together as Ned told Robert some long story and his father nodded along as if it all made perfect sense.

Robert looked up first and smiled at her.

"I swear Ned has grown an inch in a week!"

"I have!" Ned visibly sat up straighter and puffed out his chest.

"I believe you are right." Lucy smiled at them both. "Has Penelope already left?"

"Yes, did you wish to speak to her? Her son was balking at leaving. I picked him up, threw him into the carriage, handed Mrs. Fletcher back into it, and sent them on their way."

"I had nothing I particularly wished to say to her, so all is well." Lucy gestured at Ned. "Do you want me to take him back to the nursery? I swear it is the only part of the house not currently being disturbed."

"I've got to change out of this coat, but I'm quite happy if he wants to come with me."

Ned nodded and took an even firmer grip on his father's sleeve.

Robert gently set his son on his feet and took

251

his hand. "Then let's go and see how Betty and Silas are faring in our bedchamber."

It was another full day before Robert found the time to go down to the Queen's Head. He'd released James from captivity with the strict instructions that he was to remain at Kurland Hall and not visit the village or his parents. If he disobeyed, Robert had already told him he would be instantly dismissed. Robert was fairly certain there was more to the story of James being knocked out, but on the long carriage ride home, he had come to the conclusion that James wasn't a murderer.

Which left Bert Speers . . .

Robert alighted from his gig at the Queen's Head and went inside to find Mr. Jarvis. The innkeeper accompanied him down to the cellar with the key and agreed to wait outside while Robert spoke to Bert.

When Robert entered the room, Bert didn't bother to get up from his seat on his pallet. His beard had grown in, and he looked even more ferocious than before.

"You're back, are you?" Bert sneered.

"Indeed." Robert leaned against the door, one hand in his coat pocket close to his pistol. "I was in London for a few days. I made the acquaintance of your employer."

"I'm employed here by Mr. Jarvis."

"Perhaps I misspoke. Your former employer, Viscount Gravely."

"What about him?"

"I understand that you used to work in his stables, and that at one point you were responsible for driving an actress named Flora Rosa from her house in Maida Vale to the theater and anywhere else she wished to go."

Bert looked at Robert with grudging respect. "You have been busy, haven't you?"

Robert shrugged. "As I mentioned, I am the local magistrate. I take any murder committed in my jurisdiction very seriously indeed. Why did you deny knowing Flora?"

"You never asked me about any Flora."

"Are you suggesting that you were unaware that Flora, a woman you were acquainted with in London, and Polly Carter, a woman you also knew, had swapped identities?"

Bert said nothing, and the silence lengthened until Robert grew tired of it.

"You arrived on the same coach as Flora. Quite a coincidence, that."

"Whatever you're thinking, Sir Robert, you're wrong," Bert growled. "Flora wasn't afraid of me. She was running from that other man I told you about."

"The mythical man who arrived in Kurland St. Mary, murdered Flora, and disappeared without anyone having seen him but you?"

"Why don't you ask your own bloody staff a few questions, sir?" Bert retaliated. "James and your precious Mr. Fletcher were hanging around Flora that day as well."

"Yes, and they saw Flora fighting in the street with you, not some unknown man."

"Then ask Mr. Jarvis and Mr. Haines about the man who got off the coach! *That's* why she came to find me that last day. She wanted me to make sure he left her alone."

"Then tell me his *name*. You obviously know it."

Bert gave him a disgusted look. "I can't because you'll start meddling again and make things worse. I prefer to fight my own battles. When I find that scoundrel, he won't survive for long, I can tell you that."

"I don't believe you." Robert held Bert's angry stare. "I think it is all much simpler than that. You met Flora in London and wanted her for your own. When she refused to have anything to do with you, you followed her down to Kurland St. Mary and killed her."

"I bloody well did not!" Bert shot to his feet. "That's just stupid!"

"It makes a lot of sense to me," Robert replied. "Which is why I am going to have you sent to the local assizes to await trial for the murder of Flora Rosa." He waited for a moment before adding. "Unless you have any further information you wish to share with me?"

"I've told you the truth."

"Your truth, perhaps, but with no evidence to back it up, how am I supposed to believe you?"

"Did you speak directly to Viscount Gravely?"

"Yes. He confirmed that he had employed you."

"That's all?" Bert turned away and slammed his fist against his open palm. "Maybe you didn't ask him the right questions."

"What would you have liked me to have asked him?" Robert paused, half-turned toward the door, his curiosity aroused.

"Why I bothered to rush up to London to tell him what was going on? Why he chose to ignore my advice?" Bert shook his head. "The stupid besotted, old fool. He never wanted to see what was right in front of his bloody nose."

"Are you suggesting that Viscount Gravely committed this murder?"

Bert went back to his bed and sat down, his hands linked together in front of his spread knees. "He's bloody well responsible, all right."

The absurdity of the claim almost made Robert smile. "Good luck proving that at your trial, Bert. I suggest you think up a more plausible defense before you are laughed out of court for accusing a peer of the realm of murder."

"You're wrong about all of this, Sir Robert. This is all Viscount Gravely's fault."

"If I'm wrong, give me the evidence to prove it," Robert snapped. "So far, nothing you have said is worth attending to." He inclined his head a stiff inch. "Once the body has been identified—"

"I could do that for you," Bert interrupted.

"There is no need. Someone from London will be coming down to do that fairly soon."

"Polly?"

"I have not yet had the pleasure of meeting the real Polly Carter. Apparently, our arrival in the capital made her go into hiding."

"Clever girl." Bert almost smiled. "You'll be accusing her of murdering her friend next."

"Polly could help clear this matter up in seconds," Robert reminded him. "All she has to do is talk to us."

"And risk what happened to Flora?" Bert asked. "Viscount Gravely doesn't like loose ends. If he finds Polly, she'll be in big trouble for making things worse."

"Viscount Gravely is an invalid who rarely leaves his home."

"He has enough money and power to get whatever he wants," Bert argued. "And if he wants Polly dead, like her friend Flora, he will find a way to make it happen."

Robert considered Bert anew. "Is that what you did?"

"I'm not sure I follow you, sir."

"Did you murder Flora for Viscount Gravely?"

Bert had the temerity to laugh. "Now who's making things up out of thin air, Sir Robert? Do you think I'd be sitting in here if I'd killed her? If I'd been responsible, I damn well wouldn't have come back to Kurland St. Mary."

"Then why did you come back?" Robert asked, intrigued despite himself.

"Because I'm a fool, that's why." Bert sighed. "If Viscount Gravely comes down here to identify the body, let me have a word with him, eh? He'll clear my name. I'm certain of it."

"By implicating himself? Somehow I doubt that." Robert banged on the door. "Rest easy, Bert. Viscount Gravely is too ill to bother to save you"

"If it's not Polly coming, then who is going to identify the body?" Bert shouted the question at Robert's back. "Tell me!"

Robert ignored Bert and pulled the door closed behind him.

"Tell me!" Bert carried on yelling, his voice now muffled by the thick oak door.

Mr. Jarvis relocked the door and pocketed the key.

"I do apologize for the inconvenience of having a man locked in your cellar for two weeks," Robert said as they went back up the stairs. "I will soon have him removed to Hatfield for trial."

"It's been no trouble, Sir Robert. We make sure he's fed and watered just like the other guests and the horses at the inn," Mr. Jarvis replied.

257

"He's calmed down a lot in the last few days."

"I appreciate all your efforts." Robert shook the landlord's hand. "Now I must get back to Kurland Hall. I have a week's worth of farm business to catch up on."

Robert climbed into the gig but made no effort to hurry home. He idled along the county road, his thoughts occupying him until he reached the stables of Kurland Hall and relinquished the reins into the hands of one of his grooms. He had a sense that something was eluding him, that if he could just shake the pieces together again, they would somehow form a more cohesive and understandable picture.

As usual, when he felt undecided, his steps turned toward his wife's favorite sitting room at the back of the house, where the light was better for her needlework. She was sitting in a chair by the window, sewing, her head bent over some minuscule garment he assumed was for their future child. She looked well and happy. Seeing her like that brought him an unexpected sense of peace.

She looked up and smiled at him.

"Did you speak to Bert?"

"I did. I told him I would be sending him for trial."

"And how did he react to that?"

Robert grimaced and sat in the chair opposite hers. "He declared his innocence, suggested that

Viscount Gravely was the culprit, and said that Polly would be next."

She set her sewing aside. "Did you believe him?"

"I asked him to produce evidence to support his claims, and he offered me nothing."

"Which indicates that he is still lying to you," Lucy said. "Then why are you hesitating?"

He offered her a sharp glance. "What makes you think I am?"

"I know you, Robert Kurland." She met his gaze. "You are one of the most decisive men I have ever met, and yet I can still hear the uncertainty in your voice."

He sighed. "Perhaps it is because I am trying to over-complicate things and will not believe the evidence of my own eyes."

"Or maybe something Bert said made you think that things aren't so clear-cut?" Lucy suggested.

"Why the devil won't he just admit what he's done?" Robert burst out. "Why continue to deny everything, and even implicate a peer of the realm rather than accept responsibility for his crime?"

"It certainly was a strange thing for Bert to say." Lucy frowned. "From what you have told me about Viscount Gravely, he would barely have the strength to strangle *anyone*."

"I suggested to Bert that maybe he had been paid by Viscount Gravely, his past employer, to do his work for him, and he laughed in my face."

"Your idea has merit." Lucy stared out of the window and worried her lower lip before turning back to Robert. "I could quite see that happening—Viscount Gravely sent Bert down to Kurland St. Mary with Flora and told him to kill her if she refused to return."

"Versus Viscount Gravely descending on our small village, finding our nursemaid, and strangling her himself in a remote field?"

"If the viscount did insist on coming to Kurland St. Mary, maybe Bert took Flora to him," Lucy said. "Bert was seen with Flora in the village by both Mr. Fletcher and James, and we know he went off with her."

"You believe Bert marched Flora an unspecified distance to where the viscount awaited them, killed her, and then dumped her dead body in the field?"

"It's possible." Lucy paused. "If Viscount Gravely did come in his carriage, it might also explain how James was hit on the head."

"How so?"

"Maybe the viscount's coachman knocked James out and then took his body to his parents' farm for discovery."

"How would he know where James lived?" Robert demanded. "The more complicated we make this, the worse things get!"

A sharp knock on the door made them both start as Robert bade the person enter.

Foley came in and bowed low. "Sir Robert, Mr. Jarvis sent a message for you. He said that it is very urgent."

"Thank you." Robert took the note, put on his spectacles, and read it before turning to Lucy.

"Mr. Jarvis is sorry to report that while Bert was being given his midday meal, he overpowered the maid who brought it to him, and escaped from the cellar." Robert screwed up the note and threw it onto the fire.

"Now we really are in the basket."

Chapter 16

W here do you think Bert will go?" Lucy asked Robert as she followed him up the stairs to their bedchamber. It had begun to rain, and he had decided to change his coat before he returned to the Queen's Head.

"Back to London?" Robert looked absolutely furious.

"The mail coach won't arrive until tomorrow morning," Lucy reminded him. "And I doubt Mr. Jarvis will let him get on it."

"True." Robert strode into their shared dressing room and threw his coat onto a chair. "Which is why I intend to drive up the London Road and see if I can discover our fugitive before he gets too far."

He opened up his cupboard and took out his heavy caped driving coat. "Don't worry. I'll take one of Mr. Jarvis's grooms with me to manage the horses."

"You don't wish me to come with you?"

"It's not necessary." He grimaced as she helped him put on the coat. "I'm afraid that he is going to find Polly and kill her."

"I am worried about the same thing," Lucy agreed. "Is it worth sending a message to Polly's parents or Mrs. Pell, to tell them to watch out for Bert's appearance?"

"We'd do better asking Viscount Gravely, but I suspect he wouldn't be very helpful."

"What about the sons?"

Robert paused as he wrapped a scarf around his throat. "That's a good idea. Both men seem worried by their father's behavior and eager to let the matter of Flora Rosa drop. They might well be willing to intervene if Bert turns up at their place and make sure he is stopped."

"The poor girl," Lucy murmured as she tucked the ends of Robert's scarf securely in place. "If you like, I'll write to them immediately."

"There's no need. I'll do it when I'm closer to London and can pay someone to deliver the letter faster." He kissed her briskly on the forehead. "I'll try to be back before it gets dark, but it depends on what I find."

"Be careful," Lucy said.

He winked at her. "Always."

After he left, she picked up his discarded coat and held it against her cheek. She felt rather unnecessary, and she wasn't sure if she liked it. Normally, in such cases, she tended to be the one rushing around while her husband sat back and waited for her to slow down and agree with his conclusions. Now she was left behind to worry while he ventured into danger.

She replaced the coat in the cupboard and closed the door. As the worrier, she appreciated his prior concerns for her rather more acutely now.

Lucy and Anna were just finishing their dinner when Robert came into the dining room and asked Foley to fetch him up a bottle of red wine from the cellar. He didn't have the look of a man who had achieved his purpose and was limping badly. Lucy wasn't surprised when he sat down at the table, drank a whole glass of the wine Foley provided, and let out a frustrated breath.

"We couldn't find him anywhere. I went damned near halfway to London, asking every driver on the road if they'd seen him. We also went into every inn, and there was no sign of him."

"Did you manage to send a note to the Gravelys?" Lucy asked.

"Yes. They should've received it by now. I paid for a fast delivery at the last inn we inquired at."

"Oh, dear," Lucy sympathized. "I asked Foley to speak to our staff and tell them to keep an eye out for Bert on Kurland property."

"I doubt he'd come here, but I appreciate the thought." Robert attacked his beefsteak with the savagery of a starving wolf. "I'll wager he'll go straight back to Viscount Gravely, and that's the last we'll ever hear of him."

"Can't the courts in London do anything?" Anna asked.

"Not unless someone files information about the murder with a magistrate, and as it didn't happen in London, that probably won't occur. No magistrate is going to take on a peer of the realm over such a matter as the death of his young mistress." Robert grimaced. "He could've strangled her in plain view, and he'd still probably be exonerated."

"How terrible," Anna said. She wiped her mouth with her napkin and rose to her feet. "Will you both excuse me? I have to write a letter to Harry."

Robert stood and bowed. "Good night, Anna. I do apologize for my bad temper."

"On this occasion, your temper is completely justified." She sighed. "There is a vast amount of inequality in our world, that's for certain. Poor Flora Rosa."

Robert sat back down and continued to eat his dinner, while Lucy finished her dessert.

"If Bert has gone to Viscount Gravely for assistance, there is very little we can do about it, is that right?" Lucy finally asked.

"That is unfortunately true. As a magistrate, I can alert the courts as to Bert's disappearance, but as he wasn't formally charged, there isn't much else I can do." Robert helped himself to more wine. "Perhaps this is the one occasion when our attempt to find justice for a murdered soul will bear no fruit."

"That seems wrong."

Robert raised an irate eyebrow. "What else would you have me do, my dear? Go back to London, storm into Viscount Gravely's house, and demand to see Bert? The viscount already said he would have me thrown out if I dared to step foot over his threshold again."

It was Lucy's turn to frown. "I didn't say you had to do anything. I merely remarked that it seems unfair that no one will be held accountable for Flora Rosa's death."

Robert slapped the table hard enough to make the porcelain plates tremble and chime. "But you're right! I *should* be doing something. Flora was in my employ when she died, and she is my responsibility."

"Perhaps Polly will come to her senses and contact us," Lucy said hopefully.

"If Polly has any sense, she will already have left London, and she should never return." Robert finished his second glass of wine and pushed his plate away. "Bert himself intimated that if Viscount Gravely gets his hands on her, she won't survive the experience."

"Why is he so vindictive?" Lucy wondered.

"Because he can be? He is old, wealthy, and

dying, and he no longer cares about such social niceties as not murdering his own mistress."

"And if Marjory is right and Flora Rosa was about to leave him for his son again, he might well have taken such a matter very personally indeed," Lucy mused. "We have learned to our cost that jealousy is a very powerful motivator."

"Yes, perhaps looking old and foolish didn't sit well with him." Robert reached over to take her hand. "Are you ready for bed, my dear? I own to being quite exhausted after the day's unexpected activities."

"I think I will sit up for a while. I have a letter to finish to Anthony."

"Give him my best, won't you?" Robert stood and came around to pull out her chair. "I doubt there are many of my old cavalry friends left in the regiment, but be sure to ask him to remember me to them."

"I always do." She smiled up at him. "He seems very settled in India and gives no indication that he intends to return home."

"It's a very long way. He'll probably come back when he's looking for a wife, or if he inadvertently makes his fortune and can sell his commission." He kissed her gently on the lips. "Don't stay up too long, will you, my dear?"

"I won't." She searched his face, saw the lines of tiredness etched there. "Sleep well, my love."

When Robert had gone, Lucy retraced her steps

to her sitting room, where one of the maids had banked up the fire and set a branch of lit candles beside her desk. Her desire to write to Anthony had disappeared. She picked up the baby gown she had been smocking and carried on sewing. She found the rhythm soothing, and it allowed her mind to wander at will.

Poor Flora Rosa still hadn't been given a proper burial. If Robert truly believed Bert would be protected by Viscount Gravely and that the viscount was above the reach of the law, then perhaps, for the first time ever, they would have to admit defeat.

It was a lowering thought, and not one she was comfortable with. All she could do was pray about the matter and hope that, for once, her husband's instincts were proven wrong.

Over breakfast the next morning, Lucy was pleased to see that Robert looked much more the thing. She'd spent a restless night, unsettled by dreams of her nursemaid, and was more than willing to hope that this new day would prove uneventful.

"I know that it is early, but do you wish to accompany me to the Queen's Head?" Robert asked. "I want to speak to Mr. Jarvis and watch the mail coach come in."

"I intended to go into the village to visit Penelope this morning. Perhaps you could take me as far as the inn, and I could walk through the village to the Fletchers' house."

"If you wish." Robert finished his coffee. "Are you ready to leave?"

Used to her husband's somewhat peremptory ways, Lucy finished her tea with all speed and nodded. "Yes, of course."

Less than a quarter of an hour later, she was sitting in the gig as Robert guided the horse into the coach yard. Mr. Jarvis came out to greet them, his battered face a picture of misery.

"Morning, Sir Robert. Lady Kurland. There's no sign of the blighter, if that's what you've come down to ask me about." He sighed heavily. "I can't believe I let my guard down like that."

"It's not your fault, Mr. Jarvis," Robert said. "I should have formally charged him and removed him to a proper prison."

"He ran at Janie when she went through the door and then clobbered me with his tray before I could shut him in." Mr. Jarvis turned to Lucy. "I went down like a sack of grain. The next thing I knew, Mrs. Jarvis was sitting on my chest crying and screeching like a barn owl."

"Did he say anything before he escaped?" Lucy asked as Robert gave the reins of the gig over to one of the stable boys.

"He was muttering a lot when Janie went in, and pacing back and forth. I think he was disturbed by Sir Robert's visit. Maybe he knew he was about to be incarcerated and decided to make a break for it before that happened."

"Quite possibly," Lucy agreed. "But did Bert say anything specific?"

"Only that Sir Robert was completely wrong, and that the last thing any of us would want was the Gravely family, whoever they are, descending on this village."

Lucy didn't enlighten him as Robert came to join them.

"I'll be off then," Lucy smiled up at her husband. "Do you plan to stay here for a while?"

"I'm not sure." Robert frowned. "Do you want me to send the carriage to pick you up from the Fletchers' later, or shall I come and collect you?"

"If you are finished with your business here in an hour or so, please do come. Otherwise, I will wait for the carriage."

"As you wish." Robert nodded. "I think I'll take a moment to look in the cellar and see if Bert left behind anything of interest before his escape."

Robert waited until Lucy had left the inn and went down into the cellar with Mr. Jarvis. There was nothing to indicate that Bert had been incarcerated there for so long.

"Did he take a horse?" Robert asked Mr. Jarvis, who was still apologizing to him.

"I didn't think to ask, what with me being knocked out and all that." Mr. Jarvis groaned.

270

"Good Lord, I have let you down, sir, haven't I?"

"As you say yourself, you could hardly chase after him when you were unconscious, Mr. Jarvis." Robert turned to the door. "May I go and ask your stable hands if Bert stole a mount?"

"Of course, sir. I'll come with you and make sure that you get to speak to every single one of them."

They progressed out to the stables, and Mr. Jarvis called out to his head ostler.

"Did Bert take a horse yesterday?"

Fred scratched his nose. "He took his own horse, yes. He strolled in here as if he owned the place, taking us all by surprise, and off he went before anyone thought to lay a hand on him."

"Did he have any baggage?" Robert asked.

"No, and Douglas says that Bert stole his hat and coat." He nodded at the innkeeper. "I meant to tell you about that this morning, sir, but it slipped my mind."

"Better late than never, I suppose," Robert intervened, as Mr. Jarvis's face grew alarmingly red. "Thank you for your assistance."

"I wonder if he had any money." Robert stared out across the yard as the head ostler walked away from them.

"Not on him in the cellar," Mr. Jarvis said. "I took his purse away."

"Do you still have it?"

"I locked it up in my strongbox. Would you like to see it, Sir Robert?"

"I'd like to make sure it's still there," Robert replied and retraced his steps into the house.

He was rapidly coming to the conclusion that unless something extraordinary happened, he would never prosecute Bert Speers for murdering Flora Rosa and disrupting the peace, not only of the village but also of Kurland Hall and his wife.

Bert's purse was still in the strongbox, and contained rather more money than Robert had anticipated. There were at least three folded five-pound notes and lots of sovereigns.

"I didn't realize you paid your ostlers so well, Mr. Jarvis," Robert commented as he weighed the coins in his hand.

"I don't, sir." Mr. Jarvis studied the money, his eyes wide. "He either stole it or brought it down with him from London."

"I wonder who else was paying him," Robert mused. "I suspect I know, but I wish to God I could confirm it."

Three sharp blasts of a horn penetrated the silence. Mr. Jarvis relocked the strongbox and looked at his pocket watch. "Mail coach is late today."

"I'd like to watch and see who gets on, Mr. Jarvis." Robert followed his host out of the door. "I'll stay out of the way."

"Don't you worry, sir. We'll all be watching," Mr. Jarvis said.

He walked out into the yard, his expression grim, and waited until the coachman brought the team of four horses to a complete standstill before he approached the box.

"Morning, Mr. Haines."

"Morning, Mr. Jarvis. Sorry we're late. There was a herd of sheep all over the road a mile or so back. I had to slow down or kill the lot of them."

Robert, who had positioned himself near the door with a good view of the coach, paused to wonder whether the sheep were his, and how the devil they had got out. A trickle of passengers came from the inn, ready to board the coach. Robert knew all of them, and at least two of them stopped to pass the time of day with him. There was no sign of Bert, unless he'd managed to disguise himself completely.

Robert transferred his attention to the coach, where the passengers who wished to get down to stretch their legs or who were leaving the coach were emerging from the interior or climbing down from the roof.

A young woman alighted and looked around nervously, one hand to her throat, the other clutching a large bag. Something about her hesitation caught Robert's attention, and he started toward her, only to have his passage blocked by the arrival of a farm cart pulled by a dray horse the size of a small barn.

"There he is!" Mr. Jarvis bellowed so loudly that the dray horse took exception to his tone and tried to buck out of his traces, which set off the team of coach horses.

For a moment, Robert's world took on a nightmarish quality as the huge horse reared up on his hind legs, almost upsetting the empty cart. The hooves, which were the size of dinner plates, whistled past Robert's ear as he ran for the safety of the inn wall.

He fought to breathe normally as the entire yard seethed and bubbled like a witches' cauldron.

"I've got him, Simon!" Mr. Jarvis finally managed to bring the dray horse under control. "Get the leader, Fred!"

By the time everything settled down and Robert forced his way through to the mail coach, Mr. Jarvis was holding forth.

"I saw Bert, Sir Robert! He came in off the street and went straight for the coach!"

"What happened to the woman who got off?" Robert asked urgently.

"Which one?" Mr. Jarvis asked.

"The dark-haired one."

"She screamed when she saw Bert, I can tell you that," Mr. Jarvis said. "But I don't know what became of either of them because I had to attend to the horses. Did you check inside the inn?"

"I doubt Bert went in there," Robert countered.

"Sir Robert?" the coachman shouted down to him. "He took her. Bert took her by the arm and dragged her out onto the street."

Mr. Jarvis looked at Robert. "Your gig is still outside. Shall we see if we can find them? He hasn't had much of a start."

Robert was already in motion, pausing only to check inside the coach before he climbed up onto the box seat and let Mr. Jarvis take the reins.

"Which way?" Mr. Jarvis asked as they exited the yard.

"Not into the village."

Mr. Jarvis clicked to the horse, and they set off at some pace, Robert shading his eyes to look ahead, and for once thanking God that the land-scape was so flat.

"Up there, on the side of the road. I think I see them." Robert pointed. "By that open gate."

As they neared the two figures, it became apparent that they were engaged in a struggle.

"Oi!" Mr. Jarvis shouted. "You leave that young woman alone, Bert Speers, and come back here to face justice!"

Robert got one glimpse of Bert's face before he shoved the woman to the ground and made off over the grassy field. He wondered whether Bert had deliberately slowed the mail coach by releasing the sheep so that he had a chance to look inside and see who was arriving at the inn.

"Do you want me to go after him, sir?" Mr. Jarvis asked as he pulled up the gig.

"No, I think he will outrun us both, and he's probably left his horse hereabouts." Robert carefully got down from the gig and went to the woman's side. Her bonnet had been knocked askew in the fight and hid her face. He knelt down by her side and rolled her gently onto her back.

Wide brown eyes stared up at him in terror.

"Are you, by any chance, Polly Carter?" Robert asked politely.

"Bloody hell," she breathed. "Not you again."

She closed her eyes and went as limp as a newborn.

"Yes, Penelope. I will be sure to mention it to Robert when I return home," Lucy said patiently.

She was currently drinking tea in Penelope's front parlor while her hostess repeated a list of grievances about the state of the house, which was owned by the Kurland estate. Apparently, in Penelope's absence, some of the slate tiles had come loose, and there was water coming in through the roof.

"I know that such a matter means little to you, Lucy, but waking up with water dripping onto one's face is not pleasant at all." Penelope offered her a sliver of cake and another cup of weak tea.

"I'm sure it isn't." Lucy accepted the second slice of seed cake and waited for Penelope to remark unfavorably on her appetite, but for once, Penelope's attention appeared to be elsewhere.

"And when my dear Dr. Fletcher is away from home, all these decisions fall on *me*."

"Did you ask Dr. Evans to look up on the roof for you?" Lucy mentioned Dr. Fletcher's new assistant, who currently lived in the attics. "If there is water coming into the house, one might think that he would be aware of it."

"I will ask him to look tomorrow when the light is better, but I doubt he will be able to do anything. He is a quiet, scholarly man who rarely ventures outside."

"Is he settling in well?" Lucy asked. She'd hardly had a chance to become acquainted with the shy young Welshman since his arrival in the winter. "Do Dr. Fletcher's patients accept his ministrations?"

"They obviously prefer my husband's attention, but he appears to be quite satisfactory." Penelope glanced toward the window at the sound of an approaching vehicle. "Someone is driving rather fast. It usually means they are coming to see my husband."

She rose to peer out of the window. "It appears to be Sir Robert and Mr. Jarvis from the Queen's Head."

Lucy went to join her. "What on earth?"

She picked up her skirts and ran to open the front door as Robert and Mr. Jarvis carried a woman up the garden path.

"Is Dr. Evans here?" Robert called out. "We need his assistance."

Penelope turned back. "I'll go and see if he is upstairs. Bring the patient through to the back, please! I don't want blood on my best carpet."

Lucy held the door open as Robert and Mr. Jarvis came through. The woman they carried between them was unfamiliar. Her face was bruised and bloodied, and she appeared to be unconscious.

"I think this is Polly Carter," Robert murmured to Lucy as he went past. "Bert Speers attacked her."

"Bert Speers?" Lucy followed them down the hall into the doctor's study and examination room, where they carefully laid Polly on the bed. "He didn't leave?"

Robert drew Lucy to one side as Mr. Jarvis went back to make sure the gig was secured at the side of the house. "One has to wonder whether this is why he came back to Kurland St. Mary. Mayhap he realized that at some point, Polly would have nowhere else to turn except her cousin Agnes, and he decided to murder her here."

He briefly told Lucy what had occurred at the inn, and then left with Mr. Jarvis when Dr. Evans came in to examine his patient. Lucy remained in the room, as Penelope preferred not to have to deal with her husband's patients.

After a short while, Dr. Evans looked over at Lucy. "Well, she's been hit in the head at least twice and manhandled quite badly, but she's still alive."

"Thank goodness for that!" Lucy exclaimed. "Will it be all right to move her up to Kurland Hall?"

She had no intention of leaving Polly Carter anywhere Bert Speers might gain easy access to.

"I'd prefer it if she could stay here at least for one night, so I can keep an eye on her. Head injuries can be quite deceptive sometimes. A patient might insist that they are well enough to get up and later suddenly drop dead like a stone."

"Well, we certainly don't want that to happen," Lucy replied.

Dr. Evans folded Polly Carter's hands together on her chest. "She should regain consciousness fairly soon."

"Thank you, Doctor," Lucy smiled at the young man. "I will ask Mrs. Fletcher if she has a spare nightgown for our patient to make her rest more comfortably."

Lucy would also have to speak to Robert about guarding the doctor's house until Polly was well enough to be moved up to the hall. Dr. Evans had a very soothing way with him that contrasted strongly with the rather bluntly spoken Dr. Fletcher.

Lucy left the doctor with Polly and went back into the parlor, where Robert was being accosted by Penelope about the state of her roof, while poor Mr. Jarvis looked as if he wanted to be anywhere but there. Lucy had nothing but sympathy for his plight and hastened to intervene in the somewhat heated discussion.

"My dear, Dr. Evans says we should leave the woman here overnight until she regains consciousness. Perhaps you could take Mr. Jarvis home and then bring our carriage back with Betty and my night things."

Robert frowned. "I don't want you staying up all night in your condition. I will certainly bring Betty back, but she will stay up, and you will return home with me."

Lucy met his gaze and reluctantly gave in. At least she'd distracted him from his argument with Penelope. "As you wish." She turned to her hostess. "If that is acceptable to you?"

Her companion tossed her head, making her blond ringlets bounce. "It seems that as this house belongs to the Kurland family, and I am beholden to them for *everything,* that I can hardly say no."

"I'll be on my way, then." Robert gave Penelope another glare before heading to the door with Mr. Jarvis. "Thank you for your hospitality, ma'am."

Penelope shook her head and tutted as the front door was slammed shut. "Sometimes, Lucy, I am amazed that I almost married Sir Robert. Thank goodness I changed my mind and allowed you the opportunity to deal with his temper."

"Was he not helpful about the roof?" Lucy inquired.

"He suggested it was not at all important at this time, and that as the wife of a doctor, I should perhaps reassess my priorities!"

"He is rather concerned about the young woman," Lucy offered.

"And *why* is he so concerned about her, Lucy?" Penelope turned on her, blue eyes sparking fire. "What is she to him? I warned you about this, didn't I?"

Unwilling to embark on an explanation of the tangled lives of Polly Carter and Flora Rosa, Lucy was forced to hold her tongue, which was proving harder by the second.

"If you'll excuse me, Penelope. I'll go and speak to Dr. Evans about our patient and make sure she is comfortable."

Chapter 17

After two days with no sign of Bert Speers, Dr. Evans allowed Lucy to take Polly up to Kurland Hall. He was somewhat perplexed by her still being unconscious, but he reassured Lucy that Polly occasionally drifted back into some semblance of awareness, and said that she should encourage this when it occurred.

Lucy did wonder whether Polly was deliberately choosing not to remain conscious because she was still convinced that they wished ill on her. But why had she come to Kurland St. Mary if that was still the case? If she'd spoken to Marjory and accepted that the Kurlands were trying to help solve Flora's murder, Lucy had to assume Polly had come to find them.

Lucy ate her breakfast slowly as Robert read the daily newspaper. She considered whether it was worth attempting to speak to Polly even though she appeared to be insensible. Perhaps if she just talked about what had happened, Polly would instantly recover. Agnes had identified her cousin, and Lucy could see the likeness between them. She'd also volunteered to sit with her whenever Ned was napping, which had proved very helpful.

"The post, my lady." Foley deposited a silver tray beside her piled high with correspondence. Lucy set about sorting it, pausing when she noticed a letter marked urgent from Dr. Fletcher.

"Robert?"

As usual, her husband didn't immediately respond from behind the barrier of his newspaper, and Lucy raised her voice.

"Robert! There is a letter here from Dr. Fletcher. May I open it, or do you want to do so?"

"You do it." He didn't even bother to lower his paper.

She broke the wax seal, which bore her uncle's crest. He had also franked the letter.

"Robert." Lucy's voice trembled.

He lowered his paper. "What?"

"Marjory is *dead*."

"Who is Marjory?"

"The parlor maid who used to work for Flora, and who also knew Polly." Lucy passed the letter over to Robert. "Mrs. Pell came to find us at the Harringtons' and luckily met Dr. Fletcher instead. She said Marjory was found in the kitchen next door. She'd been strangled."

"Good Lord, the poor woman." Robert read the letter. "Is it possible that Bert returned to London and killed her?"

"It's certainly possible if he left the day Polly

arrived," Lucy confirmed and sighed. "Poor Marjory, she had aspirations to go on the stage, and was a good and loyal friend to Polly and Flora."

"For which she paid with her life." Robert remarked. "The more I think about Bert Speers getting away with all this, the worse I feel about my decision to keep him in Kurland St. Mary and not the county gaol."

"You did what you thought was best at the time with the information you had," Lucy reminded him.

"Don't try and exonerate me." He scowled at her. "I failed Flora and Marjory."

She reached over and took his fisted hand in hers. "You cannot change what happened, can you? Therefore, all you can do is move forward and do your best to bring their murderer to justice."

"How?" Robert asked.

"I would start by writing to Viscount Gravely, and making sure that he understands the implications of aiding or abetting Bert Speers."

"I can certainly do that."

"And I will write to my uncle, and see if he can use his influence to persuade the viscount to reveal where Bert is."

"It's a start," Robert said and raised her hand to his mouth to kiss her knuckles. "Thank you, my dear. I know I can always rely on your good sense to set me right."

Lucy smiled. "I appreciate the compliment, but I must admit that usually *I* am the one who relies on *your* common sense, not the other way around."

She pushed back her chair. "I will go and write to my uncle immediately."

"And I will write to Viscount Gravely. He might have denied me access to his house, but he can hardly object to a letter."

Lucy wrote her letter and left it with Robert, who intended to send it off with his as quickly as possible. Leaving him to finish his missive, she went upstairs and paused outside the room where Polly was being cared for. Going in, she found Betty sitting beside the bed, knitting, while she watched over the patient.

"How is she?" Lucy asked.

"She hasn't stirred," Betty replied. "I managed to get a few sips of water down her throat earlier, as Dr. Evans suggested."

"Well done," Lucy said. "Would you mind going up to the nursery and telling Mrs. Akers that I intend to come with her on her walk with Ned? I will watch over Polly while you are away."

"As you wish, my lady."

Betty was one of the few Kurland servants who had been trusted with Polly's true identity.

After Betty left, Lucy took her place beside the bed and looked at Polly's slack, unresponsive face. The left side of her head was still badly bruised, as were her upper arms where Bert had attempted to drag her away with him. Lucy wrapped her fingers around one of Polly's wrists and spoke slowly and clearly.

"Polly, if you can hear me, I want you to know that you are safe and protected at Kurland Hall. There is no need to be afraid. Sir Robert and I only wish to help discover who murdered Flora Rosa and bring them to justice. Perhaps, when you wake up, you can tell us what has been going on. I promise that we will believe you."

Lucy felt slightly foolish speaking to an unconscious person, but she was at her wit's end. And if her words could penetrate Polly's torpor, then she was certainly willing to try.

For a brief second, her hopes flared as Polly blinked and restlessly moved her head from side to side, but she subsided into nothingness again. Lucy let out a breath she had been unaware of holding, and her baby kicked hard against her stomach.

She would repeat her plea to Polly once a day and pray that, at some point, the girl would wake up. Her only concern was that by the time Polly was able and willing to tell her tale, Viscount Gravely would have concocted a story to defend himself and Bert. No one would believe a lowly servant like Polly against a peer of the realm.

Betty came back in, and Lucy rose to her feet.

There was no point in worrying about things that she could not control. She would walk with Anna and Ned down to the stables and consult with Dr. Evans when he came to visit his patient at three.

Robert looked up as he finished folding and sealing his letter to Viscount Gravely, and found his land agent had come into his study.

"Ah, there you are, Dermot. Can you arrange to have both these letters taken down to the Queen's Head and delivered to London with all speed?"

"Yes, Sir Robert." Dermot took the letters but remained pinned to the spot.

"Well, get on with it," Robert suggested.

"I forgot to tell you that I sent a man to fix my brother's roof."

"Good."

Dermot still didn't move.

"I . . . wanted to ask you something, sir." He swallowed hard. "The woman who came with Dr. Evans?"

"What about her?" Robert asked.

"Does she have something to do with the disappearance and death of Polly Carter?"

Robert set down his pen. After attempting to write a letter to Viscount Gravely that wouldn't immediately be thrown on the fire, his patience was already wearing thin. Perhaps this was a good moment to revisit his concerns about Dermot's interactions with Flora. He'd be damned if he would find the truth out otherwise.

"Why would you think that?" Robert asked.

Dermot shrugged. "I just overheard something when I was in the kitchen, and I began to wonder . . ."

"I'm still not certain why you are wondering anything when your own relationship with Polly Carter could be viewed in a very unfavorable light."

"What?" Dermot blinked at him. "I mean, I beg your pardon, sir?"

"You were angry with Polly for not returning your affection," Robert pointed out. "Shortly afterward, she was murdered on a farm that you and I had visited that very week."

"I did *not* murder her, Sir Robert." Despite his pallor, Dermot met Robert's gaze straight on, the outrage in his eyes quite visible. "I would *never* do anything so underhanded. How could you even think such a thing of me?"

"Then why do you continue to lie to me about why you didn't go after her when you allegedly saw Bert Speers dragging her off down the high street?" Robert demanded. He was tired of all the deception, particularly from members of his own damned staff, who should know better. Dermot was supposed to be his most trusted employee. "If you truly cared for her, you would've intervened, and perhaps she would be alive today!"

The last part wasn't particularly fair, but Robert was beyond that. If he was ever to work out what had happened to Flora Rosa, he had to get to the bottom of all the deceptions and lies that had piled up around her.

"I didn't go after her, because—" Dermot stopped speaking and gazed helplessly at Robert.

"Because what?"

"I . . . became distracted," Dermot said carefully. "I am not proud of what happened, but I at least attempted to do the right thing and make sure he was placed somewhere safe."

"Oh, for God's sake. That's it, isn't it?" Robert stood up, startling Dermot, and marched over to the door. He opened it and bellowed.

"James! Come into my study immediately!"

Robert waited by the door until James appeared, looking remarkably apprehensive. He guided him into his study, where his footman took one look at Dermot and almost bolted. Robert shut the door before either of them decided to make a run for it.

He returned to stand behind his desk. "Now, let's have it. Who hit who first?"

James raised his hand. "I cast the first blow, sir." His cheeks reddened. "He told me to leave Polly alone, and I came back and thumped him."

"Is this true?" Robert looked at Dermot.

"Yes, sir." Dermot admitted. "And then I hit him back, and he went down like a stone."

"I tripped over a branch!" James protested. "You hardly touched me."

"That's not correct, you—"

"Be quiet! Both of you." Robert held up a hand. "I am not interested in your claims to boxing greatness. I am merely concerned with finding out what happened next."

"I tried to rouse James, but without success," Dermot said. "I didn't want to leave him lying by the church, so I decided that the best thing to do was to take him to his parents' farm, which was where he had been heading anyway."

"Then why didn't you take him right up to the front door?" Robert asked.

"Because I didn't want them to know what I'd done," Dermot explained. "As your land agent, I am in a position of authority on this estate. I didn't want James's parents to think badly of me."

"It's a shame you didn't think about that before you acted like a jealous fool over a woman who would never have consented to be your wife," Robert said acidly.

"I agree I acted impulsively," Dermot said. "I am ashamed of that."

Robert looked from James to Dermot. "What I still don't understand is why neither of you owned up to this beforehand."

James cleared his throat. "You thought I'd murdered Polly, sir."

"So why not tell me the truth?" Robert snapped.

"Well, it was like this, sir. I thought that, being as I was knocked out and at my parents' house, that would be enough for you to realize that I couldn't possibly have killed Polly, without me muddying the waters by telling you about a stupid fight and getting Mr. Fletcher into trouble as well."

Robert digested that meandering statement and slowly breathed out through his nose. He'd dealt with a fair number of young soldiers in his military career, and their absurd logic never ceased to amaze him.

"I felt the same way, Sir Robert," Dermot piped up. "I knew that James was in trouble when you had him locked in his room. I thought that bringing up our fight might only make things worse for him."

"Did it not occur to either of you halfwits that telling me everything might have helped me catch Polly's murderer faster?"

Dermot and James exchanged an embarrassed look, and then replied in unison.

"Not really, sir."

James continued. "What could our disagreement have to do with Bert Speers grabbing hold of Polly?"

"For one thing, if the two of you hadn't been so busy fighting each other, one of you might have been able to follow Bert and make him *unhand* Polly. Did you think of that?"

Silence fell, and Robert made no effort to break it as both men suddenly looked wretched.

"Your stupid, cock-of-the-north behavior wasn't exactly that of men who were truly in love with Polly, was it?"

"I'm sorry, sir," Dermot muttered. "I let you and Polly down."

"Aye," James added. "I acted the fool, and she paid the price."

Robert made no effort to console them. He'd observed that for a lesson to hit home, sometimes it needed to settle in and burn a little.

"Now, before I send you both on your way, is there anything either of you would like to tell me about what else happened on that day?" Robert asked.

"I can't think of anything, sir," Dermot said, and James nodded.

"Then you may go about your business, and be grateful that I am not in the humor to give both of you your marching orders," Robert said.

"Thank you, sir." Dermot checked his pocket for the letters. "I promise I will never allow anything like this to happen again."

Robert nodded and watched his land agent depart in something of a hurry. James lingered, a thoughtful look on his face.

"There was one thing, Sir Robert."

"What is that, James?"

"I did speak to Polly that day. She told me

she couldn't walk out with me because she was meeting Bert. I insisted she could do better for herself. She laughed and said that I'd got it all wrong, and that she and Bert had grown up together, and that he was her best friend and worst enemy."

James sighed. "She patted my cheek, told me to be a good boy, and that she would be going back to London shortly, and I was not to worry about her."

He met Robert's gaze. "I still can't quite believe it was Bert who strangled her."

"If she truly said that Bert was her best friend *and* her worst enemy, perhaps his worst side won out," Robert suggested quietly.

"I suppose that might be it, sir." James didn't sound convinced. "All I know is that she didn't look like a woman who was afraid of him at all."

"Which might be why he found it so easy to walk away with her and murder her."

James's face crumpled. He rubbed furiously at his cheeks as tears started to fall.

"I let her down, Sir Robert. I loved her, and I let her go without a whimper."

"You did what she asked you to do," Robert reminded him. "Don't blame yourself for that." He paused. "In truth, we all let her down, didn't we?"

Chapter 18

I cannot believe that Mr. Fletcher and James were so busy fighting each other that they let Bert walk away with Polly right under their noses!" Lucy stared at Robert aghast. "And why didn't James tell you this in the first place?"

Robert, who was pacing the length of her sitting room, turned toward her again. "Because he thought admitting to fighting with Dermot would lead me to disbelieve he was at his parents when Polly was killed, and to assume he was the murderer."

She opened her mouth to speak, and he cut across her.

"I know. His reasoning is completely illogical. I barely stopped myself from leaping across my desk and knocking him out cold again."

Lucy considered what he had told her anew and sighed. "This doesn't really help much, though, does it?"

"Well, it eliminates those two fools from my list of suspects—not that I had come to believe either one of them was capable of murder—and it does clear up some loose ends."

"It certainly does." Lucy frowned. "I wonder what Flora meant about her and Bert being friends for a long time? Do you think she made it up to reassure James that everything was fine, or do you think she meant it?"

"James seems to believe she was telling the truth, but we can't forget that Flora was, by all accounts, a very skillful actress."

"Perhaps she was trying to prevent James from interfering because she knew her meeting with Bert was going to be difficult," Lucy suggested.

"That's certainly possible," Robert agreed as he finally stopped pacing and took the seat opposite her. "What if she did know him well, though?"

"Bert? I suppose she might have known him from the orphanage. I wonder if it is possible to find out such a thing?"

"Mr. Biggins mentioned that Bert was an orphan. He might know which orphanage he came from."

"Would he tell you if he did?"

"I don't see why not." Robert shrugged. "He isn't employed by the Gravely family any longer, so they have no leverage over him." He sighed. "I suppose you want me to write to him as well?"

"It might help," Lucy said.

"I don't see why," Robert grumbled as he moved to sit at her small writing desk and helped himself to her best pen and a sheet of paper. "My expenses this month are triple what they usually are after all these postal fees."

"It's still cheaper and less ruinous to your health than riding all the way to London," Lucy reminded him as he wrote his letter, sanded it, and sealed the outside with her crest.

He swung around to look at her, his face still set in a frown. "I'd still rather hear from Viscount Gravely myself than rely on the post."

"But he won't allow you in his house," Lucy said.

"There's always a way in." Robert propped up the letter against the lamp.

"I'd rather you left that part of the puzzle to my uncle David. He is very good at getting what he wants."

"So I should imagine." Robert rose to his feet. "How is Polly?"

"Much the same." Lucy grimaced. "Dr. Evans doesn't know why she hasn't regained consciousness yet."

"Dr. Fletcher will be back soon. Maybe he'll take a look at her and see if his partner missed anything."

"I did wonder if she is pretending," Lucy confessed.

"Why would she do that?"

"Perhaps she still believes she is in danger."

"From us?" Robert looked impatient. "If I'd wanted her gone, I would've left her with Bert."

He picked up the letter. "I'll take this down to the Queen's Head."

Lucy had just finished her letter to Anthony when Anna came to find her, a note in her hand. Despite the unavoidable absence of her new husband, Lucy had never seen her sister look quite so serenely beautiful.

"Aunt Rose wants us to have dinner at the rectory tonight to celebrate Father's birthday. She also asks if you could bring Ned."

"I have no objection to dining at the rectory," Lucy replied. "But if Ned is to accompany us, I don't wish to stay late."

"Rose has anticipated your concerns and suggests we arrive at five and dine well before six." Anna checked the note.

"Then as long as Robert is in agreement, I am happy to attend."

"He is. I just spoke to him in the entrance hall, and he said to ask you." Anna confirmed.

Lucy opened her desk drawer and took out a slim volume with a marbled leather cover. "On the recommendation of Uncle David, I purchased a book for Father when I was in London."

"What is it about?" Anna asked.

"Some obscure history of Greece that our father has apparently always wanted."

"In Greek, I assume?" Anna sighed. "And I just knitted him a new scarf."

"Which he will appreciate when he is out hunting in all weathers." Lucy smiled at her sister. "I do believe Ned has drawn him a picture of a horse, which will please him more than anything either of us could offer."

Anna's laughter rang through the room, and Lucy suddenly felt much better. If they were unable to capture Bert Speers, life would still go on, and moments like these with her sister made her remember that.

"I'll go and write a reply to Aunt Rose, then," Anna said. "And if you wish to come and walk with me and Ned, we will be leaving in an hour."

The rectory was ablaze with lights when Lucy and her family arrived in the carriage after deciding that the walk there and back might be too much for Ned to manage at such a late hour.

"Come on, my boy." Robert lifted Ned down from the carriage and kept a firm grip on his collar as his son attempted to run past him. "No, we don't have time to go to the stables to see your grandfather's horse. If you behave yourself, I'm sure someone will take you to see him after we have eaten."

While this discussion occurred, Lucy got out of the other side of the carriage by herself, as did Anna. She went around to take Ned's other hand.

"I have your picture here, Ned. Don't you want

to give it to your grandfather and wish him a happy birthday?"

"Yes!" Ned lunged toward the path. "Come on!"

Lucy was still smiling as they were ushered into the house and discarded their cloaks and hats in the hallway. She could already hear her father holding forth in the drawing room, his loud, jovial tone, which he used to drown out his congregation, was hard to miss.

She let go of Ned's hand as they entered the room, as did Robert, and watched as her son, who had no fear of his rather fierce grandfather, ran straight over to him.

"Happy Birthday, Grandfather!" Ned grinned up at his relative. "Papa says you are one hundred and two!"

Lucy glanced over at Robert, who shrugged innocently.

"Not quite, young man." The rector didn't take offense. "What have you brought me?"

Ned handed him the rolled-up piece of paper and hopped impatiently from one foot to the other as his grandfather slowly revealed his drawing.

"It's Apollo! Your horse!" Ned said.

"By Jove, so it is!" He looked over at Lucy. "This is remarkably detailed. Did he sneak into my stables and draw my favorite horse by eye, or did he do this by himself?"

"From memory, sir, I believe." Robert came

to stand beside Ned and dropped an affectionate hand on his shoulder. "He certainly refused to take any advice from me."

"It is perfect, Ned." The rector looked down at his grandson, delight shining in his eyes. "I will have it framed and put up in my study. Thank you."

Ned's grin was so huge that Lucy couldn't help but smile back at him. She proffered her own parcel.

"Happy Birthday, Father."

"Thank you, my dear." He undid the string and brown paper and considered the slim volume within. "Oh my word! Wherever did you find this?"

"In an antiquarian bookstore, with a little help from Uncle David," Lucy said.

"Well, well." Her father put on his spectacles, opened the book, and started reading the preface.

"Ambrose?" Aunt Rose came by, gently patted his arm, and deftly removed the book from his hand. "Dinner is almost ready. I will send Meg upstairs to hurry along our other guests, and then we will be ready to proceed."

"As you wish, my dear."

Amazed at her father's continued good humor, Lucy could only applaud Rose's way of managing her scholarly and somewhat selfish father. In the past, when her father had received a new book, he would retire to his study, eat his meals in there, and become deaf to the calls of society and his parochial duties.

"Grandfather?" Ned was tugging on the rector's sleeve. "Will you take me to see Apollo so that we can show him his picture?"

"Certainly, but after dinner."

Ned's face fell. "But—"

"Ned?" Lucy stepped forward and took him firmly by the hand. "You heard what your grandfather said. Now come and make your bow to the other guests."

She greeted the Culpeppers, who lived in the village and had two children, one a similar age to Ned whom he often played with. Mr. Culpepper was her father's curate and did most of the work of running the large rural parish. Mrs. Culpepper was Penelope's younger sister and was nothing like her at all.

"Is Penelope coming?" Lucy asked.

"She was invited, but she declined to come because Dr. Fletcher isn't home yet, and she didn't wish to come without him." Dorothea smiled. "Her devotion to Dr. Fletcher is something to admire."

"Indeed." Lucy agreed. "Did my father mention he had other guests?"

"I believe someone arrived this afternoon," Mr. Culpepper said. "An old friend of his from university."

"How pleasant for him." Lucy smiled as she

noticed Aunt Rose gathering her guests together by the door to the dining room. "Please excuse me. I must go and find Sir Robert."

With Ned firmly in hand, she turned toward the door, only to see her husband marching toward her, his expression furious.

"You'll never guess who else is coming to dinner, my dear."

Lucy raised her eyebrows as Robert stepped out of her way and pointed toward the doorway.

"Viscount Gravely and his two sons."

Lucy fought a gasp. "Now, that *is* rather unexpected."

"And somehow I doubt it is a coincidence, either. Do you?" Robert murmured. "I can't wait to find out what flimsy excuse Viscount Gravely used in order to invite himself to *my* village."

"Sir Robert." Viscount Gravely, who was seated at the rector's right hand directly across the table from Robert, inclined his head. "What a surprise to see you here."

Robert didn't bother to answer him but looked steadily back through the candlelight until the viscount dropped his gaze.

"I didn't realize that you knew my son-in-law, Gravely," the rector intervened.

"We met in London. Your brother introduced us," Viscount Gravely said. "I suppose I shouldn't be surprised to find him here at your dining table, Ambrose, when I met him in your family house."

"Kurland is married to my oldest daughter, Lucy."

Viscount Gravely looked down the long table to where Lucy was sitting with his two sons. "Ah, how delightful."

"What brings you to Kurland St. Mary, my lord?" Robert asked. "I was led to believe that you were no longer capable of leaving your house."

"When I was in India, I picked up a form of wasting fever that sometimes leaves me in a weakened condition and I have to retire to my bed." Gravely offered Robert a tight smile. "On the occasion of your visit, I was recovering from a bout of sickness."

"But that still doesn't explain your sudden desire to visit my village."

"*Your* village?" Viscount Gravely raised an eyebrow. "I suspect my friend Ambrose might take issue with that."

"Not at all," the rector said jovially. "My son-in-law is correct. All the land hereabouts, apart from that owned by the diocese, is held by the Kurland family, which has been here since the reformation of the monasteries."

"You still haven't answered my question, my lord," Robert said gently. "Why choose to come now?"

"Because meeting the earl of Harrington reminded me that I wished to discuss with my old friend Ambrose some interesting material that I had accrued on my travels through India."

"Indeed." Robert hoped his skepticism showed on his face. "How long do you plan to stay?"

"Surely that is of no interest to you?" Viscount Gravely met his gaze. "I promise not to interfere with your pursuits."

"I was thinking of bringing Gravely up to Kurland Hall tomorrow, Robert. He would enjoy seeing your munitions room and the secret passages under the stairs."

"I'm afraid that won't be possible." Robert smiled at his father-in-law and rose from his seat. "If you will excuse me for a moment?"

He left the rector openmouthed and walked out of the room into the hall, where he paused to gather his composure. The nerve of the man—to sit there opposite him, daring him to expose his wrongdoing . . .

"And what brings you to Kurland St. Mary, Mr. Gravely?" Lucy addressed her question to the younger of the Gravely brothers, who was sitting beside her at the table.

Neville glanced nervously across at his brother. "I . . . was worried about my father's health and decided that it would be better if I accompanied him."

"How very thoughtful of you." Lucy commented. "I had no idea that Viscount Gravely knew my father."

"I understand that they have been friends for a considerable time, my lady, and that visiting the earl of Harrington inspired my father to . . . to reconnect with Mr. Harrington."

Lucy glanced toward the head of the table, where Robert had suddenly risen to his feet and walked out of the room. She considered following him and then realized that would leave Ned unattended. She decided to stay seated and hoped that whatever had happened between her husband and the viscount hadn't resulted in a heated argument across her father's dinner table.

"Please excuse me," Trevor Gravely also rose and placed his napkin carefully beside his plate.

"Trev." Neville grabbed for his brother's sleeve but was shaken off.

"Is your brother unwell, Mr. Gravely?" Lucy inquired.

"No, he's one of those annoyingly healthy people who rarely even catch a cold." Neville attempted a smile.

"Did you return to England for your schooling, Mr. Neville?" Lucy attempted to set him at ease. "Or did you remain in India?"

"No, my lady. My mother couldn't abide the climate, so she came back with us while we both attended school." His anxious gaze shifted back toward the door through which his brother and her husband had gone.

"Did your mother return to India at some point?"

"She much preferred to live here and died a few years ago in our house in London."

"My condolences," Lucy said.

"Thank you." Neville looked as if he might cry. "I still miss her. She meant the world to me."

After making sure that Ned was fully engaged in talking with Anna, Lucy leaned in closer toward Neville.

"Are you feeling quite well, sir?"

"I'm . . . just wondering what has become of my brother."

"I'm sure he will return momentarily," Lucy said soothingly. "If you came to support your father, why did your brother come to Kurland St. Mary?"

"That's a very good question, Lady Kurland, and one that only Trevor can answer. The only thing I would say is that, as my older brother, he has a tendency to think that he should fix everything for me."

"I suspect that is common with older sisters and brothers, Mr. Gravely. I certainly have been accused of meddling in my younger siblings' lives," Lucy agreed.

"Yes, but Trevor"—Neville sighed—"tends to overreact to the slightest misdemeanor on my part. He still tells everyone how I 'accidentally' murdered the kitchen cat as though it is a highly amusing story."

"It certainly doesn't sound amusing," Lucy said.

"It was an accident." Neville shifted in his seat. "A horrible accident, and I wish he would just stop *talking* about it."

There was a rising note in Neville's voice that made Lucy want to reach for his hand and soothe his ruffled feathers. She hastened to change the subject.

"Did your father return home with your mother to set up the household?"

"No, he was too busy. Mother did it all herself." He smiled more normally. "As a charitable woman, when she recruited her staff, I think she offered employment to half the orphans in East London in one fell swoop."

"How wonderful of her." Even as she spoke, Lucy was furiously making connections in her head. "I wonder if she ever employed a boy called Bert Speers?"

Neville almost choked on the sip of wine he'd just been drinking and stared at Lucy in horror.

"He is currently working as an ostler in the Queen's Head. I believe he said he'd been taken straight from an orphanage and employed by a big London house in their stable." Lucy kept up her artless chatter. "Wouldn't it be wonderful if it had been your mother who had employed him?"

Neville was now shaking so badly that his wine threatened to leave the glass entirely.

"I have no recollection of such a name, my lady," he said stiffly. "It would be something of a remarkable coincidence if my mother had employed him, would it not?"

"Indeed. How silly of me." Lucy smiled at him. "My husband often scolds me for my ridiculous flights of fancy."

Ned tugged at her sleeve, and she returned her attention to him.

"What is it, Ned?"

He pointed at his empty plate. "I've finished my dinner. Can I go and see Apollo now?"

Glancing at her hostess, Lucy saw her give the signal for the ladies to retire.

"Yes, you have been very well behaved indeed. I will ask your aunt Rose if you may visit the stables immediately."

"Sir Robert?"

Robert turned to see Trevor Gravely coming after him, his expression contrite.

"I expect you are wishing all of us to the devil."

"Yes." Robert didn't bother to be pleasant. He was far too angry.

"I'm afraid it's all my fault." Trevor motioned toward the rector's empty study, and Robert followed him inside. "I made the mistake of confiding in Neville as to my intentions to travel down here and identify Flora Rosa's body." He swallowed hard. "He grew very agitated, and the more I tried to calm him, the worse he became. He even tried to hit me. Eventually, I had to enlist the aid of father's butler to restrain him."

Trevor stared out of the window. "I thought we had moved beyond such overwrought displays of emotion, but I was wrong. Neville's feelings for Flora ran far deeper than I think any of us realized."

"Is it true that Flora was thinking of leaving your father and returning to your brother?" Robert asked.

Shock flashed across Trevor's face. "Who in the devil's name told you that?"

Robert didn't attempt an answer and waited as Trevor took a hasty turn around the room, his hands behind his back.

"I don't know who said that, but yes, Neville did tell me that might happen. I must confess that I didn't believe him because . . . he does tend to daydream about Flora rather obsessively."

It seemed to be a reoccurring theme with Neville's father as well, but Robert didn't point that out. "You still haven't explained why your entire family has descended on Kurland St. Mary."

"As I said, it was my fault. After Ahuja helped me subdue Neville, he must have told Father what I planned to do—or Neville told him he was coming with me. Father decided he couldn't trust either of us and opted to join the party." He paused to study Robert's face. "He really is acquainted with Mr. Harrington. They were at school together, and they have written to each other over the years."

"What does your father hope to achieve here?"

"I'm not really sure." For a moment, Trevor looked worried. "I suspect he is concerned that Neville will insist on seeing Flora's body, and that he will somehow publicly disgrace himself and our family."

"By mourning her?"

"You don't understand, Neville isn't . . . ," Trevor sighed. "I feel disloyal even saying this because he is such a remarkable brother, but like my father, he has his obsessions, and Flora was one of them."

"How exactly does your father intend to stop Neville from seeing Flora's body?"

"I don't know," Trevor said. "This whole matter has become so complicated that I have no idea what will happen next. Is Flora's body being held up at Kurland Hall?"

"No," Robert said.

"Ah, then she's in the village." Trevor nodded. "Which is a shame, because it means that it won't be easy to shake off Neville when I go to see Flora."

"I suppose I could invite him up to the hall," Robert suggested somewhat reluctantly. "My father-in-law suggested allowing your father to visit me tomorrow. I could make sure that Neville is included in that invitation."

"That might work." Trevor nodded. "If you can stomach dealing with my father. I understand that he banished you from our house."

"Indeed." Robert half-turned to the door. "But once you have done your duty and identified Flora, I expect you to persuade your father and brother to leave this place immediately."

"Don't worry about that, Sir Robert," Trevor said fervently. "I'll have them out of here in a flash."

Robert returned to the dining room, along with Trevor, and retook his seat, only to have to stand again as the ladies left the gentlemen to their port. Lucy made a point of coming past his chair and pausing to speak to him.

"Is everything all right?"

"Not really." He squeezed her hand. "Give me a moment with your father, and then I will come and tell you all."

"As you wish. Ned is going to visit Apollo, and then we shall see how tired he is and whether we need to go home." She went out with Ned and closed the door behind her, shutting Robert in with his father-in-law and a man he was beginning to dislike intensely.

"I do beg your pardon for leaving the table so abruptly," Robert said to the rector. "I suddenly remembered that the thing I was supposed to be doing tomorrow would not be possible until Dr. Fletcher returns home. I just sent a note to his wife to apprise her of the change of date."

"Does that mean I can bring the Gravelys up to the hall?" the rector asked.

"Yes." Robert smiled. "That would be delightful."

Chapter 19

You invited Viscount Gravely and Neville to Kurland Hall?" Lucy stared at Robert as though he had grown two heads. *"Why?"*

They had just returned from saying good night to Ned in the nursery. Robert had been on the point of ringing for Silas and Betty when his wife had decided to pick a fight with him.

"Trevor needs to identify Flora's body. If Neville sees him setting out to do so, Neville might follow him and cause a scene."

Lucy considered that, her lips pursed in thought. "Neville is rather an emotional young man. I spoke to him at length at the dinner table. He denied all knowledge of Bert Speers, even though we already know that Viscount Gravely acknowledged his employment."

"Why the devil were you talking to Neville Gravely about Bert Speers?" Robert demanded.

"There is no need to shout. I went about it in a very indirect way."

"You shouldn't have mentioned him at *all*. Didn't you just say that he sounded rather unstable?"

"If we are to find out what is going on, Robert, sometimes one has to attempt to ask the difficult questions!" Lucy squared up to him. "And what were you doing talking to Trevor Gravely, then?"

"I didn't exactly seek him out. He came to apologize for bringing the whole family down upon us."

"As well he should." Lucy sniffed. "What on earth was my father thinking, inviting a man he hasn't seen for twenty years to visit him?"

"Your father was manipulated, much as we have been," Robert said. "At least Gravely's weakness and apparent inability to leave his house have been unmasked. There's no reason why he couldn't have come down here and strangled Flora, or done the exact same thing to Marjory."

"Except it would've been much easier for Bert Speers to do it for him," Lucy reminded him.

"Then, is that what we believe?" Robert asked. "That Viscount Gravely and Bert Speers conspired together to murder Flora, and then Marjory, and are still after Polly?"

"It seems the most logical explanation to me." Lucy studied him. "The problem is proving it."

"Indeed." Robert sighed and flung himself down into a chair beside the fire. "And now I have committed myself to hosting Viscount Gravely in my house."

"Perhaps you should use it as an opportunity

for some plain speaking." Lucy came to stand in front of him, her arms folded over her bosom. "Tell him you intend to prosecute Bert Speers for Flora's murder. Suggest to him that if he is harboring Bert, he should be aware that you have directed my uncle to lay information against Bert at Bow Street and set the Runners on him."

Robert smiled at his wife's resolute expression. "Bravo, my dear."

"Are you making fun of me?"

"Good Lord, no. I wouldn't dare." He caught her hand and drew her down to sit in his lap. "I am merely admiring your logic and congratulating myself on marrying a woman of such good sense."

He kissed her cheek. "My only concern with alerting him to the fact that I intend to set the Runners on him is that it will give him the opportunity to send Bert abroad, never to be seen again."

"I suppose you are right." Lucy sighed. "Because even Bow Street would balk at suggesting that a peer was involved in a murder, with no evidence to show except conjecture. Perhaps you should just tell Viscount Gravely that you intend to continue to pursue and prosecute Bert, and that nothing will be allowed to stand in your way."

"I will certainly do that." He kissed her again. "When they are here, I will rely on you to detach your father and Neville from the viscount so that I can have a quiet word with him in private."

She kissed him back. "That, my dear Robert, will be the easy part."

Despite Robert's best efforts to be a good host and Lucy's father's jovial presence, it was obvious that Viscount Gravely and his son were not entirely at their ease as they walked around Kurland Hall. Neville looked as if he expected a ghost to jump out at him from every corner, and Viscount Gravely looked bored. Robert supposed that for a man used to plundering the treasures of India, a small Elizabethan manor house in the southeast of England was rather commonplace.

The only time the viscount did show any interest was when they entered the oldest part of the structure, which had been used as a magistrate's hall for as long as anyone could remember. Lucy maneuvered her father and Neville through, into the picture gallery, and shut the door behind her, leaving Robert and Gravely alone for the first time.

"This was the original hall of the house. I hold a quarterly court for my tenants and local landowners here, and deal with the majority of petty crime." Robert stepped up onto the raised dais at one end of the paneled hall in front of an enormous fireplace. "We set the table here and allow anyone who wishes to express an opinion to offer it."

"How very medieval of you," Viscount Gravely said dryly, his gaze fixed on the stained-glass window to his right.

"It is a system of justice that works very well for the most part." Robert stared at the viscount's averted profile. "If a matter is too serious for me to make a judgment on, I send the accused to the quarterly assizes in the county town of Hertford." Robert paused deliberately. "That's what I should have done with Bert Speers instead of keeping him in the cellar of the Queen's Head while I completed my investigation."

"Bert is still being held at the local inn? Whatever for?" Gravely asked.

"Murdering your mistress. But you already knew that, seeing as Bert has been keeping you informed of his progress all along."

"What a ridiculous notion," Gravely replied. "If Bert is guilty of murder, that is on him."

"Is it, though?" Robert stepped down off the dais. "Then why would he run straight to you?"

"I thought you said he was currently incarcerated?"

"Unfortunately, he escaped a few days ago."

The viscount tutted. "How very irresponsible of you, Sir Robert. One expects better from our local magistrates."

"Then you deny seeing him?"

"Of course, I do." The viscount raised his eyebrows. "Are you suggesting that I would aid or harbor a *criminal,* Sir Robert?"

"Ah, so if he does turn up in London and comes to you at some point, you will immediately turn him over to the authorities?"

"If he is a murderer, of course, I will. But to be perfectly frank, you don't have the evidence to prove even that, or else you would've instantly charged him and sent him to the assizes."

"I'm fairly certain I know exactly where to lay the blame, my lord." Robert held the viscount's mocking gaze. "And if I ever have the opportunity to prove it, you will be hearing from me again."

"Strong words, sir, from a man who has nothing of real substance to say."

"I have the body of a young woman awaiting burial after being strangled," Robert snapped. "Would you care to see her? Or would that offend your sensibilities too deeply?"

For a moment, the viscount looked away, his expression suddenly blank. "Her death was . . . unfortunate."

"*Unfortunate?* A delay in getting to a ball is 'unfortunate.' The deliberate murder of a young woman is something else entirely."

"Then one can only hope that the murderer will soon be brought to justice." Viscount Gravely headed for the door. "I wish you all the best with your endeavors."

"I intend to pursue this matter until I am satisfied; don't you worry about that," Robert said loudly as the viscount opened the door. "I never give up on anything."

He let his guest leave and stayed where he was for a few moments to allow his temper to settle. The peace and antiquity of the venerable room spread over him. He slowly raised his head to study the image of justice depicted in the stained-glass window. One of the scales had been broken by a stray bullet during the Civil War and had been replaced by a clear piece of glass, but it hardly affected the overall sentiment of the piece.

Whatever Viscount Gravely said, Robert truly believed that at some point Flora Rosa's murderer would be held to account. With that belief firmly in mind, he exhaled and went to find his guests.

Lucy paused yet again to see where Neville had gone. He was several paces behind her, staring out of the windows looking over the front of the house. Her father had decided to go up to the nursery to surprise Ned, and Lucy had been more than happy to see him go.

"I do apologize, Lady Kurland," Neville said. "I was just looking to see if Trevor had arrived yet."

"I believe you said he had gone out riding and would join us when he was ready." Lucy offered.

"That's right, but as he doesn't know the area, I'm beginning to wonder if he's gotten lost and if I should go and look for him." Neville walked slowly toward her.

"It is very hard to get lost here, Mr. Gravely, as the fields are so flat, and the steeple of St. Mary's church is easy to navigate back toward. I'm sure your brother will join us soon. Would you like to come down to the drawing room and have some refreshments while we wait for your father?"

Neville finally appeared to remember his manners and meekly followed her back toward the landing, where they could descend the shallow oak stairway into the main entrance hall.

A scream penetrated from one of the upper stories, and Lucy stiffened at the sound of pounding feet on the servants' staircase to her right. The door burst open, and Polly, still wearing her nightgown, ran toward Lucy, swiftly followed by James.

James reached Polly before Lucy, gently locked his arms around her waist, and lifted her off her feet.

"It's all right, my lady. I've got her. Dr. Fletcher is coming to see her very soon."

"Thank you, James," Lucy said.

Lucy held the door open for James to carry the now-struggling Polly back up to her room.

She turned to her companion "I do apologize, Mr. Gravely, I—" She stopped speaking as she registered the look of horror on his face. "What is it?"

He gulped once and then stared at Lucy. "What in God's name is *she* doing here?"

Lucy braced herself. "I'm not sure what you are referring to, sir."

"That woman!" Neville pointed a shaking finger at the door. "This is a *disaster!* She's not supposed to be—"

Lucy stepped right in front of Neville as he lurched toward the door, praying that his good manners would not allow him to knock her down.

"I don't know who you think you saw, Mr. Gravely, but you are quite mistaken. That woman is one of my nursery maids. She has been suffering from a fever for the last week and is still delirious."

"I—must have been wrong." Neville looked away from her. "I beg your pardon, my lady."

Lucy touched his arm. "Will you come down and have some tea? I'm sure your father won't be much longer."

She was more shaken by the incident than she was prepared to acknowledge. What appalling luck for a member of the Gravely family to see Polly Carter, of all people. She would have to tell Robert what had happened as soon as possible.

Just after her father joined them in the drawing room and Anna had been introduced to Neville, Robert appeared with Viscount Gravely at his side. Neither of them looked as if they had come to blows, but the icy disdain between them was blatantly obvious.

On the pretense of making Robert hand out cups of tea, Lucy managed to get him close enough to whisper in his ear.

"Polly escaped her room and Neville saw her."

"What?" Robert almost dropped the cup.

"James caught her and took her back to bed. Dr. Fletcher has been sent for."

"Why did she choose to escape now?" Robert muttered.

"Just a ghastly coincidence." Lucy paused. "Unless she somehow knew Viscount Gravely was here and panicked."

"And ran straight down the stairs into his son's arms?" Robert had delivered the tea and returned to her. "I thought she was unconscious."

"And I told you I suspected she was pretending," Lucy reminded him.

"Maybe she thought Neville Gravely might save her from *us?*" Robert retorted.

"I hadn't thought of that." Lucy handed him another cup of tea. "I can only hope that Neville believed my explanation that the woman was my nursery maid."

"I somehow doubt that." Robert nudged her. "Look at his face. He can barely manage to maintain a polite conversation. He knows whom he saw, and he is dying to tell his father."

"Good morning, Lady Kurland, Sir Robert." Robert looked up to see Trevor Gravely entering the drawing room. "I do apologize for my late arrival."

Robert went over to speak to Trevor, leaving Lucy dispensing tea.

"Good morning. I'm afraid that you missed the tour, but you are more than welcome to come back another day, if you so desire." Robert lowered his voice. "Did you have the opportunity to see the body?"

"Indeed, I did." Trevor bowed. "And I can confirm that it is Flora Rosa. May she rest in peace."

Robert slowly exhaled. "Thank you for that. Now at least I can bury her with her proper name on her headstone."

"I doubt that's her real name, but I understand your relief, Sir Robert." Trevor's attention swung to his brother. "What's wrong with Neville? He looks as though he's seen a ghost."

"Perhaps he did," Robert ventured. "This is a very old house, after all." He took Trevor across the room to speak to Lucy and receive a cup of tea, and went over to where Neville was staring into space.

"Did you enjoy your tour, sir?" Robert asked.

"Indeed, it was . . . fascinating." Neville's smile wasn't convincing at all.

"I understand that you met our new nursery

maid, who has been quite unwell with a fever." Robert met Neville's gaze. "I'm sure that you and your father would hate to become unwell yourselves, which is why I was just recommending to your brother that you keep your visit to Kurland St. Mary as short as possible."

Neville nodded. "I quite agree with you, Sir Robert. In truth, I cannot wait to get away from this place."

Robert escorted the Gravely family and his father-in-law back out into their gig and waited until they all departed down the drive toward the rectory. He had a strong suspicion they hadn't heard the last from Neville and wanted to speak to his wife immediately.

She was still in the drawing room when he returned, collecting cups and placing them on the tea tray, a thoughtful look on her face.

"Robert—"

He spoke over her. "We have to decide what to do about Polly. Where would be the best place to keep her safe?"

Lucy gave him an odd look. "Here, of course."

"But that idiot Neville is bound to blurt out what he saw to his father and brother!"

"I'm quite sure that he will," Lucy agreed. "Which is why this is the best place to protect Polly and catch anyone who chooses to come after her."

Robert studied his wife. "You mean we should

set a trap and see if Viscount Gravely takes the bait?"

"Exactly." Lucy smiled approvingly at him. "You know this house better than anyone. We can make sure that Polly is placed in a room where we can observe her very closely and prevent anyone from finding her."

"The priest's room," Robert said decisively. "With the false wall and the space behind it to hide someone to watch over Polly." He nodded. "That is an excellent notion. We can have someone guarding the exterior door as well."

"James already knows about this Polly Carter, and I am certain that after his recent failures, he would be delighted to guard her," Lucy said. "We can also get Isaiah and Isaac up from the stables if we need them."

"Have you been up to see Polly yet?" Robert asked.

"I haven't had time," Lucy said. "Do you want to come with me?" She set the last cup on the tray. "I am very interested in hearing what she has to say."

They walked through into the entrance hall just as Dr. Fletcher arrived, and after exchanging pleasantries, they ascended the stairs together. As they went up, Robert explained about the arrival of the real Polly Carter. Patrick expressed his surprise at her surviving what had happened in London and at her journey to Kurland St. Mary.

"Evans says that there is no reason for her not to have regained full consciousness," Patrick remarked. "But I have seen patients who have remained comatose for weeks and then woken up with no knowledge of what happened to them, so don't expect her to be able to tell you anything."

"That's not very helpful," Robert said. "And seeing as she tried to run away earlier, one might assume that she has regained her senses somewhat."

"It depends." Patrick paused by the door where James was sitting. "She might have lapsed into unconsciousness again."

Robert snorted as Patrick unlocked the door. Betty, Lucy's maid, was sitting by the bed beside Polly.

"She's asleep, Dr. Fletcher. Do you want me to wake her?"

"Asleep or unconscious?" Dr. Fletcher came to sit on the side of the bed and took Polly's hand in his, his fingers on the inside of her wrist. "She doesn't seem very aware to me."

He leaned closer. "Polly? Can you hear me? This is Dr. Fletcher. You are quite safe here."

Polly didn't stir, and Robert watched somewhat impatiently as his friend continued to sit on the bed and observe his patient.

"I don't think she's pretending, Sir Robert," Patrick finally said. He stroked the thin tip of his pen over her skin, and she didn't react at all. "I don't know quite what is going on, but I suggest you leave her in peace."

"James said that when he was halfway up the stairs, she stopped fighting, swooned again, and didn't respond to him after that," Betty added.

"Knowing James, he probably hit her head against the stairwell," Robert grumbled rather unfairly.

"I suspect it's more that she is too afraid to face what is going on in the present," Patrick said slowly. "I've seen such cases before—usually after a person has suffered a traumatic event. They deliberately retreat into unconsciousness."

"Like almost being killed by Bert Speers?" Robert asked as he turned to the door. "Will it be acceptable to you if we move her into a different room?"

"That's perfectly fine, as long as you make sure it is secure, and that someone is watching over her at all times."

"Don't worry about that, my friend," Robert said grimly. "I'll make absolutely certain it is as safe as the Tower of London."

Robert left the room with Lucy, told James to report to him in his study after he'd been relieved by Michael, and set off down the stairs. Polly was the last remaining link to Flora Rosa's death, and Robert intended to make sure that she lived to speak her truth. He needed a plan to thwart any attempt by Neville or Viscount Gravely to contact Polly. His staff was capable and loyal to a fault. He had no doubt that if they obeyed his orders and the fates were kind to him, he might successfully catch a murderer. Who it would be, he wasn't yet quite certain.

"I'm going down to the rectory," Robert announced as he went into his wife's sitting room. He'd spoken to his staff, moved Polly to the priest's room, and made certain that she was well guarded.

"For what purpose?" Lucy swiveled around in her chair to look at him.

"To have a few words with Neville Gravely. He and his brother seem keen to take their father home as soon as possible, and I intend to encourage them."

"I thought we had decided to let matters take their course and see if the viscount dared come after Polly himself." Lucy said with a frown.

"I'd rather not risk Polly's life. If we can keep her hidden, get the Gravely family to leave, and receive her evidence when she finally wakes up, I'm happy to wait."

"But what if she has no recollection of anything before she was injured? Dr. Fletcher said that is often the case." Lucy objected.

Robert scowled. "You are being rather difficult this morning, my dear."

"I'm merely wondering at your logic. There is nothing wrong with that. And I cannot agree that Neville is innocent in this affair. His whole demeanor seems guilty to me."

"I suspect he is simply embarrassed by his father."

"You forget that several people, including his own brother, have told us Flora was planning to return to Neville." Lucy paused. "Or what if that is what she told him and she changed her mind again? He would have reason to be angry enough to murder her himself."

"He doesn't have the gumption," Robert said dismissively.

"Yet he has the look of a guilt-ridden, desperate man. Maybe his horror at seeing Polly was more on his own behalf than on his father's."

Robert glared at her. "Why do you have to bring all this up when we have already agreed that Viscount Gravely and Bert Speers conspired to murder Flora?"

"Because that is what you usually do, my dear," Lucy said firmly. "You always temper my emotional instincts with your more rational thoughts. Why do you object to me doing the same to you?"

"Because—" Robert glared helplessly at her and then let out a frustrated breath. "I just want the Gravelys to leave Kurland St. Mary as quickly as possible."

"I understand your desire completely, but I'm still worried about Neville."

Robert hesitated. "Trevor did suggest that his brother was somewhat obsessed with Flora, and that he was more worried about him than his father."

"Then maybe we should be worried about him, too." Lucy suggested. "Perhaps Viscount Gravely came down here to keep an eye on *Neville* rather than the other way around."

"I told our staff to alert me to the presence of any of the Gravely family or Bert Speers in our house, so even if it is Neville, he will not get to Polly."

"Of course, you did." Lucy smiled at him approvingly, and Robert had the familiar sense that his sometimes too clever wife was masterfully managing him. "I would expect nothing less of you."

"I'll just speak to Trevor, then." Robert found himself capitulating.

"What an excellent idea." She paused. "Or you could leave well enough alone, and wait for one of the Gravelys to expose themselves as the murderer."

Robert cast her one last scathing look and headed for the hall, where his gig awaited him. He was willing to be pushed so far and no more.

As he proceeded down the drive, his ire faded, and he found himself smiling. It was unlike him to be the more passionate one about a murder suspect, but this case felt very personal because it came far too close to his beloved son. He'd never particularly wanted to be a father, but watching Ned grow up was proving remarkably interesting. After almost losing his life at Waterloo and facing the prospect of being an invalid for the rest of his days, his hopes of having a family had evaporated. And when Lucy had struggled to conceive, he'd realized that having her was far more important than a mythical heir.

But the moment Grace Turner had placed Ned in his arms he'd been totally smitten. The boy's unguarded affection and lack of fear made Robert proud to be his father and unexpectedly willing to involve himself in his son's life.

As Robert approached the rectory, he noticed a lone horseman departing from the Harrington stables. It wasn't the rector, who was usually accompanied by several of his dogs, and it definitely wasn't Viscount Gravely. The rider turned at the last moment, giving Robert a perfect view of his face.

"Where are you off to, Neville Gravely?" Robert murmured.

Knowing how easy it was to be seen in the flat, barren countryside, he took off his hat, buttoned his coat, wrapped his scarf over his lower face, and hunkered down in the driving seat in an attempt to look more like one of the local farmers. He also kept well away from Neville, his knowledge of the area standing him in good stead.

He knew immediately where Neville was heading when he took one of the rutted farm tracks to the left. Robert increased his speed, remained on the county road, and looped around to the back of the deserted farm buildings where the Mallard family had once lived. He left the gig secured on the side of the road, scrambled awkwardly through the ancient hedgerow, and continued on foot toward the back of the barn.

It was so quiet that he easily heard Neville call out to someone inside the barn. Staying well concealed behind a bramble bush, Robert saw a familiar man emerge from the barn.

"Bert Speers," Robert murmured to himself. "Now what the devil is Neville doing with him?"

Chapter 20

Hard as it was to swallow, it was possible that his wife might have been right about Neville Gravely all along . . .

Robert retreated back to the road and got into the gig. There was no point in attempting to apprehend Bert because he would simply flee again, and Robert didn't have the ability to chase him over the fields. He reckoned his best chance to find out exactly what was going on was to go back to the rectory and wait for Neville to return.

He drove back as fast as he could, left the gig in the stables, and went through into the main house, where he discovered his father-in-law in his study, writing at his desk. The rector set down his pen and looked at Robert over the top of his spectacles.

"Good morning, Robert. What a pleasant surprise! Did you bring young Ned with you?"

"I did not." Robert closed the door behind him. "Is Viscount Gravely here?"

"I don't believe he's come downstairs, yet. Do you wish to speak to him?"

"I do," Robert said. "And his sons."

"Trevor is in the garden with Rose, enjoying a stroll, and Neville has gone out for a ride." The rector paused. "Is something the matter?"

"Nothing that need concern you, sir." Robert bowed. "But there is a matter I need to clear up with them before they leave."

"You don't seem very enamored of my guests, sir."

"In truth, I wish them gone from our village, and I hope never to meet any of them again."

"Strong words." The rector eyed him curiously. "I pray you don't intend to come to blows in my house over this 'matter' of yours."

"Not if I can help it." Robert bowed again. "I just wanted you to be aware that I was here, and not to worry if you hear shouting."

"I assume you don't wish me to mediate between the parties?"

"No, thank you. What I have to say should remain confidential. I appreciate your offer, though."

Robert went out again and stopped the parlor maid who was walking through to the kitchen.

"Fiona, can you go upstairs and ascertain if Viscount Gravely is dressed?"

"I'll go and ask his valet if you like, sir."

"Don't ask. Just look for me, will you?"

"Yes, sir."

Fiona went up the stairs and came down again

quickly. "He is dressed, sir, and sitting by the fire eating his breakfast."

"Thank you." Robert smiled at the girl. "If either of the Mr. Gravelys comes in, will you ask them to meet me in the drawing room?"

"Yes, sir."

Robert went up the stairs and straight into Viscount Gravely's room. There was no sign of the valet, which meant there was no one to prevent Robert from marching up to his prey.

"Good Lord, not you again. Can't a man eat his breakfast in peace?" Viscount Gravely murmured.

Robert sat opposite him and waited until the viscount met his gaze.

"Even though I am unlikely to ever achieve a prosecution in this matter, I think I deserve to hear the truth from you."

"The truth about what?"

"Flora Rosa's murder." Robert sat forward. "If you didn't kill her yourself, did you order Bert Speers to do so?"

"Why would you think I would answer that question now?" The viscount's smile was all teeth. "What possible benefit would that be to me?"

Robert shrugged. "Well, it might prevent me from arresting one of your sons."

"On what grounds?"

"Meeting with a known fugitive. If Neville has

been helping a wanted criminal from avoiding arrest, he is complicit." Robert shrugged. "If I can't get Bert, a Gravely will do just as well."

"Neville?" The viscount's knife clattered down onto his plate.

"Yes, the man who first met Flora Rosa, and who was supposedly willing to take her back, even though she had been bought by his father."

"Who told you that piece of nonsense?"

The viscount's indolence had disappeared, replaced with obvious annoyance.

"Did Neville bring Bert here to finish off the last remaining witness to his crimes?" Robert asked.

"I don't know what you are trying to suggest," the viscount said. "Didn't you tell me yourself that Flora is dead?"

"And what about Marjory?"

The viscount frowned. "I have no idea who you are talking about."

"Then help me understand this tangle! If you didn't kill Flora, did Neville? Or did you pay your loyal employee Bert Speers to do the job for you?" Robert waited, but the viscount merely stared at him. "And what about Polly Carter?"

"The woman Flora Rosa impersonated?"

"Ah, you remember *her?*" Robert asked.

"Of course, I do. She and Flora were very good friends." The viscount nodded.

"Did you set Bert to watch the mail coach for

her arrival here? If I hadn't been in the inn yard that morning, watching for Bert, I would never have known that she had arrived, or seen Bert try and abscond with her."

Viscount Gravely slowly put a hand to his throat as if he was choking. "Polly Carter is *here?*"

Robert stared at him in consternation. "Of course, she is! Why else are *you* here?"

"I should have known . . ." Viscount Gravely grabbed for the bell and rang it vigorously until his valet appeared. His color was worsening by the second. "Send my sons up to me immediately."

Robert rose to his feet. "Please don't pretend that Neville didn't tell you he saw Polly Carter at our house yesterday."

"Oh, dear God . . ." The viscount raised his face to the heavens and started to gasp for breath. "This is a nightmare. Where are my *sons?*"

The door opened, and Trevor came in.

"What the devil is going on?" He rushed to his father's side. "Father, *please.*"

"Where is *Neville?*" The viscount wheezed. "I told him not to leave your side!"

Trevor turned to Robert. "Have you seen him? He said he was going for a ride."

"I saw him briefly. I am surprised he has not returned yet," Robert replied, his worried gaze on the viscount, who was growing more agitated

337

and breathless by the second. "Your father does not look well. I will ask the rector to send for my physician immediately."

He turned to the door.

"Wait!" the viscount wheezed, his hand outstretched toward Robert. "Don't let him get to her, *please.*"

"I'll do my best," Robert said and went down the stairs, stopping only briefly to report to his father-in-law and ask for his assistance.

He had to assume that the lack of Neville's appearance meant that he was already headed up to Kurland Hall. He needed to return home with all speed.

"Sir Robert!" He turned as he reached the stables and saw Trevor running after him. "Let me come with you. If anyone knows how to stop Neville, it is me."

"Come, then, but if your brother is attempting to hurt anyone in my house, be aware that he will first answer to me," Robert said grimly.

Lucy was in the nursery, rearranging her cupboards, when something crashed to the ground in the room next door, followed by a female scream.

"Where is she?"

Lucy stifled a gasp, crept toward the half-open door, and peered through the gap.

Bert Speers stood in the center of her nursery, brandishing a wicked-looking knife at Agnes.

"What on earth are you playing at, Bert?" Agnes demanded. "If Sir Robert catches you here—"

"Where's your cousin?"

"I don't know what you are talking about." Agnes raised her chin. "And keep your voice down, or you'll wake the young master from his nap."

"Where is Polly? I know she's here. Just take me to her, and I won't hurt a hair on your head."

"I don't—" Agnes gasped as Bert grabbed hold of her arm. "Let go of me!"

"Take me to Polly—or else, you stupid cow!"

"I'll take you to her room, Bert, but it won't do you no good. She's guarded night and day."

"Let me worry about that."

Lucy let out a very shaky breath as Bert forced Agnes to walk in front of him and out the door. She ran and checked that Ned was indeed still sleeping and slipped down the back stairs as fast as she could.

"Foley! Bert Speers is here, and he has Agnes." Lucy gasped, her hand pressed to her bosom as she entered the kitchen. "Where is Sir Robert?"

"He hasn't returned from the rectory yet, my lady. Mr. Neville Gravely just presented himself at the front door, and per Sir Robert's orders, I turned him away."

That might explain how Bert had managed to

get into the house undetected while Foley was occupied. It also led to Lucy wondering whether Neville and Bert were working together.

"Did he leave?"

"I'm not sure, my lady." Foley paused and, for the first time, looked every one of his years. "What do you wish me to attend to first? Ensuring Agnes's safety, or finding out what has happened to Mr. Neville?"

"Is Isaac here?"

"He's guarding the priest's room, my lady."

"Then where is his brother Isaiah?" Lucy asked.

"Inside the hidden room."

"And James?"

"I'm right here, my lady." James had just come into the kitchen. "What may I assist you with?"

"Bert Speers has Agnes and is demanding to see Polly."

"The blaggard!" James slapped his fist against his thigh. "In broad daylight, too!" He turned toward the door. "I'll make sure he understands he is not welcome here."

Lucy grabbed his sleeve. "Don't fight him if he still has Agnes in his clutches. Just hold him at bay until Sir Robert comes back."

James didn't look particularly happy at her request, but he nodded. "As you wish, my lady."

Michael appeared from the garden, carrying a basket of herbs and followed by Anna.

"What on earth is going on?" she asked and came to Lucy's side. "You look as if you are about to swoon!"

Lucy had noticed that herself and had a firm grip on the edge of the table. "Anna, can you go up to the nursery and stay with Ned?"

"Yes, of course!" Her sister didn't ask any further questions and disappeared up the stairs.

"And Michael? Can you find Sir Robert and make sure he comes home immediately? I believe he went to the rectory in the gig. Tell him that Bert Speers is in the house and that he has a knife."

Lucy paused to breathe as spots appeared in front of her eyes. Cook patted her sleeve.

"You should sit down before you fall down, my lady."

"I . . . can't do that." Lucy forced herself to stay upright. "Bert Speers is in my house, and I cannot allow him to hurt another member of my staff!"

Despite Foley's best efforts to dissuade her, she left the kitchen and returned to the upper floor, straining her ears to hear Bert's rough voice or Agnes's tart replies. Did Agnes know that Polly had been moved to a different room? She had been occupied with Ned all day and hadn't been able to sit with Polly.

Acting on instinct, Lucy headed toward the room where Polly had previously been held.

The door was now flung wide open, and within the room, Bert was getting angry.

"Where the bloody hell is she, Agnes?"

"I . . . don't know. She was here last night, I swear it," Agnes replied.

"I don't believe you."

Lucy winced at the sound of a slap, and Agnes screeched.

"You bloody bastard!"

Lucy gripped the handle of a cooking pot she'd taken from the kitchen and deliberated her next move. Should she go in and confront Bert, or wait until she gathered reinforcements?

Even as she took one uncertain step forward, a hand curved around her neck and gently pulled her back. Her weapon slid to the floor with a clang.

"I do apologize, Lady Kurland," Neville said in her ear as he pressed the blade of a knife against her skin. "But it is absolutely imperative that you take me to Polly Carter, or your life will be in danger."

Bert came out of the room with Agnes and stopped short at the sight of Lucy and her captor.

"About bloody time you showed up, Nev," Bert growled. "Take us to Polly, Lady Kurland. Now."

Robert abandoned the gig at the front of the hall and went in through the front door, Trevor at his heels. James was just coming down the stairs and rushed toward him.

"Sir Robert! Bert Speers is here, and he's got Agnes!"

"Damnation!" Robert said. "Is Mr. Neville Gravely here, too?"

"He tried to get in, but Foley wouldn't let him," James reported. "Did you see him on the drive?"

"I doubt he's left if he thinks Polly is here," Trevor entered the conversation. "How about I look around and see if I can find him while you deal with Speers, Sir Robert?"

"Please, go ahead." Robert nodded, and Trevor set off toward the kitchens. "Where is Lady Kurland?"

"I'm not sure, sir." James had already turned back toward the stairs. "Bert came into the nursery and took Agnes. Her ladyship came down to the kitchen to tell us. I'm just going up to see whether I can find Bert."

"I'll come with you," Robert said grimly as he checked that he had his pistol in his coat pocket. "Does Agnes know we moved Polly last night?"

"Probably not, sir. She might have taken Bert to the wrong room, which might buy us some time," James said. "Shall we go there first?"

Robert's gaze had already moved between the two corridors that radiated from the upper landing and alighted on what looked like a mob scene at one end.

"There's no need. I can see them heading toward Isaac." He went down the corridor, almost tripping over Agnes, who was sprawled on the floor. Motioning to James to slow down, he advanced toward the group of figures currently arguing outside the locked and guarded door to Polly's room.

"I don't want to hurt you, lad, but I need to get in there," Bert Speers said.

"I take my orders from Sir Robert, not you," Isaac replied. "And he told me to sit here and guard the door." He folded his arms across his massive chest. He was probably a foot taller and twice as wide as Bert.

"Would you like to give that order, Lady Kurland?"

As Neville joined the conversation, Robert went still as he realized his wife was locked close to Neville's chest and that there was a knife at her throat.

"I cannot," Lucy said, her voice clear and steady. "Isaac is correct. Only Sir Robert can open that door for you."

"Not even if I slit your throat?" Bert asked.

"You wouldn't do that, now, Bert!" Isaac blurted out. "Why hurt Lady Kurland? What's she ever done to you?"

"For God's sake, Bert. Don't make things even worse than they have to be," Neville pleaded with his conspirator. "I have no intention of—"

Robert stepped out into the center of the hall and aimed his pistol straight at Neville's head.

"Then you will kindly let go of my wife."

"Gawd, now his bloody lordship's here," Bert said. "And the cat really is among the pigeons." He held up a hand. "You don't understand nothing, Sir Robert. Let me take Polly, and we'll say no more about it."

"You, be quiet," Robert snapped at Bert and turned to Neville. "And you, unhand my wife, or I will shoot."

"And risk her getting hurt in the process?" Bert asked. "I don't think you want to do that now, do you?"

It was Neville who moved first and released Lucy before he sank down to his knees.

"I can't do this anymore. I'm sorry, Bert. I just *can't*—" He burst into noisy sobs, his head in his hands.

Bert's expression was resigned as he stared at Robert. "I should've known not to trust a toff."

Robert kept his gun on Bert and spoke to Lucy. "Are you unharmed, my dear?"

"Yes, I am." There was a wobble in her voice that someone would pay for later, but his pride in her resilience increased anew.

"Would you do me the kindness of attending to Agnes and taking her up to the nursery?"

"Yes, of course." Lucy went by him, taking a moment to squeeze his shoulder as she passed.

"Do you wish me to send for Michael and any of the other male servants in the house to assist you?"

"Yes, send Michael."

Robert waited until he heard Agnes respond to Lucy, and until the two women walked away, before he addressed Bert and a still sobbing Neville.

"I am not going to make the mistake of letting you go again, Bert. You and your companion will face justice at the assizes for the murder of Flora Rosa and the attempted murder of Polly Carter. Surrender your weapons."

Bert sighed dramatically and glanced down at Neville. "It seems that I've been caught well and good, Sir Robert. Now will you hear what I have to say?"

Neville slowly looked up and staggered to his feet, swaying like the wind. "No, don't tell him, don't tell him *anything!* It will kill my father!"

"Your father is already dying," Robert said bluntly. "Perhaps he needs to understand the legacy he has left the world in his youngest son. Isaac, will you escort Mr. Gravely down to my study, and James, will you accompany Bert? Mr. Harrington has already sent for the local constable. He should be awaiting us downstairs."

Bert took a hasty step forward. "What about Polly?"

"She is none of your concern anymore." Robert stared him down.

"You don't understand!" Bert shouted, and James stepped forward, grabbed hold of Bert, and slapped a hand over his mouth.

"I've got him, sir."

"Good," Robert said. "Then let's get them both down to my study."

Lucy walked Agnes slowly back toward the nursery and settled her in bed before returning to the main room, where Anna was playing with Ned on the rug in front of the fire. Lucy wanted to go to bed herself and forget about the terrible day, but as the mistress of the house, she had to make sure all her staff were content, and that her husband was no longer in any danger.

"Anna, I—"

She stopped talking as the tableau in front of her, which defied sense, slowly registered.

"Lady Kurland, how nice of you to join us," Trevor Gravely said heartily. Her sister lay motionless on the floor. Ned was currently being held tightly in front of Trevor, who had a gun to her son's head.

"Mama—" Ned tried to come to her, and Trevor yanked him back hard.

Lucy somehow found her voice and looked directly into her son's frightened eyes. "Stay still, my love. Don't give this man any excuse to hurt you."

Ned's lip quivered. "I don't like him. He hit Auntie Anna."

"That's because he is not a good man," Lucy replied. "But if we do as he wants, I suspect he won't hurt us and make matters worse."

"How well you understand me, Lady Kurland," Trevor said. "Now, take me to Polly Carter so I can end this ridiculous farrago once and for all."

"If you release my son, I will willingly take you to her," Lucy parried.

"No." Trevor stood up, taking Ned with him. "He comes with us."

"If you insist." Lucy briefly closed her eyes as nausea gripped her, and turned to the door, her limbs shaking so badly that she wasn't certain how she remained upright. She knew she should be asking Trevor to explain himself, but her terror for her son jammed her throat and threatened to overcome her.

Despite her hopes for rescue, the house was surprisingly quiet as she walked ahead of Trevor toward the priest's room where Polly lay. She needed to think of a plan to free Ned, but her mind was too sluggish. To add to her consternation, there was no one sitting outside Polly's room guarding it and no sign of Robert, Bert Speers, or Neville Gravely.

She stopped and looked back at Trevor. "I don't know where the key is."

"I doubt that." He met her gaze, his own eyes cold. "Find it, or I will hurt your son."

Ned whimpered and turned his face away, straining his body against his captor's hold.

"I am not lying. There is usually someone sitting outside this door who holds the key, and they are missing." Lucy paused. "I suspect they are with Sir Robert and your accomplices."

"My *accomplices?*" Trevor chuckled. "I suppose you are talking about my brother and Bert. I consider them more as my jailers, attempting to thwart all my schemes and make things so complicated that here we are, Lady Kurland, with you having to make a choice between sacrificing that baby in your belly and yourself for your son or letting me kill him."

"I—" Lucy glanced desperately at Ned, who had started to quietly cry. "I can go and find the key if you wish."

"Don't be stupid, Lady Kurland. The moment you walk away from me, you will alert the house to my purpose, and hope that *somehow* you will save your son, Polly, and yourself. Please be advised that will not happen. If you want to save your family, you will have to offer up the sacrifice of Polly. And why not do that? What does a stupid serving girl from London owe you?"

"No one deserves to die at your hand," Lucy said shakily.

"They do if they insist on interfering with what is mine," Trevor replied and tightened his grip on Ned. "This is an old house; there must be another way into this room through the servants' stairs. Find it."

Lucy took a deep, steadying breath and pointed to the end of the corridor. "We can access the servants' stairs there and enter the end room, which links through into this one."

"Well done, Lady Kurland." Trevor smiled down at Ned. "Your mother is quite remarkable, isn't she? Lead the way, ma'am."

Lucy walked slowly down the hallway until she reached the door. If Trevor wanted to kill Polly, he would have to let go of Ned. Perhaps in that instant she could shove her son to the side and attempt to stop Trevor in some way. If she died in the attempt, then so be it. At least Robert would have his son.

She opened the door, and it almost hit someone coming the other way. Even as she registered Foley's presence, he held his fingers to his lips, and she stared straight ahead as if he wasn't there.

As Trevor stepped into the small dark landing behind her, squashing Ned between them, she pointed to the left. "We can go through this door, and—"

Even as she spoke, Foley threw the chamber pot he held at Trevor's head, and the gun went off, the explosion loud in the enclosed space. As Trevor cursed and attempted to right himself, Lucy tore Ned from his grip and shoved Trevor hard until he lost his balance and fell down the stairs with a series of loud thumps.

"Mama!" Ned burst into tears as Lucy gathered him to her bosom and held him for dear life.

She was shaking so hard she could scarcely breathe as a growing commotion erupted behind the door, which was suddenly wrenched open.

"Where is he?" Bert demanded.

Lucy wordlessly pointed downward, and Bert clattered down the narrow stairs, cursing as he went. Robert appeared, his expression frantic as he drew Lucy and Ned out of the small space and into his arms.

"God . . . I thought I'd lost you . . . ," he muttered into her hair. "Thank *God.*"

"Thank Foley," Lucy managed to reply. "Is he all right?"

"He's . . ." Robert met her gaze. "He's been shot. Dr. Fletcher is on his way."

"He saved us," Lucy whispered. "He hit Trevor with a chamber pot, which threw him off balance and allowed me to get Ned and push Trevor down the stairs."

"You were your usual remarkable and resourceful self," Robert said, his voice still shaking. "And thank the good Lord for that."

Eventually, Robert drew Lucy and Ned to their

feet. "I think we should put Ned to bed, make sure that Anna is recovering, and reconvene to the drawing room to hear what Bert and Neville have to say for themselves, don't you?"

Chapter 21

⟨⟩

"Trevor's not right," Neville blurted out. "He's never been right. We had to leave India because he was caught torturing animals, and then we went through three different schools because he was so wild."

Robert was sitting beside his wife on the couch in the drawing room. He had his arm around her shoulders and didn't give a damn about what anyone thought of such a public display of affection. His butler had been shot, his wife and son terrorized, and he wanted answers.

Bert, who was standing in front of the fireplace, nodded. "I first met Trev when he tried to kill one of the stable dogs. I beat him up, and he never tried anything again. He was afraid of me." Bert shifted his feet. "That's why when she was alive, the viscountess asked me to keep an eye on him when he was home from school."

"Of course, you worked at the Gravely stables after you left the orphanage," Robert said. "You knew the viscount's sons better than he did."

"Yes, sir. I left for a while to try and become a boxer, but it was a dangerous life. I came back and asked the viscount for a job when I heard he'd returned home for good." Bert paused. "Why isn't he here, by the way? I told you that if you'd just let me talk to him, we could sort this muddle out."

"I offered Viscount Gravely the opportunity to tell me the truth several times, and he declined," Robert replied. "I suspect he was quite happy to allow you to take the blame for any murders committed by his son."

"Of course, he was, the cold-blooded bastard," Bert muttered. "But why isn't he here attempting to clear his son's name?"

Robert grimaced. "He's currently under the care of my physician and had to remain at the rectory."

"What's wrong with him?" Neville asked tremulously.

Robert grimaced. "When I spoke to your father this morning, I didn't have the full facts in my possession. He grew very agitated when he realized that you were my suspect."

"He would," Bert said.

"As I left, he was gasping for air. I've since had a note from Dr. Fletcher to say that he thinks the viscount had some kind of a seizure." Robert paused. "But Trevor spent a few minutes alone with his father before he came after me. It's also possible that he tried to silence your father permanently before his valet came back and prevented him from completing his purpose."

Neville collapsed onto a chair, one hand over his mouth. "Dear God."

"Your father is hardly blameless in all this, sir." Robert glared at Neville. "Perhaps you would care to start at the beginning and explain exactly how Flora Rosa ended up being murdered?"

Neville looked apprehensively over at Bert, who nodded. "Might as well spill everything, Nev, and make sure that your brother is held accountable."

Neville bowed and got to his feet.

"Trevor met Flora first, and he became obsessed with her." He swallowed hard. "I'd seen this play out before, and the women usually ended up being . . . hurt, and I would have to pay them off. But Flora wasn't interested in Trevor and kept him at bay until I became worried that he would lash out at her. I told Father what was happening and asked him if he could help because Flora wasn't some prostitute who would easily be forgotten, but a rising star of the theater with many men vying to be her protector. She'd become afraid of Trevor, and she willingly agreed to accept my father's offer of a house and his protection as long as she could continue her career in the theater."

Neville sat back in his seat and surveyed the room. "We thought that Trevor would back down, that Father asserting his power would make him find another, easier target, but he wouldn't stop pursuing her. I ended up spending a lot of time at her house because she was so afraid Trevor would appear, and he ended up getting jealous of me *and* my father."

Bert started speaking again. "One night, Mr. Trevor followed Flo home and tried to choke her. She was absolutely terrified, and after Viscount Gravely declined to believe her, she knew she would have to get out of the relationship."

"Which is when I assume her friend Polly Carter suggested that Flora take her place as our new nursery maid?" Robert asked.

"Yes, sir," Bert nodded. "As soon as she could, Flo escaped from the house and went to my place, where Polly was waiting for her."

"Your place?" Lucy suddenly sat upright. "*You* own the house in Paradise Row in Bethnal Green?"

"I don't own it, my lady. I rent it from the Gravely estate," Bert replied. "It kept Flo safe for a day or so while Polly sold off some of her stuff to bribe Agnes and to pay Flo's fare down to Kurland St. Mary."

"And you accompanied her," Robert said slowly.

"Yes, sir." Bert looked down at his boots. "Someone had to keep an eye on her. I pretended to be in love with her so that no one would question me always hanging around and asking impudent questions."

"You were certainly very adept at that," Robert commented dryly. "How did Trevor discover Flora was here?"

Neville raised a hand. "I fear that was my fault. I decided to visit Bert's house to see if Flora was safe, and Trevor must have followed me. Flora had already left for Kurland St. Mary, but Trevor must have gotten the key to the house from our land agent and found out something that led him to your village. He boasted that he knew where Flora was and that he would soon find her, whatever I did."

"I wonder if Polly still had Agnes's letter with our address on it?" Lucy looked up at Robert. "Trevor could have found that."

"Seeing as Polly wrote that note to Flora, telling her that she had been unmasked, one has to suspect she did," Robert said. "So, at some point, your brother Trevor gets away from you, comes down to Kurland St. Mary, and waits for the opportunity to murder Flora."

"Yes, Sir Robert." Neville nodded.

Robert looked over at Bert. "And what were you doing when Mr. Trevor Gravely abducted and killed her? Weren't you supposed to be protecting her?"

A tremor passed over Bert's face. "I met with her in the village on her day off. She showed me Polly's letter and said she thought she'd seen Trevor on the mail coach. I told her to go straight back to Kurland Hall and not leave the grounds until I gave her permission to do so."

He grimaced. "She never liked being told what to do, and we had a bit of a fight. She was thinking about running away again, and I took her purse off her so she couldn't go anywhere." He paused to look over at Robert. "That's why it was hidden in my boot, sir, but I couldn't tell you that because I knew what you'd think. I marched Flo back toward the hall, arguing all the way, and waited until she entered the grounds before I left to get back to work and see if I could find any trace of Trevor.

"He must have grabbed her just after I left." Bert slowly exhaled. "The bastard. I was halfway back to the inn when I heard someone yelling. Thinking it was Flo, I ran back toward the church." He nodded at the door, where James stood guard. "I saw your footman and land agent having a fight over who Flo liked more. I admit, I stopped to watch the mill, which meant I didn't get back to Flo in time. As soon as I couldn't find her, I knew what that evil bugger had done, and I went back to London to confront Viscount Gravely. I was even stupidly hoping that maybe Trev had just taken Flo with him and I could rescue her." He cleared his throat. "Instead, I lost the person I loved most in the world."

Silence fell as Bert's voice cracked, but Robert

wasn't in the mood to be conciliatory or sympathetic quite yet.

"If you had just told me the truth, Bert, we could at least have discovered who killed Flora earlier and stopped Trevor from murdering Marjory as well."

"At first, I thought Flo might still be alive." Bert raised his head. "I was working for Viscount Gravely, sir, and I was honor bound to tell him what was going on. I couldn't betray him in case he could find Trevor and make him release Flo. I soon realized that the viscount was more interested in protecting his son than in bringing him to justice, and we parted ways." He shot Robert an angry glare. "Why do you think I came back to Kurland St. Mary the second time?"

"I don't know."

"To make sure Trev didn't come down here again without someone being here to tell him to leave you all in peace. But that didn't work out too well, did it?"

"Yes, why *did* you all end up in Kurland St. Mary again, Mr. Gravely?" Robert turned back to Neville.

"Because you invited Trevor to identify Flora's body. He was delighted by that notion," Neville's mouth twisted. "At that point, Bert and I didn't know where Polly had gotten to, and we were scared to let Trevor out of our sight. I reluctantly decided I had to tell Father what was going on.

When he realized that he had a connection in Kurland St. Mary, he decided we would both accompany Trevor and make sure he behaved himself. We thought if he identified Flora, that might be the end of it."

"Did Trevor know that you suspected him of killing Flora?"

"He was far too arrogant for that," Neville said. "He thought it was all an amusing game and that he was in charge of it." He paused. "He'd watch me sometimes with such malicious glee in his eyes that I'd feel like my life was worth nothing to him. He wanted Flora, Father and I had tried to prevent him from having her, and he was going to do his damnedest to make all of us suffer."

"Which brings me to my last point," Robert said. "Why in God's name didn't you identify yourselves when you came up to the hall today and ask for my help rather than scaring my wife and knocking out my child's nurse?"

Neville cast an accusing glance at Bert, who shrugged.

"I can't say you've endeared yourself to me, Sir Robert, what with locking me up in a cellar for weeks and ignoring all the hints I gave you. I must confess I thought a bit of a scare might pay you back a little."

"A little?" It was Robert's turn to glare back. "You *deliberately* kept me in the dark so as not to anger your employer, and even if you didn't actually murder Flora or Marjory, you damn well didn't help them much, either."

"I *thought* that after proving to Viscount Gravely that his son was a murderer, he would deal with Trev once and for all, but he chose not to do that." Bert held Robert's gaze, his throat working. "I was wrong, sir, and I paid dearly for trusting the family that gave me a home after the orphanage. No justice for Flo or for me. All I wanted to do was help Nev stop Trevor getting to Polly, and then I was going to wash my hands of the lot of them."

"Were you in the same orphanage as Flora?" Lucy asked.

"Of course, I was. She's my bloody sister!" Bert looked affronted. "I held her in my arms five minutes after she was born. She was beautiful even then." Bert's voice cracked again. "Our mother died when Flo was five, and we were all taken into the orphanage in Bethnal Green. I kept an eye on her as much as I could, but it wasn't easy."

He met Lucy's gaze, tears glistening in his eyes. "She was beautiful and clever, and didn't deserve to die at the hands of Trevor bloody Gravely."

"That is something we can both agree on, Bert," Robert said. "Would you be willing to testify against Mr. Trevor Gravely at his trial for murder?"

Bert glanced over at Neville. "No offense, Nev,

but I think it's time Trevor got what he deserves, don't you?"

"Yes," Neville whispered. "I've spent my whole life trying to stop him, and I still failed. I am exhausted. Poor Flora Rosa, poor Marjory."

Robert rose to his feet. "May I suggest that you both stay here at Kurland Hall until I have arranged for Trevor to be charged and placed in gaol."

It was less of a suggestion and more of an order. Both Bert and Neville looked too drained to argue with him. Robert wasn't certain if he could charge them for lying to him in his capacity as local magistrate. He wasn't about to mention that line of investigation before he carefully studied the law and consulted with his colleagues. The thought that they might get away with inflicting such damage on those in his household didn't sit well with him.

"Will I be able to see my father?" Neville asked unsteadily. "He'll want to know what is happening."

"Your father is in no state to receive you or such news," Robert said firmly. "In truth, it might even make him worse. I will send Dr. Fletcher to speak with you at his earliest convenience, and I suggest you follow his advice to the letter."

Neville subsided into his seat again. If Robert had his way, it would be a very long time before Viscount Gravely was informed about his oldest son's current position. Hopefully, that meant there would be little time for aristocratic meddling with the justice system.

"Is Trevor all right?" Neville asked, causing Robert to reluctantly admire his dogged determination.

"He suffered a few bruises and was knocked out when he fell down the stairs," Robert answered him. "Dr. Fletcher says there are no bones broken. Trevor is currently locked up in my cellar, with Isaac and Isaiah guarding him, and no one will be allowed to see him."

Neville shuddered and looked over at Bert. "I don't want to see him. He's a persuasive devil."

Bert held open the door. "Then come along, Nev. We'll muddle through this together, eh?"

Robert offered Lucy his arm. "Perhaps you might care to take a tour of our various patients. I swear this place feels more like a hospital than a home today."

"I would be delighted to accompany you," Lucy said and looked over at James. "Perhaps you could escort our guests up to their bedchambers and make sure that you and Michael are available to wait on them."

"Yes, my lady."

Bert might have snorted, but he quickly concealed it and obediently followed Neville out of the room, with Michael shadowing him, just in case he changed his mind and decided to make another run for it.

Lucy leaned heavily on Robert's arm as they went up the stairs. "What a tangled mess."

"Indeed. I suspect that we will never have answers to all our questions, but if I have anything to do with it, Trevor, at least, will stand trial."

"If Viscount Gravely allows it," Lucy said.

"From what Dr. Fletcher told me, the viscount was already ill and, after this seizure, might never regain his ability to speak."

Lucy nodded. "Then, perhaps there is some sort of justice in that he will never again be able to defend the indefensible."

They walked in silence toward Anna's bedroom and found Dr. Fletcher making his rounds. He had tended to the small cut on her head and expressed his hope that, apart from a lingering headache, she was on the mend. She was currently sleeping, with her maid watching over her. He also reported that Polly was awake and willing to talk to them, and that Agnes had bruised ribs and was sleeping well after a dose of laudanum.

"Thank you, Dr. Fletcher," Lucy said.

He smiled at her. "I think I'll stay here tonight, if that is all right with you, my lady. I have more patients to tend to here at the hall than in the entire village."

"You are most welcome to stay," Robert

answered for both of them. "I hope you'll deduct your bed and victuals from the rather large bill I'm anticipating."

Dr. Fletcher winked at him. "As we are acquaintances of long standing, I will certainly bear that in mind when I do my calculations."

They went on down the corridor to see Foley, who had been settled in great state in one of the guest bedrooms.

The old man was propped up against his pillows with his arm in a sling. Lucy went over to the bed and bent to kiss his wrinkled and bruised cheek.

"Thank you, Foley. You saved our lives."

"It was my pleasure, my lady," Foley said stoutly. "I couldn't allow that blaggard to hurt you or our precious young master."

Robert reached over and carefully shook Foley's undamaged hand. "I suspect you are more than ready to retire now, aren't you? Just say the word, and I'll find you a nice peaceful place on the estate where you hopefully won't ever be shot at again."

"I'll wait until Christmas, Sir Robert, if that's all right with you, and until James has proved satisfactory," Foley replied. "I am a man of my word."

"As you wish," Robert smiled at his oldest retainer. "Now, we'll leave you to your rest, and we'll see if James is capable of managing this household without you."

Foley sniffed. "I doubt that, sir, but I'm sure he will do his best."

Lucy was still smiling as they proceeded down the corridor toward their bedchamber.

"What if it was our son?" Robert suddenly said.

"Who was like Trevor?" Lucy asked.

"Yes." His brow creased. "Would I not do everything in my power to save his life?"

Lucy looked up at him. "You, my dear, have a strong sense of justice running through your veins. I suspect that, even though it would break your heart, you would do the right thing."

"I suspect I would." Robert sighed. "I *hope* I would."

"What did Viscount Gravely protecting and indulging Trevor for all those years actually achieve?" Lucy asked. "Nothing except the unnecessary deaths of two women and the gradual blurring of Viscount Gravely's own morals into accepting and ignoring the inexcusable."

"You are right, as always, my love." Robert gently kissed her nose. "You should take yourself off to bed."

She hesitated. "I have to see Ned before I sleep. There is no one in the nursery except Betty this evening, and he is *quite* unsettled."

Robert gave her a wry look. "Then why don't you take him to sleep with us tonight? I'm sure he'd appreciate it."

His wife frowned at him. "You've always

insisted that children and dogs have no place in your bed."

He wrapped his arms around her and drew her close. "Well, just this once, I will relax my rules. Tonight, I will truly appreciate having all my family together in one place."

"Amen," Lucy whispered.

"Unless Ned starts kicking me as much as the babe in your belly, at which point I will either eject Ned or leave myself."

Lucy pressed her forehead to Robert's waistcoat and finally allowed herself to smile. She was safe, her family was secure, and she would never, ever take that for granted again.

| Books are produced in the United States using U.S.-based materials | Books are printed using a revolutionary new process called THINKtech™ that lowers energy usage by 70% and increases overall quality | Books are durable and flexible because of Smyth-sewing | Paper is sourced using environmentally responsible foresting methods and the paper is acid-free |

Center Point Large Print
600 Brooks Road / PO Box 1
Thorndike, ME 04986-0001 USA

(207) 568-3717

US & Canada:
1 800 929-9108
www.centerpointlargeprint.com